MW00759702

OCTOBER'S GHOSTS

A CALENDAR GIRLS BOOK

STEPHANIE ERICKSON

CHAPTER 1

"Oh no dear. That's far too purple. I need a red or I'll just look…well dead." Mrs. Catrakas looked over October's shoulder as the old woman went through the drawer of lipstick.

"How about this one?" October held up a modest red and Mrs. Catrakas frowned.

"No. My shade is called Roxanne," she offered.

October knew just the one. Race car red. "A bold choice," she said as she fished it out, and swept it across the woman's cold lips.

"You have to be bold, dear. Better than being boring."

October's father, Steve, chuckled as he watched her work. "Boo is anything but boring."

Mrs. Catrakas gave a single nod, conceding his point. "I suppose an undertaker would have layers of interest."

October snorted. "That's one way to put it." The phone rang and Mrs. Catrakas scowled.

"You'll never do a good job with all these interruptions," she declared.

"Yes well. I'm a one-woman operation since Dad joined

your kind." Picking up the phone, October shook her head as she spied the old ghost's disapproval.

"Manning Funeral Home, how can I help you?" It was the hospital calling to schedule an appointment for a family, which they didn't often do. Well, a son apparently. He was on his own, which explained the hospital going the extra mile. Mr. Davis, the woman said.

Davis. The name sounded familiar to her, but she couldn't place it. "Certainly. I have him down for 3 o'clock tomorrow. Send him my condolences will you?"

"Back to the business at hand," Mrs. Catrakas said curtly as October hung up.

"I'm sorry. I never was very good with the hands on stuff. I was better with, well folks like you."

Steve laughed at that. "That's the truth. They never had to tell me how they wanted to look."

"Not like you would've heard them if they did," she needled.

"Fair enough. You were always better with the families. I liked working down here. It's quiet," he said as he looked around the sterile space.

October had Mrs. Catrakas laid out on the silver table, dressed in the outfit her family brought. Mrs. Catrakas hated it. October made a note to call them later and ask for a green jumpsuit.

"Much more comfortable to spend eternity in than this frilly dress," she'd said.

October couldn't disagree. Although, what was put on her body didn't matter. Her ghostly form was dressed in flowy palazzo pants and a white knit top.

"What about what you're wearing now?" October asked. "You seem to like that."

She chuckled. "Dear. I didn't own hippie pants like this in

life. I just wanted to try them. And you know what? I quite like them."

"Well, they look very smart on you," October said with a smile.

She jammed her hands in the pockets. "Look! They even have pockets!"

October laughed. "Nice to know the small pleasures transcend death."

"Well, what's the point if they don't?" She snapped.

October shook her head. "No idea."

Mrs. Catrakas raised an eyebrow at her. "This is the part you're good at?"

Steve laughed even louder and October glared at him.

"Not all ghosts are as vocal as you," she said as delicately as she could.

"I suppose not."

Just as October was finishing with Mrs. Catrakas, Mrs. Davis' body arrived.

Joe rang the bell at the back door, and October greeted him gratefully. He always went the extra mile helping make their new guests comfortable.

Aurora Davis, according to her paperwork, died of natural causes. When October looked at the woman lying on the table, she knew exactly why she recognized the name. October knew her. She sighed sadly as she donned gloves and set to work.

Mrs. Davis was the polar opposite of October. Short, silver hair, tan skin, thin lips October knew were vibrant red in life. Long beautiful eyelashes, and a perfect button nose. She'd aged beautifully.

October, on the other hand was approaching 35, had stringy black hair she kept in a constant, but practical bun. In school they had called her Wednesday, after the girl in the Addam's family. And they weren't that far off the mark. After all, the daughter of the funeral director did carry a certain air of Wednesday Addam's with her.

She set the paperwork on the counter behind her and looked down at Mrs. Davis' neutral face. "Oh Mrs. Davis. What happened?" But her ghost was nowhere to be seen, and the bodies never talked. Which was probably best, now that October thought about it. She had enough on her plate with the opinionated ghosts that surrounded her. No need to add zombies to the party.

Mrs. Davis was an elementary school teacher before she retired and volunteered at the library where she and October met. They had so many wonderful talks about books they read. Mrs. Davis never understood October's affinity for horror books. But, she respected October as a reader just the same. She always set the newest horror novels aside for October to have first dibs on when she came in.

Mrs. Davis preferred Jude Deveraux. They'd even traded genres once, but it had been a disaster. October couldn't buy into the Hallmark style feel good schmaltz, and Mrs. Davis was truly traumatized by the book she'd recommended. The Stand. Too much gore. Neither had made it to the end of their respective books, and agreed to just appreciate one and other as readers.

Even though October never saw her outside the library, she considered her a friend. And she didn't have many living friends. Or...any living friends if she was honest. Staring at the woman on the table made her realize, she wasn't in the mood for introspection, so she set to work. The familiarity of the tasks set her grieving mind at ease.

Her dad wasn't around as she finished getting Mrs. Davis comfortable, and she assumed he was somewhere chatting with her. As she turned off the lights and walked out, he startled her from behind the door.

"I hate it when you do that," she chided.

"What's the fun in being a ghost if you can't spook people occasionally?" He asked with a sly grin.

"Have you seen Mrs. Davis?" She asked as she methodically went through the building turning lights off and locking doors.

"No. She wasn't with you?"

Instinctively, October looked around, hoping to catch a glimpse of her. "No. I thought you were with her. Did you know, I used to chat with her at the library?"

"I didn't. I'm sorry, Boo."

"Yeah. Me too. I hope she turns up soon. I like her."

Her dad sighed and October couldn't help her own sigh. Those that hung around their loved ones instead of their bodies were the most difficult. She never knew just how to help the families, because their ghosts usually wouldn't talk to her. She thought Mrs. Davis mentioned her son, but October couldn't remember. Their conversations centered mostly around books.

"I'm meeting with her son tomorrow. Maybe we'll meet her then," she said hopefully. Although it was almost impossible to tear a ghost away from their family once they'd latched on. She could always try.

"Night dad." She blew him a kiss, and he caught it and held it to his heart, as he'd done ever since she could remember.

"See you in the morning, Boo."

October's apartment wasn't far from the funeral home, and most days she walked. Unless it was raining, or miserably cold. The early October air nipped at her face and she shoved her hands deeper into her pockets, wishing she'd brought a coat.

As she put the key in the door to the duplex she shared with an older woman who lived alone just like her, she could hear Queso screaming his little heart out.

5

She opened the door and the orange cat purred almost as loudly as he'd been meowing a moment ago.

"Nice to see you too, Bud." She picked him up and carried him to the chair by the window, as was their ritual when she got home.

She'd bought the place years ago. Before her father passed. He lived in the suite above the funeral home. After he died, she considered moving into it. It made the most sense. She did own the building after all. Why pay for another place? But it just didn't seem right.

The apartment was home. She assumed dad stayed in his apartment when she wasn't there, but she didn't know for sure. She never asked, and he never offered. He did still come over on Sundays though, to join her for dinner. He didn't eat anymore but he was always good company, and he seemed to enjoy spending some of his afterlife maintaining their traditions.

Queso ran over to the table, where a woman was sitting, and rubbed up against her legs, but she didn't seem to notice. Queso loved everyone, but especially ghosts. She had no idea if Queso was special, or if all animals could see and interact with ghosts. But she was always jealous of his ability to touch them. One thing she missed most was her dad's hug.

The woman had silver hair cut into a very trendy pixie for her age, and she wore jeans and a t-shirt that read "this is fine," but the expression on her face said otherwise.

"Mrs. Davis." October crossed the room going to her unexpected guest. Although she was dressed differently than when October had seen her on the table, there was no mistaking her gorgeous friend.

Mrs. Davis looked up as if she hadn't known October was there until just that moment. "I'm worried about Wilder."

"I'm sorry to hear that." October figured Wilder must

have been her son. For the life of her she didn't think the woman had ever mentioned his name.

"He's not used to being on his own. Not that he's a momma's boy, mind you. His friends are just horridly selfish. They won't be of any use. They'll all be busy with work, or their own families. I'm afraid I filled the gap more than I should have. He's had a tough life so far…" She didn't elaborate, and October didn't push.

A desperate tear ran down her cheek as she looked up at October.

Feeling like she had to do something for her friend, October scooped her keys off the table. "What kind of food does he like?"

"The brisket from Mission is his favorite."

"Perfect. What's the address?"

She rattled it off, and October put it into her phone.

"I'll go drop off some food right now. Will that make you feel better?" The relief in the ghost's eyes was all the answer October needed. "Wonderful. In the meantime, you might go and meet my father. He'll be sure to help you feel better."

"If it's all the same to you, I'll just go with you."

October nodded. "That's fine too."

She went to the car, and Mrs. Davis was already in the passenger seat when she got in. She looked out the window quietly, and October let the silence stretch comfortably in front of them while she drove to Mission BBQ on Main Street.

Mrs. Davis smiled widely as she got back in the car with a bag full of food, sauces, napkins, and utensils. "You didn't say what kind of drink he liked so I guessed and got him a Coke."

"That's perfect, dear. Thank you."

"Of course." October hesitated. Normally she didn't like

7

to push the ghosts. But Mrs. Davis had been a friend. She had questions. "Mrs. Davis, what happened?"

"Heart attack, I think. Which is a shame. That's exactly how Wilder's father died over twenty years ago. Poor kid shouldn't have to go through that twice."

October's heart broke for him. But Mrs. Davis didn't let her dwell on it.

"Wilder's a good boy. He deserves happiness. I really appreciate you doing this."

"It's the least I can do, Mrs. Davis," October assured her. She parked the car on the street and left it running. "I'll be right back."

"You're not going to go inside?" She acted like a knock and drop was out of the question.

"I hadn't planned on it."

"Well, what if he doesn't eat it?" She chewed the inside of her cheek and October turned to face her.

"Mrs. Davis. I only got one meal. If he's the gentleman I expect him to be, he wouldn't want to eat in front of me anyway. And, I expect he won't waste his favorite food, don't you think?"

"Yes. I hope you're right."

She nodded encouragingly as she went to deliver the package. She knocked on the door and left quickly, keeping her back to his doorbell camera. Last thing she wanted was him recognizing her at their meeting tomorrow and thinking she was some kind of stalker.

When she got back in the car, Mrs. Davis was gone. October could only assume she'd gone inside to be with Wilder, and there was nothing wrong with that. Sometimes, the dead needed more time to say goodbye. Sometimes it was the living who needed that. October hoped by the time her meeting with Wilder was over tomorrow, she'd know which was which.

CHAPTER 2

"I saw Mrs. Davis," October said the next morning when she found her father sitting in his favorite highbacked chair in the hallway reading a paper from two years before he passed away. He never read anything current, even though October kept a subscription to the local paper just for him. She never had the heart to ask him if he could, so she kept the paper coming just in case.

He folded the semitransparent paper and set it on the table next to his chair and looked at her from behind his gold rimmed glasses. "And?"

"She's anxious."

He nodded. "I figured as much, since she's yet to reunite with herself."

"I took food to her son last night at her request."

Dad raised an eyebrow at that. "You don't usually do that before the service."

She shrugged. "She was a friend of mine, Dad. And, she was at my kitchen table when I got home. I knew she wouldn't leave until she felt like her son was taken care of."

"You're getting soft in your old age."

She laughed and tossed a rose at him from a nearby vase. It landed flatly on the chair, as if he wasn't sitting there at all.

"And you're getting cheeky in your death," she retorted.

"Ha. Says you. I was always cheeky."

"True enough."

She spent the morning doing paperwork, getting ready for Mrs. Catrakas' service later that evening, and her meeting with Mrs. Davis' son.

Mrs. Catrakas fussed about the flowers people had delivered, and specified which ones she wanted at the front. "Joey. That old cheapskate. Don't put that measly thing by my head. Move that to the back. George. Now he always had an eye for me. Look at that beautiful bouquet," she smiled warmly, and October knew the feelings were mutual. "What songs did my son pick out for the viewing?"

October rattled off a few titles, but Mrs. Catrakas stopped her. "Oh no, that's such a boring list. Keep his of course, but add a few won't you? How about *We are Young*, and *Stronger* by that Kelly Clarkson? You know the one?" I nodded. "Of course you do. I'd like a bit of irony. Keep them laughing. And how about *It's a Great Day to be Alive*?"

"The Travis Tritt song? A bit on the nose don't you think?"

She giggled. "Exactly."

"No problem. I'll add them now."

At 2:40, October went downstairs and visited Mrs. Davis. She hadn't expected to find her ghost, but was pleasantly surprised. At least until she saw the dire expression on her face.

"We have a problem," she said.

October looked at her body. She hadn't done much prep work yet, but she had lots of time. She'd be ready for the service, so October was a little lost. "With what?"

"There's a ghost."

"Are you talking in third person like a queen again?"

Mrs. Davis blinked at October. "Again?"

October smiled, trying to lighten the mood, but the stress pulling at Mrs. Davis' eyebrows wouldn't let go.

"There's a ghost hanging around Wilder."

"I assume that's you?" October asked cautiously.

"Not just me. When you dropped me off last night I saw her. And she has the strangest impact on him. The closer she gets, the darker his mood."

Now it was October's turn to frown. "Who is it? Do you recognize her?"

She nodded. "It's Wilder's girlfriend. Abby Lennox."

October pulled a rolling stool over and sat down, but Mrs. Davis was too upset for sitting. "She died years ago. They were sixteen. Wilder was driving. He never really got over it. Now I know why."

October covered her mouth, which she only just realized had been hanging open. "That's awful."

"Her parents blamed us. We stayed for a little while, but it became almost dangerous for Wilder. The bullying. I lost count of how many times his car was vandalized."

"Why?"

"They wanted revenge. They called him a murderer."

"Was it his fault?" October asked before realizing how blunt her question was.

Mrs. Davis shook her head no. "But he still felt responsible. As you can imagine."

"Of course," October agreed.

"He didn't need her parents and friends giving voice to his dark thoughts." Mrs. Davis looked at her carefully. "He tried to end it once…"

"I am so sorry." October skooched her stool closer, and wanted so badly to take the ghost's hand. But Mrs. Davis was looking out the small window in the door.

"Me too. That's when we moved here. I wanted to offer him a fresh start. Where people didn't know our story."

"Well, it worked. I had no idea. He and I graduated the same year, didn't we?" She nodded, and October went on. "I didn't really know him. I was a weirdo, and he was new. Our paths never crossed in the class of almost five hundred kids. But there weren't any rumors I heard about him. You did a good job."

"And thank goodness. But apparently not as good as I'd hoped. She followed us."

"Where is she buried?" October asked.

"Back home. In Ohio."

"And she came all the way to Kingston? I've never heard of a ghost traveling so far from their body."

"What do you think it means?"

October tried to put the pieces together, but couldn't. She couldn't see the big picture. Why would she follow Wilder across the country like that? Why not stay with her parents if she was going to hang around?

"Have you heard from her parents? How are they doing?"

"No," Mrs. Davis' expression turned hard. "I wanted to make a clean break. They were grieving parents, and needed someone to blame. They were...unreasonable at best."

"I can understand that. Burying a child is very unnatural," October sympathized. "I just wondered if they'd moved on better than Wilder, because Abby wasn't hanging around them. I've found in some cases when the ghost hangs around their family, it can make it difficult for the living to properly grieve."

"That makes a lot of sense. And now that I know she's been hanging around for almost twenty years..." She paused and looked up at October with tears in her eyes. "Twenty years, October. She's been bringing this black cloud to him. I can't believe it. She's torturing him."

It was horrible. October had never heard of such a thing. Most ghosts moved on within a month. Her father was the only one she'd known to hang around as long as he had, and he wasn't hurting anything. He was helping her.

"Could she be helping him in some way?"

"Absolutely not. He's a shell of himself. Made worse because of my death I'm sure, but helping is the exact opposite of what she's doing. Every time he gets upset, she almost clings to him. This bluish grey haze settles on him, and he slumps over like the weight of his life is just too much."

She looked up with terror in her eyes. "What if it *is* too much. What if…"

October held up her hands. "Wilder is coming to see me in half an hour. You'll see for yourself he's functional."

She knew she shouldn't have said that. She had no way of knowing just how functional he was, nor should she make promises she had no influence over. But Mrs. Davis was working herself right into a proper tizzy. Frankly, October couldn't blame her.

Mrs. Davis looked up at October with pleading eyes. "You have to do something."

October pushed her stool back reflexively. "Like what?"

"I don't know. You can talk to her. Tell her to leave him alone. It's clear she's making him unhappy. Why would she do that to him? She was such a nice girl in life. A bit selfish and vain, but who isn't at sixteen?"

October's frown deepened. "Realistically, when do you want me to do this? If she follows him here, I can't exactly speak to her like I am with you. We're alone. Wilder would think I'm a total whack job if I just start ignoring him and addressing his dead girlfriend."

"Mmm." Concern etched Mrs. Davis' face while she chewed on their predicament.

"I can't exactly go to his house and expect to be able to

talk to her there either. He'd think I'm an absolute stalker showing up at his house, not even wanting to talk to him. Undertakers are given some allowances to be nutters, but not that much, I assure you, Mrs. Davis."

She threw up her hands in frustration. "Well, you have to do something. No one else can see her. Not even Wilder."

"You can. Did you try talking to her?"

"I did. I asked her why she was there. Told her it was good to see her after all those years. Tried to be motherly with her. But she got upset when I suggested she move on. She said she couldn't abandon him. That they were soul mates, can you believe that? Soul mates wouldn't hurt each other so much."

Deeper into the rabbit hole I go, October thought to herself as she chewed the inside of her cheek searching for a solution. Only once had she had a ghost angry enough to flicker the lights on her. And that had been after some long-lost ex showed up at the service and spoke to her husband. The ex said he was sorry he ever let her go, and that he never stopped loving her. He even implied a part of her still loved him. Mrs. Fielding was so angry that the ex would plant that seed in her poor husband's mind, the lights went out in the room for a full thirty seconds. October politely, but sternly, asked the ex to leave, and then spent an hour trying to calm Mrs. Fielding down, all while soothing the ghost's poor husband. She ended up telling him she didn't believe it for a minute. That she thought the ex was just being manipulative, which was all things Mrs. Fielding was feeding to her. He looked at her with such gratitude in the end. Mrs. Fielding hung around for about a week after that, making sure her husband was all right. And October still sent him brownies every year, on the anniversary of her service. Mrs. Fielding said they were his favorite. He always stopped by to thank her, and every year he had a little more color, was a little more relaxed, and had a little bigger smile.

Maybe this could work out that way too. October just didn't know how to get there.

"Well. Wilder will be here shortly. Stick around, and maybe we will see a way to help," she offered.

Mrs. Davis looked over at her, daring to hope. She reached out her hand, and October reached back, but passed right through the ghostly figure.

"I'm so glad you're here," Mrs. Davis said at the same time October was thinking it.

CHAPTER 3

*P*romptly at 2:55, Wilder Davis awkwardly walked into the funeral home followed closely by a teenage girl. She was lovely. Long blonde hair cascaded angelically around her shoulders, and she clutched Wilder's arm as if he was leading her inside, without him even knowing. She watched the girl fawn over Wilder, as if no one else existed in the world except them. Only problem was, her beau couldn't see her.

Mrs. Davis snuck in behind them with a disapproving scowl on her face. She made pleading eye contact with October, and October took a deep breath before greeting Wilder at the double doors.

"Mr. Davis. I'm October Manning. Can I get you anything? Water, beer, wine?"

"Water's fine," he said. His voice was scratchy as if it hadn't been used in awhile. Or maybe was raw from crying? Maybe both.

"Perfect. I'll meet you in my office with it in just a moment." She gestured toward her open office door and watched as he found his way inside.

As she added a little lemon to his water Mrs. Davis accosted her. "See? See what I mean?"

October hoped her startle wasn't visible. "I do. I believed you, I promise," she whispered, hoping not to draw attention to the fact that she was talking to no one visible.

"What's your plan?" The ghost looked eagerly at the door, ready to spring into action.

"I'm afraid I don't have one." Mrs. Davis shot her a look, so she amended her statement. "Yet. Let me talk to him and see if inspiration strikes."

"You're just going to wait for inspiration to strike? That's your master plan?"

She put her free hand on her hip. "If you have a better idea, I'm all ears."

Mrs. Davis frowned. "Fine. But I'm coming with you."

October shrugged, giving up. "The more the merrier."

She found Wilder sitting on the couch looking out the front window, Abby sitting by his side stroking his leg, although October knew he couldn't feel it in a conventional way. He might get a chill, or goosebumps without knowing why, but it wouldn't feel like the ghost meant it to. She refused to acknowledge October's existence, only having eyes for Wilder. It creeped October out.

Wilder had short, brown hair, and a scraggly beard she wasn't sure was always there or if he just hadn't shaved in light of what had happened. Although he'd worn a dress shirt and slacks, he hadn't ironed them, and his beautiful green eyes were red-rimmed.

October followed his gaze out the window and noticed the color had already settled in nicely, and the street outside was lined with reds and yellows. But she didn't think Wilder was looking at that.

She set his drink down on the coffee table in front of him, and sat in the armchair nearby, saying nothing. Cars going by tousled the leaves that had already fallen, twirling in their wake. She found herself hoping the magic of the season could crack the walls Wilder, and maybe Abby, had built around himself.

Mrs. Davis sat on the couch next to him. Abby glared at her, and October tried to telepathically tell Mrs. Davis to tread lightly. Of course, that wasn't one of the talents she possessed. Ghosts couldn't hear her thoughts, which she generally appreciated. Only then did she see how handy that little perk would've been.

After about ten minutes of companionable silence, he finally reached for his water, took a long drink, and looked at October. "I'm sorry Ms. Manning. I don't mean to take so much of your time. I just...I don't know how to do this."

"You're doing just fine," she assured him.

He snorted, and October knew he didn't feel just fine. "How do we proceed?"

She guided him through the particulars. Urn, cremation, service, all the things. That part never took long. It was the part after. The part where they were done making decisions, but still had to execute them that was tough. The limbo before the closure that the service would bring.

"So, we're all set for Monday at two for the viewing, six for the service, and then she'll be cremated, as requested," she confirmed.

"And that'll be it." His voice was small and distant. As if a part of him wasn't here with her.

"Well. Yes and no I suppose." He dragged his eyes away from the window to October's face with some effort, and Abby followed suit, looking at October for the first time. "This isn't the hard part you think it is."

"Well, that's encouraging," he said.

October ignored his sarcasm and pressed on. "It's the living. Once this is over, people will be less patient. They'll expect you to start to go back to normal. As if you haven't just lost a limb, an essential part of your being. It's not a very nice expectation."

He blinked at her, as if he hadn't even considered what would happen on Wednesday, or Thursday, or any of the days after. He probably hadn't. To him, they didn't exist.

She reached across and laid a gentle hand on his arm. Abby revolted, and tried to push her hand away, but couldn't make contact. So, she pushed Wilder's water over instead, and left in a huff.

Both of them stood and she went to get paper towels. He apologized profusely and didn't understand. "Neither of us were near it," he insisted.

"I must have bumped the table when I reached over," October explained calmly, although she was more than a little worried about Abby, and her powerful impact on Wilder and his environment. It was rare to see a ghost actually move an object in the living world. And Abby seemed to have done it without a second thought. What else could she do? October worked to push her growing concerns aside and focus on Wilder.

He sat back down and watched her wipe up the water, a confused expression on his face.

"Penny for your thoughts?" October asked.

"I'm sorry. I just…never mind," he wiped his hand back and forth in front of him, as if wiping his slate clean.

"No really. Is there something I can do?"

"No. Just, all of a sudden, I feel as if a weight is off my shoulders."

Mrs. Davis and October shared a telling look.

"I haven't felt like this in…well. It doesn't matter how long." He looked up at her with such gratitude, and for the first time in a long time she felt uncomfortable around a client. She hadn't done anything, except run a jealous ghost off by touching him.

"Grief is a funny thing. It comes in waves. Enjoy the ebbs while you can. I'm not going to tell you it will be okay. Because it probably won't for a while. And that's okay. Let that be enough," October offered.

He turned to the window and the leaves outside, but October could tell his posture was much straighter than he was when he walked in. As if a weight had been lifted off his shoulders. Mrs. Davis was right. Abby was doing a real number on him.

"How much time did they give you off work?" She ventured. He seemed hesitant to disturb this newfound lightness he felt, and she didn't need to do anything else for at least another hour, so she could indulge him. Although she knew Mrs. Catrakas was probably pacing around out there ready for the attention to be on her.

"I own the business. I can go back when I want. I probably should go back sooner rather than later. I just…" He dragged his eyes away from the leaves outside. "I can't seem to focus." October thought she caught a hint of anger in his voice, but she didn't comment on it.

"That's understandable. Like it or not, your life is different now, without this key person. Even if you didn't talk to her every day—"

"I did," he interrupted. "I mean. I didn't call. I don't like talking on the phone. But we texted a lot."

October smiled. "That's sweet. So, it's even more of an adjustment. You'll think of something you want to tell her, and take out your phone. Not until you're part way through sending it will you realize she won't get it."

"I've sent a few."

October nodded. She'd done that too when she was alone in her apartment. It was so easy to forget her dad was dead and didn't have a phone anymore. Those times when it smacked her in the face weren't her favorite.

Wilder looked at her with those green eyes October thought would pierce her soul, and she sat up a little straighter, hoping she passed inspection. "How do you know all this?"

"I'm around grief a lot." She didn't like to share with her clients that her dad died. Sometimes that would lead them to question her abilities, since he'd started the funeral home before she was even born.

"I suppose that's true. But I'd think that would make you rather jaded toward it."

October thought about that. "That could be true for some people. But I've also experienced it first-hand. My dad died ten years ago, leaving me to run the business by myself." She didn't know what it was about him that made her tell him something so personal. Her desire to help him, combined with the familiarity of his grief disarmed her more than she'd like to admit.

"Where's your mom? Doesn't she help out?" He asked.

She shifted uncomfortably.

"I'm sorry," he held up his hands in surrender. "That was inappropriate. You don't have to answer. It's just...easy to talk to you." He seemed surprised by his own admission.

She smiled. "It is easy to talk to you." She didn't try to hide her own surprise.

He smirked, and she liked how relaxed he looked when he did it. "You say that like it's odd."

Mrs. Davis clapped, startling October. "October! It's working. Look, he's smiling. I knew you'd be able to help."

October grabbed her chest and tried to slow her racing heart. She'd nearly forgotten Mrs. Davis was there.

"Are you okay? What happened?" Wilder asked, reaching out for her.

She tried to think on the spot, but she wasn't the best liar. "Sorry. I just...two cars almost hit each other out there. It was close."

"Nice cover. I'm so sorry dear. I didn't mean to startle you," Mrs. Davis said, and October couldn't look at her.

Wilder was clearly confused about the change in mood, so October worked to pick their conversation back up. "Sorry. What were we saying?"

"That it's easy to talk to me? But maybe you spoke too soon," he teased.

She forced a laugh, but he could tell it wasn't genuine and stood up. "I'm sorry. I should go. I've gone over on our time quite a bit." He stuck out his hand for her to shake.

"It's fine. The dead are surprisingly patient," she said with a wink, and it was his turn to look startled.

"Are we now?" Mrs. Catrakas yelled from the hall, and October fought the urge to roll her eyes.

"Sorry. I guess you're not ready for undertaker humor." She cringed and let go of his hand like it was on fire, and he barked out a single laugh.

"Is *that* what that was? Ok. Well, that's kinda funny then." He chuckled once more. "Anyway, thank you for making this part easy."

"Of course, Mr. Davis."

"Wilder. Please call me Wilder."

She smiled warmly at him as they walked to the front door together. "Wilder. I'll see you Monday."

"Great." He stammered. "Well, not great. But...you know what I mean."

"I do. Go enjoy the rest of your day."

"I will." As she watched him go, she noticed he was walking taller than he was when he came in. But how long would Abby leave him alone? Where had she gone? Had she ever left him like that before? She sighed. Her questions would have to wait. She had work to do.

"That went well," Mrs. Davis said as soon as she turned around to come back inside.

"Except for the part where you scared me half to death."

"I know. I'm so sorry." She reached out for October but passed right through. How did Abby touch Wilder so easily? Maybe it was a skill that came with time. She was clearly a powerful ghost, tipping over water glasses like that. Her dad couldn't really do much of any of that. Then again, he'd never really tried. The first time they'd tried to hug, it upset them both so much, he never did it again, and reverted to blowing her kisses, like he did when he was alive. October resolved to ask him about it the next time she saw him.

"Don't worry about it. We just have to try to remember he doesn't know you're there. Do you think Abby will leave him alone now?" October asked hopefully.

"No. That would be way too easy."

October frowned. Hearing her concerns voiced out loud wasn't exactly the comfort she was looking for.

"Why the frowns? Boo, you making friends again?" Steve asked.

"Apparently. Since I'm so good at it."

He laughed and stuck out a hand. "Mrs. Davis, so nice to finally meet you."

She took his hand hesitantly, and October watched while they made actual contact with each other. Her dad's expression changed to one of absolute delight, and he put his other hand over hers while they shook. He never got over those rare occasions when he could have physical contact with another ghost.

"Steve Manning. I owned this place before. Now my daughter runs it for me, and I help her when I can, with ghosts like you." He turned to October.

"Dad I need to talk to you about something."

"In a minute," he said while he looked at Mrs. Davis. "I hear you have need for an exorcism."

Mrs. Davis let a giggle escape, and October looked at her, startled. It was a sound she'd never heard from her friend. Far too girlish for the distinguished woman.

"Well. She's not a demon. Just a teenager."

"Potato, potahtoe." Steve winked at Mrs. Davis knowingly, prompting another giggle from her. October looked between the two of them, trying to decipher what was going on.

"Hate to break up the love fest here, but my body's getting cold up there." Mrs. Catrakas always did know how to make an entrance.

"Oh, there are more." Although Mrs. Davis seemed shocked, she didn't seem bothered. She was almost glad for more company.

"Miriam Catrakas. My service is tonight, and it's going to be good. You should hang around for it."

"Thank you, but I think I'll pass. I have a few things on my mind." October looked to her dad, who missed her cue entirely because he was too busy looking at Mrs. Davis' profile.

October rolled her eyes. "Dad. Maybe Mrs. Davis would like somewhere quiet? Maybe you could explain all this to her, like you should've done yesterday?"

"Well, she didn't come around. Not like I could've," he defended himself.

"No time like the present," October insisted.

He held out his arm. "Might I interest you in a quiet spot and some light conversation?"

"Don't let him fool you. We had loud music and a few laughs," Mrs. Catrakas interjected.

"If you'd prefer a distraction, I can offer you that too," Steve said.

Mrs. Davis hesitated and looked back and forth between the two ghosts, but October tried to ease her worries. "Mrs. Catrakas is right. Our little...problem will have to wait. Her guests will be arriving soon. Go upstairs with my dad. Talk it out. Maybe he can offer you some insights."

"Maybe I could use some company too, Steven." Mrs. Catrakas refused to call her dad Steve, and he'd stopped correcting her after the third time. October was proud of him. In another time he would've kept at it like a dog with a bone.

Mrs. Catrakas put her arm around Mrs. Davis, and shepherded her down the hall, toward her dad's upstairs apartment.

October could only hope the two of them might have a solution.

MRS. CATRAKAS' service went off without a hitch, and while a few naysayers commented on the music, or the fact that their beautiful arrangement was relegated to the back, most people, the ones who knew her best, said it was a very fitting service.

The ghost debated lingering after, to help Mrs. Davis. After all, a renegade ghost sounded like fun. Or so she'd said. October had her own thoughts about having a renegade ghost around. But October's dad said he had things well in hand, and she shouldn't linger unnecessarily. So, off she went.

October always tried not to think about where they went too hard. It led to thinking about where her dad should be. And guilt soon followed. Best not to zero in on it at all. Guilt made it very difficult to be productive.

As the week went on and Mrs. Davis' agitation didn't subside, October hoped her service would bring some solutions.

"Dad, she's relentless," October said as she closed her computer down and pushed back from her desk. "She wants me over at his place every night. I had to put my foot down. He'll think I'm a stalker."

He watched her from the couch where Wilder had sat days ago. "She's just upset. Her son is being stalked by a ghost that's been hanging around longer than me." October thought he looked a little green at the idea.

"She can touch him. Did Mrs. Davis tell you?"

He looked at her, and October didn't miss the longing in his eyes. "Aurora mentioned it. Yes."

"How do you think she does that?"

He stood up and went to her bookcase, looking at the books she had, closing some of the distance between them. "I'm not really sure. Mrs. Davis is so new, she didn't have any thoughts. She didn't really know we couldn't touch people. Especially after your odd little cat rubbed up against her."

"I don't know what's so special about Queso. Maybe all animals can do it for all I know."

"I swear a bird flew right through me the other day." Her dad indignantly put his hands on his hips.

"I was there."

Her dad scowled. "I remember your laughing."

October cringed at the memory. "That woman in the parking lot thought I was laughing at her."

"No more than you deserve." He walked closer to her. They were close enough to touch, if they could.

"So maybe not *all* animals," she amended with a smile as her dad watched her.

"Maybe with a little practice." He reached out for her, his concentration drawing a deep line between his eyebrows.

But no luck. As soon as his hand began to pass through hers, he withdrew it like he'd touched a hot stove and retreated back to the couch.

Before he could apologize, October spoke up. "One thing at a time, Dad. We have a bigger problem here. I've never seen a ghost impact someone like that for so long before. What can we do?"

"I don't have an answer for that either, I'm afraid. Except to keep doing what you're doing. Maybe, the more time you spend around him, the more she'll vanish, and eventually, she just won't come back?" It was a question, a hope he was offering, not a solution.

They sat in silence, pondering what to do. October came up empty and looked over at her dad, who was wearing a serious expression on his face. "Do you think that fear of the unknown is why that young ghost won't leave? When Mrs. Catrakas left, where do you think she went?" He asked.

"Geeze, Dad, I didn't think about it like that. You don't know where the ghosts go?"

"Do you?" He demanded.

"No. I just assumed since you were one of them, you knew."

"Well, I don't."

October didn't know what to say. The conversation had taken such a turn. "You're not afraid, are you? That's not why you've stayed all this time is it?"

A small smile pulled at the corner of his mouth. "No, Boo. That's not why I've stayed."

"Do you want to know?" She asked quietly.

He looked up at her, all reservation gone from his face. It was replaced with tenderness as he closed the distance between them. Okay, he walked through the table, which even after ten years October wasn't used to.

He held his hand above hers, and it looked like they were

touching. She couldn't feel him though, and it made her heart ache. "I do want to know. Someday. Not today though."

"Tomorrow?" She felt like a five-year-old kid, seeking reassurance from her daddy.

"Not tomorrow either, Boo. I won't go until you are ready. I promise."

"What if I never am?"

"Then we can find out where Mrs. Catrakas went together."

"I love you, dad."

He smiled warmly at her. "I love you to, Boo."

CHAPTER 4

*W*ilder could not settle. He wasn't sleeping well, nothing sounded good. Although he did appreciate the mystery meal left on his doorstep a few days ago. He felt the most at ease in October Manning's office. Which was just weird.

Maybe it was the closure she offered. Once the funeral was over, he'd have to move on. But was he ready for that? It had always been he and his mom. His dad had a heart attack when Wilder was so young, he barely remembered him. His mom said she always wanted more kids, but without his dad that wasn't going to happen now, was it? So that left the two of them. Peas in a pod she said.

But he wasn't a momma's boy. He had his life. His landscaping business. His friends. But she was always there. He took care of her. Fixed the house when it needed repairs mostly. Drove her to the doctor when she turned her ankle. And she took care of him.

Dinner at her house at least twice a week. Best meals he had all week. And she always went with him to garden shows. She tended to reign in his spending when he wanted all the things. New breeds of flowers. New equipment. New software systems to manage the back end better. He hated that part. And since the business had blown up, there was more and more of it. He couldn't think of the last time he'd actually gotten his hands dirty.

All kids expect to outlive their parents. It's the natural order of things. And Wilder knew that better than most, he expected. But perhaps because his dad died so young, he thought his mom would live forever. Like the universe's payment for stealing his father away.

Tomorrow. Tomorrow was the day he'd say goodbye to his mother. And he'd be one pea, alone in the pod.

As he laid down in bed with the TV on to give him something to focus on other than his dead mother, he knew he was not at all ready to move on.

THE DAY dawned annoyingly bright and cheerful for early October. Where were the clouds and cold that made you want to put your head down and fold your arms across your chest? That matched his mood. Nope. The day was sunny, and the air was crisp making the sky a beautifully vibrant blue. It was the kind of weather Wilder liked to work in. Why couldn't the weather ever cooperate?

With every step closer to the funeral home, he got grumpier and grumpier. Until October greeted him at the glass double doors.

"Welcome Mr. Davis." Her voice was hushed, and calming, and completely disarmed him. He didn't know what to do with himself. His dress shoes were already rubbing on his heels, and he wanted to stay mad. Because when he wasn't, he felt like crying. And he didn't cry in front of other people. So, he focused on the pain in his heels.

"I asked you before to call me Wilder." It came out more

gruff than he intended, but he couldn't bring himself to apologize.

"Of course. Wilder. Can I take your coat?"

He noticed she was looking at something next to him as he handed it to her, and he looked but he didn't see anything. She smiled at him as if it was nothing, and hung his coat in a closet in the hall filled with hangers and Wilder's lone coat. He expected that's where everyone would hang their things. His friends. His mom's friends. They had no family left. Her parents had died when he was in his twenties. And his dad's parents never tried to be involved after he died. They said he was too much of a reminder of their son who, in their opinion, refused to follow the natural order.

He questioned it when he was a kid. Sent them drawings. Tried. Because he didn't know how to deal with another loss. But soon the things he sent them came back with a yellow "Return to Sender" sticker on them. So, he stopped. He didn't even know if they were still alive.

Both his parents were only children, so he'd never had aunts or uncles. He was a lone pea, rolling across the floor and under the piano. Forgotten and left to shrivel.

October must have seen the despair on his face. She put a warm cup of coffee in his hands, and held it with him for a beat.

She looked into his eyes and laid a hand on his shoulder. "This will be a day."

He offered her a weak smile. "This will be a day."

He liked that she never offered him false comfort. She never said it would be okay. Or he'd get through it. He knew he would. That wasn't what he wanted to hear. But his friends were so full of those kinds of words. October was so different, he found himself drawn to her.

He thought he heard the front door click closed, and turned. "People already?"

She frowned but schooled her face into a more comforting expression so fast he thought he'd imagined her initial displeasure. "No. I need to get that door fixed. It gets caught in the wind sometimes. Makes it tough to heat the lobby in the winter."

He nodded. "So, what now?"

"Would you like to see her?"

No. Not even a little bit. "Of course." The words were automatic, and his feet followed suit. The traitors forced him to follow behind October like a sad puppy.

She opened a set of white double doors next to the closet and gestured for him to go in.

"It's um…pink," he commented.

There were pink walls, and a strange green carpet. The couches were scattered around, and folding chairs were set up in rows around them. Floral arrangements lined the walls on pedestals and high tables. He looked everywhere at everything until he had nothing left to look at except the front of the room.

"Yes. I wanted to change it, but my dad says it complements the flowers."

"Ten years and you still talk about him like he's here with you."

She laughed nervously and shifted her weight. "I suppose I do."

Reluctantly, he turned to the front of the room. Two huge arrangements flanked the casket he'd rented for the occasion. The casket. Where his mother was.

He was frozen to his spot. He couldn't move forward, and he couldn't get away. His heart raced and he gulped air like he was drowning. He was drowning.

October put a hand on his elbow, and he was snapped back to the present. He looked at her and only her. Her blue eyes felt like the ocean he was drowning in. But somehow, he found comfort in them. Like maybe he wouldn't drown at all. Maybe he would float.

"Wilder? Would you like me to go with you?"

He didn't need her to go with him. He was a grown man. He could do it. But he nodded his head anyway.

"Most people have spouses, or siblings to go with them. You shouldn't feel less than because you don't want to go alone. That's not fair at all," she offered.

And again, she'd found just what he needed to hear. He found himself clutching her hand as they walked toward the front of the room. He held his breath with every step they took. If he didn't breathe, it wasn't real.

Before he was ready, they were close enough that he could see her. She looked peaceful, as if she was sleeping. October had done a lovely job with her makeup, and that almost made it worse. She didn't look...like she was gone.

The tears came hard and fast. So fast he didn't have time to be embarrassed. She held him, and it was almost like a reflex. Like she'd done it a hundred times before with grieving family members. And she probably had. And yet, he still felt like she cared.

He had no idea how long he stood there in her arms, but she didn't rush him, or push. It was Tim from work that broke up the moment.

"Wilder?" He called tentatively from the back of the room.

Wilder straightened and looked at October horrified at his outpouring. But she wasn't ruffled. She produced a tissue from who knew where, and went to greet the guest, gently turning his back to his employee.

"Hello Mr..." she trailed off, giving him an opportunity to fill in his name.

"Tim McDee. I work for Wilder." They shook hands.

"Can I get you a drink? Coffee or water?"

"Oh yeah. Coffee sounds great."

"Why don't you join me? We have a wide selection of those pods so you can pick out what sounds good."

"Of course." He turned to Wilder. "Back in a bit, Wilder."

Wilder nodded, afraid to turn around. What had happened? He hadn't cried like that in a long time. Not even when he heard the news. The call came early that morning. It had been quick. A heart attack, just like his dad. It had hit him so hard, he'd gone numb. Yes, he'd cried when the news sunk in. But not like that. Not like he had in October's arms. Like he was safe there, and he could let it out. He cleared his throat and turned to his mom.

"What am I going to do?" He asked her, but she didn't respond. "Oh of course, the one time in your life you have nothing to say."

He'd gathered himself completely by the time October returned with Tim and a dozen others. She smiled at him, and he nodded back, letting her know he was okay. And he didn't even have to fake it. He *was* okay.

Tim was great. Didn't even acknowledge what he'd seen, which Wilder wasn't sure if it was because he was his boss, or because that's just the kind of kid Tim was. At twenty-four, he'd been working for Wilder about five years, and he'd always been steady, on time, and a hard worker. But after that moment, Wilder appreciated his discretion the most.

The service was...the service as October would say. Wilder couldn't call it nice. Nice was a word you used for things like daisies, and warm days, and soft blankets. Funerals weren't nice. It was a funeral. End of story.

Lots of people came. Not just his friends, but her friends too. Friends from Bunco, which was apparently some dice game she played on Thursday nights. Wilder was convinced it was just a reason to get together and drink a glass of cheap wine and giggle. He'd walked in one Thursday when it was at her house to fix the faucet, and the things he heard. Well, let's just say you don't forget Betty's comments about pigs in a blanket easily. Especially when the pig was her husband.

Wilder had a hard time looking at Betty with a straight face while she tried to offer her condolences that day. But he did his best. He played it safe and completely avoided eye contact with her husband.

Besides a few stand outs, like Betty, it was a sea of faces to Wilder. The "I'm so sorry for your loss," and "my deepest condolences" became a blur, and he felt like a bobble head, just nodding along while he tried to be polite.

By the end, he felt numb again. Nothing like he did after his outburst with October. So, he lingered. After the last person left, he just couldn't bring himself to leave.

October checked on him about fifteen minutes after their last visitor left. She didn't ask how he was doing. Or what he thought of the service. She just stood with him. Of course, she busied herself repairing an arrangement that had gotten a bit mangled, but she didn't push him to speak, or leave.

"You can take any of these arrangements home with you, if you like. Or I can donate them."

"Where?" He asked, as he looked at the one nearest his mom's head.

"Hospice will usually take them. Some patients like flowers in their room."

He frowned. "Isn't that a little morbid, sending flowers from a funeral to a Hospice patient? Like, you're next?"

October laughed, and then cleared her throat, as if catching herself. "I never thought of it that way. I'm not sure they know where the flowers came from, Wilder. And you have to admit, they are lovely. Seems a waste to just toss them."

"This one here, from the funeral home. It's the only one with iris.' How did you know that was her favorite?"

October smiled. "I knew your mother, Wilder. I met her at the library."

"I didn't realize that. But of course you did. She knew everyone between her job teaching and the library."

"And most of them were here tonight. It was a very nice turnout."

He nodded numbly. "I think I'll take that one home. Donate the rest to whoever you think will appreciate them."

She turned back to him and offered him a comforting nod. "Consider it done."

"October, I just want to say thank you. For…" For what? Not bolting over his inappropriate show of emotion? For being a bit of a rock through this whole thing? For helping him in ways he didn't know he needed? "Well, for everything," he finally settled on.

"Of course, Wilder. I'm so happy I could help."

"I just. I don't know how I would've gotten through this without you."

"You would've. Times like these reveal amazing strengths you didn't know you had." She looked over at his mom and smiled sadly. "I was alone when my dad died. I had to do everything. Run the service, greet everyone, arrange the burial, everything."

"Oh." Suddenly, Wilder felt stupid for feeling sorry for himself. She'd been through everything he had, and she'd done it alone.

She looked over at him and saw his horrified expression. "Oh no. I didn't tell you that so you'd feel sorry for me." She shook her head. "I was just saying it's not me that made the difference here. You'd have gotten through it whether I was here or not."

But Wilder wasn't so sure about that.

CHAPTER 5

October sat in her dad's apartment after the service, drinking a cup of tea with two ghosts. "Where were you?"

Mrs. Davis fidgeted. "Steve thought it best if I stayed away during the service. He said it can be odd to see your own body. Although, didn't that Catrakas woman go to hers?"

"Mrs. Catrakas marched to the beat of her own drum," October offered.

October wished she could hold Mrs. Davis' hand. She was trying to tear a piece of paper sitting unbothered on the table in front of her. It was something she did at the library when she was working out a problem. She'd make fringe on the edge of a discarded scrap until she'd arrived at some solution. October asked her about it once, and she said it helped her focus, and settled her nerves. But she couldn't seem to make contact with the paper she was trying to tear.

"How did it go?" Mrs. Davis finally asked after sighing and giving up on the paper.

"Your service was lovely."

"Not the service. I'm sure you did a fine job. With Abby," the ghost insisted.

October stole a look at her father, who was watching her intently. He'd been just as curious about the ghost who was so powerful. "She left."

"She what?" Mrs. Davis said.

"And Wilder sobbed in my arms."

"He *what*? We are talking about *my* son right?"

October nodded.

"Tell me everything."

October did her best to regale them with the tale, but there wasn't much to tell in the end. "Abby didn't hang around. She seemed put out when I was trying to comfort him and slammed the door behind her."

Mrs. Davis frowned at that. "Always did have a flare for the dramatics, that girl. But I thought she'd grow out of it. Not sure I knew a sixteen-year-old girl who didn't."

"She never got the chance to grow out of it, did she?" Steve asked. "It's sad."

"Don't tell me you feel bad for the ghost that's been terrorizing my son for over twenty years." Mrs. Davis folded her arms over her chest and glared at her dad. October hid her giggle behind a cough.

"What's so funny?" She demanded and October straightened.

"Nothing. I just, don't think my dad has ever met his match before."

Steve shot her a glare but quickly schooled his face when he caught Mrs. Davis looking at him. "It's all right to have a slightly different opinion, isn't it, Aurora?"

"Depends on if your opinion is wrong."

October didn't even try to stifle her laugh when she got up to refill her tea.

"Now, don't get me wrong, Aurora. I don't like how she's hanging around. It seems unhealthy." He looked away from October when he said the word 'unhealthy.' "But you can't deny what happened to her was tragic."

"No one said it wasn't. I lived through it, Steve. I watched that tragedy unfold."

Her dad reached out for Mrs. Davis' hand and October was glad he could give her some tangible comfort. He never had trouble making contact with other ghosts. Just the living.

"She slammed the door, you say?" Steve asked.

"She did."

"Do you think I could learn to do that?"

October puzzled at her dad. "Why would you need to?"

He shrugged. "Might be a fun parlor trick."

"Oh sure, pull it out at all the best funerals. Really set the mood." October rolled her eyes.

He looked over at her. "If I could touch the door, maybe I could...maybe I could touch you."

"Oh," October said quietly. "I hadn't thought of that."

"What do you think, Mrs. Davis?"

"I'm not sure. In all my years as a teacher, and volunteer at the library, I never read anything about new ghosts, or ghosts having to learn skills. They always just...knew what to do."

It was Steve's turn to roll his eyes. "Yes well. Isn't that convenient?"

"Well. If a sixteen-year-old girl can pick it up, I'm sure you can, Steve Manning. Quit sulking," Mrs. Davis scolded. Steve straightened and Mrs. Davis nodded. "Maybe I could help you try to figure it out, and you and October could help me evict the ghost that's haunting my son?"

October held up her hands. "Whoa. What if I don't have any luck? I don't want to enter into any kind of agreement here. What if I can't hold up my end of the bargain?"

"The same could happen with us. I'm just a baby ghost."

Steve raised his eyebrow at her. "Don't look like a baby to me."

October wasn't sure how she felt about the way he was looking at Mrs. Davis, and cleared her throat.

Mrs. Davis took that as her cue. "My point is, will you be angry and dissolve our agreement if we don't have any luck?"

"No. I would *try* to help. I was already trying to help. The keyword there is try. There are no guarantees. Especially if she won't hang around so I can talk to her."

"Mmm," Mrs. Davis agreed. "That is a problem. One we have time to solve." She brightened considerably. "Thank you both. I feel better having the beginnings of a plan."

October wasn't so sure. They had nothing, except an agreement to try. But maybe that was enough. And maybe October Manning would sprout wings and call herself a hummingbird. It seemed just as likely.

TWO DAYS LATER, October called Wilder to let him know his mother was ready for pickup. Even though she'd told him to expect her call, he seemed surprised to hear from her. Almost excited.

"Wilder? Hi, it's October."

"Oh hi. What can I do for you?" She could hear the smile in his voice, and she hated to be the one to take that away.

"I wanted to let you know, your mother is ready to be picked up."

"Oh." She could picture his shoulders slumping as the weight of what she'd said settled over him.

"You can pick her up whenever you like."

"Okay."

"I will tell you, if you come after six tonight, no one else will be here." She liked to offer this to families, just in case they needed privacy. Like a burial, the process of picking up your loved one can be tough. Some people aren't ready for the closure it brings.

His tone picked up a bit. "Oh. Sure, that would be great."

"Okay. See you then?"

"Sure." He didn't sound sure, like he'd agreed to something he wasn't quite ready for.

"If you're not ready, there are plenty of times when there's no one here," she offered, giving him an out if he needed.

"No. That'll be fine. See you tonight then."

"Okay. Looking forward to it." It was out before she could stop it.

"Sorry, I can't say the same."

"Of course not. I apologize. I shouldn't have said that." She smacked her forehead as silently as she could.

He chuckled. "See you around six."

"Okay then." She hung up before she could make it any worse, and looked over at Mrs. Davis who'd been leaning against the frame of her office door. "Not a word. I'm a professional."

"Oh absolutely. Judging by that call, a professional of the highest caliber," she needled. "Perhaps I should've asked a different undertaker who talks to ghosts to help. Someone with better social skills?" She grinned, and October knew she was teasing, but still.

"I think you'll find anyone who talks to ghosts to be impaired in the social arena."

"Is that so? Maybe you need Wilder just as much as he needs you then?" October didn't like the look of Mrs. Davis' self-satisfied smile one bit. "What an interesting thought."

October launched a tissue box at her, and it hit the wall

directly behind her. Mrs. Davis cackled and walked away, leaving October alone with her thoughts.

WILDER WALKED in at 6:01 with bags in his hands, and Abby on his arm. October brought his mother's urn up after her last appointment and had it on her desk along with a small arrangement she'd kept from her service.

"What's all this?" She asked as he set the bags on the coffee table by the couches.

"Dinner. I figured you hadn't eaten." He began unpacking the food, and Abby sat on the couch next to him, glaring at October.

October worked to ignore the ghost. She didn't know what to say. Usually she took care of her clients, not the other way around. "I actually have not eaten. Thank you." She walked around her desk and sat down.

"I got Mission. I hope you like bar-b-que. It's my favorite place."

"Don't shoot me, but I've never eaten there."

He stopped unpacking the food and looked at her like she'd just sprouted a second head on her shoulders, and it was spouting Latin at him. "You've never eaten at Mission? Why not? What's wrong with you?"

"I don't care much for bar-b-que," she admitted.

"Oh. Well, this was the perfect meal to curb your hunger then," he said as he started putting stuff back in the bag.

She reached out and touched his hand, stopping him from packing up. "No, I appreciate the gesture, and frankly, beggars won't be choosers. You got what sounded good to you, which is exactly what I would've done. I'm grateful you did. Now, let's see what all the fuss is about." She started to unpack the bag closest to her when Abby knocked a drink over, soaking October to the skin with Coke.

"Oh my gosh. I'm so sorry. Here." Wilder sprang into action, grabbing napkins and dabbing at her pants, which only sent Abby into a bigger tizzy. The lights flickered, and he stopped, looking up. "Electrical problem?"

"Not sure," she said through clenched teeth. "Could be a wayward spirit who doesn't know how to keep her place." Abby vanished right in front of her, without slamming any doors that time.

He looked at her, a bit startled. "Undertaker humor?"

She laughed and dragged her eyes back to Wilder. "Of course. This place isn't haunted. I had it checked by Father Johnson years ago."

"Oh my God. Are you serious?"

October stopped dabbing at the Coke on her pants. "No, Wilder. I'm not. That's not really a thing." She went back to wiping. "I mean, I guess it could be. But I've never felt like it was necessary."

"Well," Wilder looked up at the lights, now holding a steady warm glow over their heads. "Maybe you should consider it."

She tossed the spent napkins on the coffee table and dug into her own food. "Noted."

Wilder watched her intently while they ate, and she looked around nervously, thankful her ghosts were giving them some peace for the moment.

"Yes?" She finally asked.

"Well? What's the verdict?"

She chuckled. "Why is this so important?"

He set his sandwich down and then she knew it was serious. "What if I hated your favorite place? Then what?"

"Yes, then what, Wilder? We're different people with literally zero obligations to each other. We're allowed to have different opinions." She smiled, but she could tell she'd popped some bubble she hadn't seen.

"I just thought...oh never mind. You're right. I think it's the texture," October admitted.

Wilder nodded and finished his sandwich quickly. Whatever magic they'd had, she'd ruined it. Again.

October ignored Mrs. Davis, who'd walked in while they were eating, as she looked out the window wondering if that was why she didn't have friends. Not because she was a funeral home director. Clearly Wilder didn't mind that. And not because of her ghosts. But because she just couldn't go with the flow. She couldn't just say she enjoyed the meal, even if she didn't like the food. She had enjoyed his company. At least until she ruined it.

She picked at her fries and at the garlic bread, which was delicious. "Well, thank you for dinner. I really appreciate it."

"It's the least I could do. After everything you've done for me."

He stood, and October knew this was it. And it bugged her this time. And not because Mrs. Davis was waiting for her to do something, or because she had a ghost to get rid of. Because she actually enjoyed spending time with him.

"Is that her?" He gestured toward the urn on the corner of her desk, next to the flowers she'd kept from the service.

"It is."

He picked up the urn awkwardly, first carrying it like a football, then a baby. "Well, I guess we'll be going then."

"It was very nice to have met you, Wilder."

He looked at her with his emerald-green eyes, and she wanted to take a step closer to him. To remove some of the hurt she saw there. But she held her ground. She wasn't his friend. She was the funeral home director. A necessary, but temporary fixture in his life.

As much as she wanted him to, he didn't speak to her again. October decided not to comment as she watched him adjust the urn one more time while he walked out the door, and out of her life.

"This won't do," Mrs. Davis insisted as she followed after him.

For once, October agreed. But she had no idea what to do about it.

CHAPTER 6

The next day, Wilder went back to work. He had another week off, but he couldn't sit around sorting through his mother's things anymore. He needed familiarity. Purpose that meant something. The house could wait.

Nikki was surprised to see him when he walked in. "Wilder. I wasn't expecting you until next week. All the mail that can wait is on your desk. I'm sorting through the things that need attention now."

"Thanks Nikki. I'm sure you're doing a great job." He went into his office without making eye contact and closed the door behind him.

He knew coming to work was a dumb idea. As he stared at his computer, the focus he needed was still out of reach. The peace he'd felt with October was gone, right along with her poor taste in food. He hadn't even asked her what she did like. That was dumb. Why hadn't he—

Nikki interrupted his train of thought. By the look on her face, she regretted it immediately. "Wilder? I'm sorry. I have Mr. Jansenville on the phone. He wanted to know if we could expand the hedge across his back fence. I'll handle it."

"Thanks," he said, still avoiding eye contact.

She didn't bother him again, just let him sit in his office doing nothing, blessed woman that she was. He surfed the internet some. Played a little solitaire. But he let her answer the phone, and apparently any emails that came in, because he didn't even open that window on his computer.

It had been ages since he felt that...listless. He knew it was dangerous territory. Last time he'd let his mind wander too deeply down the road he was on, it didn't end well. It was after Abby. His life was defined by her. Before Abby. And after. And after had seemed so...long.

He stood up, knowing full well he couldn't do that again. His mom wasn't there to save him this time. He just needed to get his hands dirty. So, after Nikki left, he grabbed a truck and went to the Manning Funeral Home.

HE HADN'T DONE it on purpose. Well, he had, but he hadn't meant to be weird about it. He wasn't stalking her. He just wanted to feel comfortable again. That peace he'd felt with her. So, when he found himself sitting in the parking lot that evening, he wasn't sure what he meant to do. He didn't want to bug her. It seemed like there were a few cars in the lot. Maybe she was meeting with a grieving family.

And, he hadn't necessarily wanted to chat anyway. He'd noticed a few hedges that were getting lanky when he'd been there yesterday. Not terribly so. She obviously had someone who came and took care of things. But, he wanted something to do.

And it had been so long since he'd done the real work. Once the business blew up, he'd hired people like Tim to help out so he could focus on the business end. Scheduling, billing, landscape design, things like that. But his heart was outside. That's why he'd picked an office building with huge floor to ceiling windows that faced the park. If he was going to be trapped there, he wanted to have a good view.

His mom suggested hiring a business manager so he could go back outside. Nikki had been the next best thing. He just didn't feel right handing all the reigns over to her. His mom said it was a control issue, but he didn't put too much thought into it. In that moment though, he knew he wanted to go back to his roots.

So, he parked the truck as far from the other cars as he could, and grabbed some tools from the back. The air was cool and refreshing and energizing. He pulled weeds, trimmed bushes that didn't really need it, did edging that looked like it had been done a week or two ago, and wouldn't need to be done again any time soon with the cooling temperatures.

He walked by her office window more than once, and he did catch her watching him, but she didn't come out to stop him. He appreciated that small gesture more than he could say.

It got dark on him before he was ready to quit, so he got out a head lamp and kept on working. His favorite thing about landscaping was, there was always something that could be done. Weeds to pull, things to trim, stuff that needed watering.

He puttered around for two hours, and October never came out, nor did he go in and say hi to her. He didn't know how. He knew he should tell her thank you. But he didn't. He went home feeling genuinely tired for the first time since before his mom died.

. . .

IN THE MORNING, he woke up energized. He went to work with a renewed sense of purpose, and after only a few hours, he'd finished everything he needed to do. Signing checks, filing permits, things like that.

A few people stopped in and made small talk. That threatened to derail his good mood. Tim was one of them. But he was the only one, besides Nikki, who didn't act different. Like Wilder was broken. When people acted that way it made his skin feel prickly, like he wanted to climb out of it. It was too familiar. Too much like when Abby—

But Tim had saved him from his dark thoughts. "Hey boss. You want lunch? You could come with us, or I can bring you back something." He asked it like everything was so normal. Like he expected him to say yes, and that felt good to Wilder.

"That sounds good, Tim thanks. Bring me a burger or whatever."

"Sure thing." Tim looked up at him, and Wilder found he was able to look back. He didn't see any pity there. Just... stability. A consistency Wilder found comforting and unusual for someone so young.

After lunch, there wasn't much left for him to do, so he left early and went to his mom's. The house was dark and quiet, and he regretted going as soon as he opened the door. He'd been having such a good, productive day. That was exactly why he reasoned he should go. He didn't want to lose his momentum.

When it came down to it, sorting through her things, and deciding what to do with the house was overwhelming. He'd tried to take it one room at a time, starting with the living room, but he hadn't made it past her shelf of VHS tapes before he popped one in and lost ninety minutes watching The Lion King in all its non-digital glory.

His house was smaller than hers, and he couldn't keep

everything, but he found it hard to part with anything. It all held such memories. Okay, that wasn't entirely true. She had a horrid collection of porcelain cats she kept on the windowsill in the kitchen. He'd tried to talk her into getting rid of them ages ago. She'd found them at an antique store and fell in love. But they were kitschy at best, mostly just tacky and a little creepy looking with their big eyes.

He decided to start with those. But as he walked through the kitchen, he noticed something. It didn't smell like anything. Nothing had cooked in it for almost two weeks. He'd never been in her kitchen when it didn't smell like something. His mom was such an amazing cook, and her food was an expression of her love.

He looked in her fridge and realized immediately he should've started there. Grabbing a trash bag, he didn't even try to save containers. Everything got tossed. The freezer was another story. There was frozen meat, and seafood he'd eat eventually, so he saved everything he could identify and wanted. Everything else went the way of the fridge contents and he made a mental note to set the can down on trash day.

When he was done, he sat at the table with a bottle of water, eyeing the cats. He'd hidden them on her once or twice. Or a hundred times. It had become a thing. Every time he came over, he'd hide at least one of them. And every time she found them, she'd send him a picture.

Reunited, she'd caption her message once the set was complete again.

Only once did she get mad when he hid one next to the trash can. He hadn't dared to put it in the can. But even next to it was too close. He'd gotten a stern talking to over that.

As he sat there despising them, he knew he'd never get rid of them.

. . .

HE LEFT his mom's house feeling drained. He'd meant to go home, but when he pulled into the parking lot, he felt better. Despite how much he'd puttered around the night before, there was more he could do. He started with the leaves out back. That side of the property didn't seem to get much love. There were no windows on the back of the building, only a rather industrial looking set of double doors with a driveway in front of it.

Wilder decided not to put too much thought into those doors as he raked. It would've been faster to mow it, and bag the leaves, but he didn't bring the trailer. He had his own truck and his own tools. That meant a rake.

In an hour, he had several piles, and started working to bag them up. He felt renewed, and he wondered at the fact that he only felt comfortable at a funeral home.

CHAPTER 7

*O*ctober peeked out her office window, looking for Abby but didn't see any sign of her hanging around Wilder while he worked. She knew he'd seen her watching him but she couldn't help it. Once her last client left, she took a cup of hot chocolate out to him.

"Thought you might be getting cold out here." Her breath fogged in front of her face as she held the mug out to him.

"Thanks. I hadn't noticed."

"Lost in work?"

"Ideally." He seemed relaxed, and she couldn't help but wonder if that was because of Abby's absence. "Thank you."

"For what?"

"For giving me a space to work."

"You didn't need a space to work, Wilder. You could work anywhere. The world is your canvas." A small, and disarming, crinkle appeared in the corner of her eye as she sipped her hot chocolate. "You needed a space to grieve."

He nodded, not willing to acknowledge that's what he was doing. She reached out and squeezed his hand. The small, but intimate gesture took him by surprise, and he found he enjoyed the warmth of it.

When she let go, he finally felt the coolness of the evening, and grabbed the mug with both hands.

"How was your day?" She asked.

"Good. Productive." He sipped his hot chocolate and held it out in toast to her. "This is good."

"It's the real milk. I'm so glad you were productive," she said.

He nodded. "I finished up at work early, so I went to my mom's to start...cleaning out I guess. But I'm having trouble doing that. I don't know what to keep, and I end up watching a movie or something. I did clean out the fridge today. Should've done that awhile ago. There were new biological systems growing in there."

She laughed. "The fridge is a great place to start. I don't remember much about cleaning out my dad's apartment. I left most everything untouched."

"You did? So, you're still paying rent on his place? How long ago did you say he died?" Wilder was clearly horrified. And she probably would have been too if she didn't know her dad still lived there.

"No. His apartment is above the funeral home. So, there's no rent or anything." She pointed to the windows on the second story.

"Oh. I wondered what was up there, but didn't want to think too hard about it."

She laughed again. "Nothing but ghosts I'm afraid."

He missed her joke, and she smiled to herself as she sipped her hot chocolate. "You didn't want to move into it?"

"You know, I considered it. It would be easier to be here all the time. But, I'd bought my place long before he passed. It's home. The apartment is his home." She shrugged.

"I understand. But you could use the space for storage or something. Seems like a waste."

October shrugged. "It's serving its purpose for now." She looked up at the window and thought she saw Mrs. Davis watching them from her dad's apartment and her eyes narrowed.

"What?" Wilder asked.

"Hmm? Oh nothing. I just…" She looked back at the window but nothing was there. "I thought I saw something."

"Ghost?"

"Definitely," she confirmed.

He laughed. "As a funeral home director, you must have a pretty firm belief system when it comes to ghosts. So, let's hear it. Are they real or not?"

She watched him, wondering just how much of the truth she should tell him. She'd been teasing him before. She did that a lot with people. Told them the truth without them comprehending what she'd said. But no one had ever asked her flat out if *she* thought they were real.

"My belief in them doesn't make them exist. Either they do or they don't. My opinion is irrelevant," she said diplomatically.

"Are you a politician? Because that was the slipperiest answer I've ever heard," he needled.

"It's the truth."

"Spoken like a true congresswoman."

"Well, what do you think?" She asked.

"I'm not sure. I've never really thought about it before. I hope people have peace. I'd hate to think about them lingering around with unfinished business they can't do much about."

She bit the inside of her cheek but said nothing.

"Wow. That was a real conversation stopper wasn't it?"

He laughed, and October found she liked the sound of it. "Sorry. I promise I'm not always so doom and gloom."

"As an undertaker, I make no such promise," October joked, making Wilder chuckle again.

"You are a very unique person, October Manning." She couldn't help but notice the sparkle in his eye when he said it.

"Captain Obvious to the rescue," she teased. "I'm afraid no one ever accused me of being ordinary, or dull."

"No. I bet they didn't."

They looked out at his work, and she found she felt more at ease with him than she ever had around any other living person. Except maybe for her dad.

"Thank you for coming around, Wilder. I've enjoyed this."

"I should say the same thing to you. Listen would you…" he trailed off, letting his thought die. "Never mind."

"What?" She prodded.

"No. I'm sorry. I'm being inappropriate." He stiffened, and October spotted Abby lingering around the edge of her property.

"Maybe I should be inappropriate," she ventured boldly, not taking the time to wonder where her courage had come from. "I wonder if you might want to have lunch or something. Maybe let me pick the place this time, so you can criticize my favorite food?"

He brightened, and she watched Abby disappear into the woods. "I would like that very much."

They started walking back to his truck. "Can I tell you something, Wilder?"

"Of course."

"Your mother was my only friend."

"What happened to your others?" He asked.

It was a normal question. And she had no idea why she was telling him something so personal. Except that she didn't know what else to do. Getting close to him seemed to be what kept Abby away. And dang it, she actually liked him. Mrs. Davis was right. He was a good guy.

"I never had any friends. Your mom was my first."

Wilder stopped walking. "What? Do you have cooties?"

She nodded. "I think so. Undertaker cooties."

"Really? People wouldn't be friends with you because of all this?"

"Can you blame them? It's weird."

He shrugged. "It's a necessary part of life. People can't shun you because you do a job they don't want to."

"And yet."

When they reached his truck, he turned and stuck out his hand. "I'd love to be your friend, October Manning."

"Thank you, Wilder Davis. I think I'd like that too."

He took out his phone and asked her for her number. She rattled it off, and almost instantly heard a message for an incoming text. She hadn't even known what the tone sounded like.

It was a gif of a whale breeching, and it said, "whale hello there."

She smiled in spite of herself. "Nice."

"Gifs are my language."

"Noted."

"Text me where you want to go, and when."

She'd nearly forgotten she'd asked him to dinner. She'd asked him out. How could she have done that? "Not a date, right?" She panicked.

He folded his arms over his chest and leaned against his truck with a smirk, clearly enjoying her terror. "You tell me. I've never been asked out by a girl before."

"Oh please. I'm sure you've been asked out loads of times."

He shook his head. "Nope. I'm the one that does the asking."

"Well, if that's the case, then this definitely isn't a date. We're friends, after all," she insisted.

His smirk softened. "I like the sound of that."

He hopped in his truck. "I'll come back tomorrow to finish picking up the leaves. Hopefully they don't blow all over in the meantime."

"Sounds great. I'll text you later." She'd never said that to someone before. She'd never needed to text anyone.

He waved as he drove off, and October noticed a second person sitting beside him once he turned onto the road.

SHE HADN'T WANTED to text him right away. She didn't want to seem desperate. But he texted her that night. It was a gif of a ghost, with the caption:

Don't you dare ghost me. I know where you work.

Queso protested when she stopped petting him so she could text Wilder back.

Meet me at Spice Thai Friday for lunch? I have services Friday night and Saturday all day.

Sure. Sounds great.

She responded with a sushi gif, which he laughed at. She'd have to figure out how to laugh at texts or gifs. But she wasn't sure she was willing to reduce herself to asking Wilder. He'd make fun of her. She wondered if Mrs. Davis would know.

That night, they exchanged messages until she went to bed, and rather forcefully had to tell him goodnight. He texted her twice more after that, but she didn't answer. She had to get some sleep. Even if her excitement was making it difficult.

· · ·

57

THE NEXT MORNING, Mrs. Davis met her at the double doors of the funeral home. "What are you doing?"

"Well, good morning to you too. Actually, I have a question for you," October started to ask, but Mrs. Davis wouldn't let her. She wouldn't even let her take another step inside, and October had a hard and fast policy about not walking through the ghosts. It felt like an invasion of their personal space. Not that she'd never done it by accident when one popped up behind her. But then she considered it their own fault.

"What are you doing?" Mrs. Davis asked again, more forcefully.

"I'm…coming to work?" October offered.

"With Wilder?"

"Oh. Yeah, I asked him to lunch tomorrow."

She smiled as wide as a Cheshire cat. "I knew it. I just knew you'd done something. He was smiling all evening. Smiling, October. And Abby was so sour. She sat on the opposite side of the couch from him. She tried to break his phone at one point, but I got in her way. She didn't thank me for that. Luckily, I don't think we can hurt each other."

"He was texting me. That's what I want to ask you. He laughed at a few things I said. How do I do that?"

"Oh, just hold your finger on the message, and the option pops up."

She took out her phone and tried it. "Huh. Yeah that works. Thanks. You know, I figured out the gifs right away. The icon is right there. But that one was beyond me."

"I would've thought you young people would know more about the technology than someone like me."

"Yes well. I've never had a need for that feature."

A text came through. *Delayed reaction to that one, huh?* Wilder said.

Maybe the joke wasn't good enough to laugh at right away.

She got a gif of Donkey from Shrek saying, "You cut me real deep just then," and laughed out loud.

"What's going on?" Steve asked as he walked up.

Mrs. Davis didn't even try to hide her glee. "Wilder and October are texting."

"Oh? What's that?" He asked. "Is that some new slang term? Are you using protection?"

October put her phone down, completely mortified. "Dad."

Mrs. Davis lost it. "Steve. It's typed messages they send with their phones. Look." She could barely get her arm up to gesture toward October's phone she was laughing so hard. "Are you using protection. From what? A computer virus?" She cackled.

Steve cleared his throat as October showed him the thread. "Huh. Why not just call? And why haven't you texted before?"

October shrugged. "Who would I text? And I guess Wilder prefers this."

Mrs. Davis nodded. "That he does. He'll talk to you on text for hours. But don't ask him to talk on the phone for more than five seconds. You might as well ask him to sign over half his business."

October laughed. "I'm learning that."

Mrs. Davis finally let her walk by as she told Steve about how their plan was working. She shut her door on the two ghosts, hoping she could concentrate on the work for the day, but Wilder must have had some time on his hands, because he texted her about a dozen times before lunch. Telling her about his day, that he decided to have lunch with Tim and the gang, and of course, silly gifs.

By the afternoon, her dad settled down next to her as she worked in the basement on a new person. Mr. Johnson. He'd already moved on earlier that morning. Right after he'd been dropped off. It was always nice when they did that, moved on right away. They saw their body was in good hands, and left.

Her phone went off again, and she resolved to find a better sound for that alert. The current one was echoing around the room.

"He sure texts you a lot."

"Mmm," she said as she trimmed a few out of place mustache hairs on Mr. Johnson.

"It's nice to see you making friends with the living." He paused, and October didn't comment. She wasn't sure she liked the tone. Felt like a lecture was coming. "Do you think it might be…more?"

"More than what?"

"Texting, or whatever this is?"

"We're friends dad. Just like you and Mrs. Davis. That's it."

He looked away. "It's just. It might be nice to see you settled is all."

"Settled? I am settled. I have my own place. And Queso."

"Yes. Queso."

He was quiet so long, she thought he'd let it go. But of course, he couldn't bear to let her off that easily.

"You have no support system, Boo. And what if…" He didn't finish his thought.

"What if what?"

"Never mind. It's not like I age, and I sure don't seem to be going anywhere." She caught the bitter edge to his comment, but didn't know what to do about it.

"Dad. You know why I can't make friends with the living? They wouldn't understand any of this."

"What? The business? The right person will," her dad insisted.

"Oh right. Like mom did?"

"Your mother was different."

"Really? Because in my experience she seems to be the

normal one. And that doesn't even bring the ghosts to the party." She was raising her voice, and realized, she was mad.

"Just, give Wilder a chance. He may surprise you."

"And if he doesn't? If he's the same as all the others? Then what? Remember what happened with Rosie? I told her I could see ghosts. It didn't go well. She wasn't allowed to play with me anymore, and frankly I don't think she wanted to. She was scared of me."

"She was also a child," Steve offered. "Wilder is a grown man, capable of making his own judgements."

"She wasn't the only one."

"I know. But Wilder is different too. Just like you. He's had a tough go of it. You might find you have more in common than you think."

"Just because we both have ghosts hanging around?"

"That too," her dad encouraged.

"Dad. Please. Even the well-intentioned people think I'm crazy and need help. I think Wilder would probably fall into that category. I can't let him get that close to me."

"What his ghost problem isn't all that complicated?"

"Oh, like our relationship isn't all that complicated?"

"It's not," he said simply. "I'm your father. That's it."

"Well, if we simplify it that much, he's not free to be dating me anyway so this conversation is moot."

"Except he doesn't know she's there. She needs to move on."

October raised an eyebrow at him. "So, tell me how his ghost problem isn't complicated again?" He scowled at her, and she pressed on. "I can tell it's not what you want, but we'll just have to be friends, and hope that's enough to solve his ghost problem. Honestly, I'm excited to have a friend again. A real friend. Not that Mrs. Davis wasn't a real friend. But someone my age. Ya' know?"

Her dad nodded, but she could tell it wasn't the answer he

wanted. He'd never pressured her into dating, or finding someone to spend her life with. Or even making friends for that matter.

"A friend you keep secrets from apparently."

"Dad," she said flatly.

He didn't turn to look at her, instead he looked at a cabinet along the back wall, studying it as if he'd never noticed it before. "Hm?"

"Why now?"

"Why now what?"

"Why do you suddenly want me to have a friend, or maybe more?"

"I don't know. Aurora has made some good points. And Wilder just seems like a good fit, that's all."

"My best shot, you mean?"

"No, that's not what I mean. There are plenty of fish in the sea, Boo. I just think there's potential there. That's all."

He started to walk away, and October stopped him. "Dad?"

He finally turned and looked at her, and she blew him a kiss. He gave her a sad smile, but still caught it before he disappeared through the door.

CHAPTER 8

October got to the restaurant first and grabbed them a table. She knew they'd be busy on a Friday with everyone wanting a long lunch at her favorite lunch spot. She ordered Wilder a Coke and got water for herself.

He walked up with a brown bag in his hand and sat down smelling like fresh cut grass. "Hey. Sorry, am I late?"

"Nope. I like to be early."

"Noted." He handed her the bag.

"What's this?"

"Just something I picked up for you."

She pulled a yellow book out of the bag. "Friendships for dummies?" She raised an eyebrow at Wilder who grinned innocently.

"Thought it might help."

"It's not heavy enough to do any real damage if I smacked you with it."

He sat back in the booth. "Good thing for me. Never pegged you for a violent one, October Manning."

"Don't peg me for anything, Wilder Davis."

She liked the mischievous sparkle in his eye a little too much, so she distracted herself with the menu.

"What's good here?"

"I like the green dragon roll, but I add cream cheese, because really what's the point of sushi without cream cheese?"

"Glad we can agree on that."

After they placed their orders, Wilder turned serious. "I'm sorry I didn't realize you were friends with my mom. It was a bit insensitive of me. Her death must have been hard for you too."

"It was. Is," she corrected.

"What did you guys talk about?" He asked. October was happy to answer. She knew he was just trying to get to know a different side of his mom, and keep her alive in some way.

"All kinds of things. Books mostly. She thought I had terrible taste in books."

Wilder choked on his Coke. "Why? What do you read? Slasher books?"

"They are *not* slasher books."

"You do! Oh my gosh. What's your favorite one?" His delight surprised her, and she couldn't figure out if it was because he liked horror books too, or because she'd gone against his mother's opinion on something.

"Oh. It's hard to choose I suppose. *The Haunting of Hill House* is amazing."

"The Netflix series was superb. Is the book anything like it?"

"Mmm, they took some liberties. But, it's also great!"

"See? It's fun when you share a love of something," Wilder said as the waitress set their food in front of them.

"Is that in the book you gave me?"

"I don't know. I didn't read it," he admitted.

"Ok mister know-it-all who doesn't need any more friends."

"Now, I never said that. I just understand how to make them."

"And how's that? By doing yard work at the local funeral home until you wear the owner down and she comes out with hot chocolate for you?"

"It worked, didn't it?"

He had her there. Rather than admit defeat, she picked up her chopsticks and started eating.

"My turn to find out about you," October said between bites.

"You know plenty about me. You know I own my own landscaping business, and that my mom just died. And that I like horror movies."

"That's true Mr. Charisma. Tell me about your friends, if you're so good at making them."

"They...don't know how to act. They quit calling me about a week ago actually."

"They what?" Now it was her turn to put her food down. Mrs. Davis was right. His friends were idiots. "Why?"

He waved her off. "Don't get the wrong impression of them. They're good people. They just don't know what to say or do. And honestly there's nothing they can say or do. So, they're giving me some space, and I'm letting them."

She frowned as she picked up another piece of sushi and popped it into her mouth. "I don't know about that."

He bristled a little. "Hey, don't judge. Grief is your job. You know how to handle it. It's in your face every day. My friends aren't used to it. Certainly not from me."

"What does that mean? You're usually such a positive happy guy, and you're not allowed to have emotions around them?" She watched him, and he didn't respond. "You're right. They sound great."

He looked down at his sushi and poked at it with his chopsticks. "Tell me how you really feel why don't you?"

"I just think, what's the point of having friends if they aren't there when you need them?"

"What do you mean?"

"I don't know. Isn't that their purpose? To be there for each other?"

"I guess. But it's more than that. It's someone to laugh with." He held up a chopstick. "Share food with. Common interests. You know," he insisted. But she didn't know. And she didn't want him to know that.

"I take it you don't have a girlfriend? Or did she bail before the service?" She asked, desperate to steer the conversation away from her once again but regretting venturing into Abby territory as soon as she saw the sickened expression on his face.

He exhaled in what October thought was supposed to be a laugh but sounded a little more like a punch to the gut. "Uh, no. I haven't had a girlfriend for a while. I don't date."

"Well, that works out well for me. I don't date either." She tried her most disarming smile on him, and he tried to smile back but it looked more like a grimace.

"Ok, my turn," he said. "What's the worst family you've ever had to work for?"

"Oh gosh. The Hillford family for sure."

Wilder shook his head. "Hillford. Do I know that name?"

"Probably. There was suspicion of foul play, but no one pressed charges. Everyone hated Mr. Hillford so much. Honestly, I've never seen a happier family at a funeral. They had a downright party. Complete with a DJ if you can believe it. My father hated it."

"How long ago was that?"

"Oh, gosh. I'm not sure," October said trying to cover her tracks. Her father had been a ghost at the funeral just spitting mad at what they were doing in his funeral home. They'd even brought a disco ball and hung it up over the casket. She had to pay the cleaning crew extra to get the room turned around for the next service.

She didn't even tell Wilder what a mess Mr. Hillford's ghost was. He did not go in peace, that was for sure. But he couldn't do anything about what they were doing, so he left before the end of the service spitting mad, a little bit like her dad. But based on some of the nasty things he'd said about his family members, she wasn't sure she could blame them.

"Seemed like there was no love lost between the Hillford's that's for sure."

They ate in silence for a few moments, and October loved that it wasn't awkward. It was natural and unstrained.

"With a name like October, I bet you're looking forward to Halloween," Wilder said after taking a drink. "I usually just go to a party my friend hosts every year. What do you do?"

She couldn't help but light up. "I love Halloween. It's my favorite holiday. It's the one time of year it's okay to be creepy."

"You aren't creepy." He seemed a little affronted. "I am not friends with creeps."

October couldn't help but be charmed. "You have to admit my Wednesday vibe is real."

"It is. But I choose to find it charming." He nodded, as if solidifying his statement. "Lots of people like Wednesday. Heck, she just got her own show on Netflix."

She looked down and smiled at her plate, hoping to hide her delight. "She's a bit bolder than me I'm afraid. That piranha gag was genius, but I could never do it."

"Yes, well. You carry a certain amount of compassion she may lack."

"I don't know about that. She's very compassionate toward the people she loves."

"True." He blinked at her. "We got off topic again. How do we keep doing that?"

She shrugged. "I didn't think we did."

"I was asking you about Halloween. What are you doing?"

"Oh, I build a haunted house every year for the neighbor kids. They love it. Last year there were so many kids, I'm pretty sure they were coming from other neighborhoods. It's a good time."

"Wow, that sounds like a blast. You know, if you want, my mom's house would be a pretty good haunted house? It's an older brick house in the middle of a great neighborhood. There are lots of kids around. Mom used to complain about seeing her students when she was out walking. Nowhere was safe, she said."

It sounded great to October. But she shook her head. "I'd love a fresh canvas. But my neighborhood would wonder what happened, and where I'd gone. Better stick with home for now."

"Well, if you change your mind, it's there." He set his chopsticks down on his empty plate. "I'd love to see it, if you don't mind."

"You offering to help?"

"Well, I…" He hesitated. "Apparently, I am. Yes."

October was relieved. "Great. I haven't had time to do much for it yet. Most of it will come together that day though." She talked a mile a minute. "I don't get to decorate the funeral home, ya know? That would be macabre. So, this is a big deal. Did you know my dad loved October too? That's where my name came from."

"Shockingly, I'd guessed one of your folks had an affinity for it. Not surprising it was the undertaker," he joked.

"Mmm," she sipped her water. "Oh my gosh. I'm so excited. Thank you. My dad used to help me with it, but since he died—"

"You've been on your own?" Wilder interrupted.

"Sorry. I guess I say that a lot."

Wilder smiled. "Doesn't make it any less true. I'm happy to help you."

"Thanks, Wilder. Really." She sat back in her seat, feeling a little overwhelmed. Was this friendship? Was it this easy all along and she'd been too afraid to let someone in? No. She'd been burned before, and the memory of it almost made her want to back away from him. This was too good to be true.

He smiled at her, genuinely. But what if it wasn't? What if she needed Wilder Davis just as much as he needed her?

THAT NIGHT, October walked home from work after dark. She knew her walking days were numbered as the weather turned colder. But she loved fall and the way the world shed its skin so something new could grow in its place.

As she walked up to her stoop, she noticed an officer parked out front, and immediately picked up her pace, concern for her neighbor growing. But her neighbor met her outside. She was dressed in a long skirt, and dark purple cardigan, and her long curly hair had a mind of its own, but Mrs. Babcock didn't seem to care.

"Oh October. I'm so sorry. I called the police when I heard the racket. They said there was no sign of forced entry, but your place..." Mrs. Babcock was holding Queso in her arms, and he meowed loudly at October as she walked up.

"What happened?" October looked at her front door, but it seemed unscathed. It was open, and she could see an occasional person walk by, and voices inside, but nothing else.

"Someone trashed your place."

"How did you know, if there was no sign of it?"

"I heard it. Plates crashing. Banging around. I knocked on your door but there was no answer. I was scared to death for you, so I called the police. They heard the noise too. But it stopped as soon as they got inside. I gave them your key, I hope you don't mind." October shook her head. "I'm afraid poor Queso is pretty spooked."

"I bet he is." She hugged her cat tighter and he purred. "What happened buddy? Who did this?" He meowed loudly at her, and she wasn't sure she wanted to know the answer.

"Will you take him to your place until I can get the police out?"

"Of course." Queso had some choice words to scream at October when she handed him back, but October wasn't taking him into a live crime scene.

She knocked on the door frame and carefully stepped across the threshold of her home. "Hello?"

"Mrs. Manning?" An officer asked her. He seemed younger than her, but still had a very authoritative air about him, with his buzz cut, and arms so muscley he couldn't hold them straight by his sides.

"Yeah..." She was distracted by the mess. Things were everywhere. Pictures were knocked off the walls, books were open and upside down on the ground, dishes were in pieces on the kitchen floor. The more she looked, the more over-whelmed she got. Her breathing came in short gasps.

"Now, slow your breathing down for me." The big officer put a hand on her shoulder, but it felt like a fifteen-pound weight and she nearly crumpled under it. He jerked his hand away, and called for help. "Stephens!"

A woman in uniform walked over and put her arm around October, guiding her to a kitchen chair. "You're safe."

October looked up at her as a glass of water appeared in her hands. The officer had kind brown eyes, and she wanted to believe her. But who would've done this?

The officer urged her to drink, and let her sit for a moment. Once she'd taken a few sips, the woman, Stephens apparently, started asking questions. "I know this is difficult, but we need to you to tell us what's missing. Were you keeping important, or incriminating documents here? Valuables?"

She gave the room a cursory glance. The tv was broken but still there. Her Nintendo was there. Those were probably the most valuable things in the house, aside from her rare books. She saw at least one of them on the floor, its spine cracked and tears formed anew.

The burly officer emerged from her room with her broken laptop in hand. "Seems theft wasn't the goal here."

"Do you know anyone who might do this?" Stephens asked her, keeping her voice soft and low to soothe her nerves.

October shook her head.

"Any...unhappy clients? You're the local undertaker right? Anyone with a chip on their shoulder?"

Abby. Abby was the only one she could think of with a chip on her shoulder, but she wasn't living. She couldn't tell the officer about her, so she shook her head again.

"It's probably just random. But bold with your neighbor home. I'm going to suggest you both sleep elsewhere tonight. Do you have somewhere you can go?"

She nodded her head. Her dad would have to put up with her. And she needed to talk to Mrs. Davis.

"All right. We're about done here. I don't know how they did it. No windows broken, no damage to the door. No one else has a key, except your neighbor, right?" The burly officer asked.

October shook her head no. Words just wouldn't come.

"We heard someone inside when we put the key in. Then the destruction stopped as soon as we got the door open. It was like the person vanished. Like a ghost." He chuckled at his own foolishness. "Well. It's nearly Halloween. Probably just some dumb kids trying to get a rise out of you," the burley officer theorized logically.

Stephens shook her head. "The local kids love her. She does the best haunted house in the neighborhood. Isn't that right, Ms. Manning?"

October nodded again.

"Well, whoever it was didn't leave anything in the way of evidence. I'm afraid this will be a tough one. We'll get you all the documentation for your insurance company by tomorrow, Ms. Manning. And I'll send an officer to circle the block twice a day for the next week or so. Okay?"

"Thank you," she croaked.

Could a ghost have done that much damage? And if they could, how much deeper should she go with Wilder?

AFTER SHE'D SIGNED some papers with the police, packed an overnight bag, collected Queso and made sure Mrs. Babcock would be all right, she headed to the funeral home. Mrs. Babcock refused to leave, and said she wanted to be around if the scoundrel came back. Although Mrs. Babcock had always kept her distance, she'd been civil, and almost kind when they had interacted. October was grateful the older woman didn't hesitate to care for Queso until she got home.

She climbed the steps at the funeral home slowly, with Queso purring in her arms, and knocked on the door before she opened it. "Daddy?"

The apartment was dark, so she flipped on every light she walked past, feeling more spooked than she ever had. And she'd seen ghosts her whole life.

"Boo? What are you doing here?" He took one look at her face, and she started sobbing. He went to her, and for the first time ever, he put his arms around her, and she felt it.

She leaned against him and sobbed even harder. He held her tightly, in a way he hadn't been able to in ten years.

"What's happened?" Her dad asked once her sobs had subsided.

"Abby trashed my place. Like trashed it. I don't think she left anything untouched."

"She what?"

"Go see for yourself if you want. Except, don't leave me," October amended quickly.

His face turned serious. That papa bear expression that only happens when someone messes with a father's child. "Aurora is here too. You won't be alone. I'll be right back."

Mrs. Davis stepped out of a shadow. "He touched you."

October nodded, words failing her again. But only for a moment. "Abby," she squeaked.

"Are you sure it was her?"

"There was no sign of entry. And she kept going until the police went inside. They said they heard the person breaking stuff inside. And when they went in, guns drawn, it was like they had vanished. 'Like a ghost,' the officer said."

Mrs. Davis frowned. "When Steve gets back, I'll go check on her. See what that nasty little tart has been up to."

"If my dad hasn't gotten to her first."

"I can't believe he touched you," Mrs. Davis looked at October with awe.

She reached up and grabbed her own shoulder, where he'd last touched her, as if she could feel it again. "I know."

"How did he do it?"

October shook her head. "He was very emotional. Might have been adrenaline?"

"Do ghosts have that?" Mrs. Davis asked.

"I have no idea. And I don't know if he'll be able to dupli-cate it. I hope he can. But if he can't, I can live with feeling his arms around me that one more time. I suppose the price I paid for it wasn't so steep if I think about it like that." She smiled through her tears, and Mrs. Davis reached out for her, but her hand passed through. She left it there though, and October fought the urge to pull back. It felt like a fog on her hand. Cool and damp, but easily ignored if you didn't know it was there.

"Mrs. Davis. What are we going to do? How can I fight this kind of anger?"

Mrs. Davis looked at her with no worry, no fear, nothing that felt like it was threatening to swallow October whole in that instant. "With love, my dear. With love."

CHAPTER 9

A chime on her phone snapped her back to reality. She was still sitting with Queso in her lap and Mrs. Davis' hand over hers, lost in her thoughts. The chime sounded again and she blinked, unable to register the sound.

"I think it was your phone, dear," Mrs. Davis offered.

She reached into her pocket and pulled it out. She had five messages from Wilder. A few gifs, and then two asking her if she was okay and why wasn't she answering.

"It's Wilder." October set her phone on the table between them.

"Aren't you going to answer him?"

"I don't know what to say. Your dead girlfriend destroyed my house to the point where I can't stay there tonight?" She looked at Mrs. Davis accusingly. The anger had risen up hot and unexpectedly. But Mrs. Davis didn't flinch.

"Well. No, I suppose you can't tell him that."

"I don't want to lie to him."

"You can hardly keep this from him," she pointed out.

"He said he'd come help me with the haunted house. How am I going to be ready for it now?" She put her face in her hands, and started crying again. That's when the video door-bell sounded at the front door of the funeral home.

"October?" Wilder asked into the camera.

"Oh my god." She swiped at her face and Mrs. Davis stood up.

"Don't leave him out there."

"Are you here?" Wilder asked.

She activated the ap on her phone so she could talk to him while she walked down. "Yes, I'm here. Sorry I missed your texts."

"What's wrong? Why are you still here?"

She didn't answer him. It was faster to just unlock the front doors and let him in.

He looked her over once, and she felt very exposed. She pulled her off-white cardigan even tighter around herself and turned away, assuming he would follow her up to the apartment.

"What happened?" He demanded.

"Glad I kept my dad's apartment in order, that's all I can say."

"Are you staying here tonight?" He asked as they stepped inside. She sat back down at the table. Mrs. Davis stood by the counter, just in case Wilder wanted to sit. Didn't want him sitting on her, after all. Her dad scowled next to Mrs. Davis, but October couldn't address him. Not with Wilder there.

"I am."

"Why?"

Queso rubbed up against his legs as he sat down in the chair, and he absently reached down to pet the orange tabby.

"My place was wrecked today." That was the truth.

"By who?"

"Police don't know." Also true. Maybe she could keep this up. Mrs. Davis nodded at her encouragingly.

"What did they take?"

Another easy question to ask. "Nothing."

He frowned at her. "Nothing?"

"You heard me." It came out shorter than she meant, but she was at the end of her rope.

"What do you have tomorrow?" He asked.

She blinked at him. It was such a change in gears, she didn't compute.

"Appointments? Services? What?"

"Oh. Um. I have services all day. But after that not much. I haven't had an intake in a few days, so I have a break."

"Okay. Great. I'll meet you at your place tomorrow when you're done, and help you sort it out." It wasn't a question. It was a statement.

"Oh, Wilder. I don't know..." It wasn't that she didn't want his help. She needed someone to help if she was going to be ready for Halloween. But she didn't think she could face it.

"Come on. You've done a lot for me these last few weeks. It's the least I can do. Plus, I want to see your place, get a feel for what we're working with on Halloween." He smiled at her, and seemed genuine.

"Wilder. Everything is destroyed. I don't know if I can..." Tears choked the end of her sentence.

"You won't have to. I'll do it. Just come and be a project manager. Tell me what goes where, and I'll do the heavy lifting."

"Better to have his help than do it alone, don't you think, Boo?" Her dad asked.

Her eyes flickered over to him, and he smiled encouragingly at her. Wilder kept his eyes on her though, willing her to accept his help.

"Are you okay here tonight? You can always come stay with me if you don't want to be alone. I can sleep on the couch."

October thought of Abby. "I don't think that's a good idea." Again, honest but vague.

"Why? Because you want to get into my pants already? Why, October Manning, you flatter me." He batted his scandalously long eyelashes at her, and she swatted him.

"No. We're friends remember? Friends don't get in each other's pants, Wilder."

He winked playfully at her. "Says you. Did you even read that book I gave you?"

"That book…" she trailed off. She'd left it at the office that night, and suddenly she was glad. Surely Abby would've destroyed it first if she'd been able to find it.

Wilder held up his hands. "It's fine. Who needs to read something potentially super helpful? You seem to be doing fine on your own. One whole friend already."

She glared at him but he only smiled back. As much as his teasing annoyed her, she found herself relaxing. The urge to sob was no longer lingering at the back of her throat. In fact, a giggle had threatened to escape after that last joke he'd made. Maybe he was good for her.

Eventually, she nodded. "Yeah. Okay. I'd appreciate the help I guess."

"You guess? Listen sister, this kind of help doesn't come along every day." He leaned back in the chair like he thought he was pretty hot stuff. Steve walked up behind him and pressed down on the back of the chair, leaning him back just enough that it startled him. Her dad laughed out loud, and so did October. She stood up and clapped. Her dad was moving things.

"No need for applause. I'm a klutz every day," Wilder said as he leaned forward, trying to counteract Steve.

October grinned, and her dad beamed at her. "I believe you," she said to Wilder.

By the time Wilder left, she was feeling relaxed again.

Safe. She walked him to the front door around midnight. "Sorry to keep you out so late. But thank you for coming to check on me."

"I was getting worried when you weren't answering me."

"So you said. But you could've just called."

"I don't do phone calls. And why would I think you'd answer a phone call if you weren't answering my texts?"

October shrugged. "Might have saved you a trip out here."

"But then I wouldn't have had this delightful evening with you." He pulled her into a hug, and she didn't know what to do. She stood their stiffly, panicking a bit. He smelled like grass and outside, and she relaxed a little, but not much.

"This is the part where you return the hug, October," Wilder encouraged.

Jerkily, she raised her arms and patted his back gently.

"Wow. That needs work," he teased as he pulled back. "Don't you hug people?"

"Only my dad."

Wilder cringed. "Been awhile huh?"

She smiled, in spite of herself. "Seems like not that long ago."

He smiled back at her, his voice quieter than it had been. "I hope I can remember mom that way soon. Without the hurt."

She reached for his hand and squeezed. "You will."

"See? You do that so well. Why are hugs weird?" He demanded.

"Comforting a grieving person is what I do. It's familiar."

He eyed her. "But getting comfort yourself is where you draw the line?" He shook his head. "More and more Wednesday all the time. Except she would never be caught dead in off white. Black all the way."

She tucked her cardigan around her tighter against the

cool fall air. "True enough. But, an undertaker who only wears black is a bit on the nose, don't you think?"

"Mmm. Probably." He hopped into his truck. "Hey, text me your address. I'll pick you up here around six ok?" He pulled the door closed and rolled down the window.

"Thanks Wilder. For tonight. And tomorrow too."

"Don't mention it. That's what friends do."

"Clean up giant messes?"

He nodded seriously. "Absolutely. All kinds of messes. Murders. Arson. Even emotional messes, but I have to admit, as a guy I may not be very skilled at that one."

She laughed. "Noted."

He seemed satisfied and put the truck in reverse, so she stepped back. "See you in the morning. And answer my texts."

"If I'm awake, I will," she promised.

She watched him drive away, flanked by Mrs. Davis and her dad.

They walked up the stairs in silence, until Steve gently closed the door behind them.

"Shut the front door," she yelled.

"Don't mind if I do!" Steve yelled back.

"How?" Mrs. Davis asked.

"At first, it was emotion. I was so upset to see you like that Boo. I needed to do something. I needed to hold you. Then, when Wilder was being so cocky, I just wanted to take him down a peg. Dad stuff, ya know? Now, I know the feeling."

He sat down at the table and looked at October's empty mug. With a determined expression on his face, he reached out for it and picked it up successfully. October marveled as he held onto it and toasted her.

"You should know, that'll look very odd to someone who can't see you," October cautioned. "Don't be doing parlor tricks during services, please."

"You're no fun," he argued and set the cup back down.

"You did it without me," Mrs. Davis said with a bit of a tear in her eye. "I'm so proud of you."

"I didn't do it without you. Without your son, and his brat of a ghost, I never would've found that raw feeling I needed."

Steve's face changed, like a lightbulb had gone off. "Abby is just hurt. She's been hurting for over twenty years. That's why she's so powerful. You need something to counter that."

"Love," October and Mrs. Davis said at the same time.

"But, loving Wilder is only making it worse. Look what she did to your place," Steve pointed out.

"First of all, I don't *love* Wilder Davis," October protested. Mrs. Davis grinned so wide you'd have thought she won the lottery. October ignored it. "Second of all, I have no idea how to show love to a ghost who's so destructive and downright bratty."

"The same way you would to a toddler going through his terrible twos," Mrs. Davis suggested.

"Seeing as how I'm thirty-five and childless, you'll have to elaborate," October pointed out.

"You keep showing up."

It was so simple. But could October do it? "What about my house? Queso? How can I show up when she's so destructive? She has no consequences."

Mrs. Davis screwed her mouth to one side while she chewed on that. "True. We'll have to think on that. Meanwhile, we'll stay with you at your place, until you feel comfortable again. Okay?" She looked at October's dad. "Steve?"

"Oh, of course. I don't mind hanging out with Queso a bit more."

"Maybe start bringing him here when you're at work?" Mrs. Davis suggested. "I don't think she'd hurt him on purpose. Obviously, or she would have tonight. But if something fell on him..."

"I'm sick at the thought," October admitted.

"Okay. That's a plan." Mrs. Davis was clearly feeling satisfied with something actionable out in front of her. "We'll crack this nut yet."

"I hope so. Before she can do any more damage."

THE NEXT EVENING, Wilder showed up alone at the funeral home with dinner. "I didn't know what you were in the mood for, so I got a little bit of everything." He held out the bags to her, and she took one of them and directed him upstairs, grateful Abby hadn't been willing to show her face. October wasn't ready for that confrontation yet. She still wasn't sure how to sort through her feelings about the whole thing. Anger and sadness felt so similar sometimes, it made it hard to want to help her at all. October needed time.

When they walked into the apartment, she found her dad and Mrs. Davis chatting, and she felt bad intruding, so she hesitated in the doorway. "Something wrong?" Wilder asked.

"Come on in," her dad insisted.

She gave him an apologetic look, and then remembered Wilder couldn't see him. "Sometimes it's hard to remember he doesn't live here anymore. I feel like I'm imposing, being in here."

"Oh stop that right now. You were here one night. You are absolutely *not* imposing," her dad insisted.

"I'm glad you had this place to take refuge in. I imagine sleeping on the couch in your office wouldn't have been very comfortable," Wilder offered.

"Would've been more comfortable than the basement," she joked, and Wilder choked on his sandwich.

"I'll take your word for it." She laughed, and he shook his

head. "Warn a person before you unleash that undertaker humor on the world. I had a half-chewed sandwich in my mouth that's now lodged in my lungs."

She patted his arm. "Aww, poor baby."

"We'll see who's laughing when I get pneumonia from that little joke."

Mrs. Davis chuckled and tutted behind him. "Tell him not to be such a drama queen and lighten up."

She raised an eyebrow and tried it out.

He stopped eating and looked at her carefully. "You sound just like my mother."

Mrs. Davis laughed out loud, so much so that the curtains she was standing near fluttered. Wilder noticed but turned back to his meal while October dug into a delicious wrap he brought. It came with some kind of pink dressing that was divine, and probably defeated the healthy purpose of the wrap, but October couldn't bring herself to care.

"Straight for the good stuff. I like it." He grabbed a container of sauce for himself and dipped his sandwich in it.

"Were you trying to make a good impression with this spread?" She asked as she grabbed a package of chips from the bag. He'd gotten quite an assortment, not something they'd be able to finish. She also discovered warm cookies at the bottom of the bag and smiled.

He shrugged. "Maybe."

"You care what I think?"

"Don't you care what I think?"

She thought for a minute. She did. But that never seemed to matter. "Well, yeah I do. But all this time, it's never mattered if I care what other people think of me. No matter what I do, they still keep their distance. Even my neighbor. She's very sweet, and took care of Queso for me before I got there, and while I sorted things out with the police. But she

83

was very glad to have me take him and leave. I don't think she'd miss me if I left."

"I hope that's not true," he said honestly, and she appreciated him for it. He didn't try to tell her she'd read her neighbor wrong. He was starting to understand her reality. Maybe. And she liked having someone she could share that with.

They finished dinner quickly, and headed over to her apartment, leaving their ghosts behind. Her dad wanted to meet Abby, so Mrs. Davis offered to introduce them, but warned him that she wasn't very receptive to comments on her behavior.

"I bet she isn't," her dad had said. "No sixteen-year-old is."

"Good luck," October mouthed to them both as she left with Wilder in his truck. Queso stayed behind, having the run of the funeral home. He'd hold down the fort just fine until she came back for bed.

"I'm afraid there's too much to do before the day's over," she said as she put her key in the door, noting the caution tape still hanging from one door jam.

Wilder pulled it off and crumpled it up. "Let's just take it in small..." he stopped talking as he followed her through the door taking it all in. "Chunks."

It looked just as bad in the daylight as it had in the darkness.

"Um..." Wilder took a few beats to gather his thoughts.

"Yes. That," October said.

He shook his head, as if trying to shake himself into action. "We can do this. Take it room by room. Let's start here, and work our way back, okay?"

She nodded.

They spent three hours in the living room alone. At first, they worked in silence. He righted the shelving and all the big stuff while she sorted through her books, trying to assess the damage. Pages were bent, covers were slashed, spines were cracked. Her collection was destroyed. She lovingly looked at a signed first edition of *The Shining* that had the cover torn right off it.

"Do you know anyone who can repair these?" Wilder asked.

"No. Is that a thing?"

"I don't have any idea. Might be worth Googling later though."

The thought gave her hope as she replaced the books on the shelves. Once the floor was clear, she felt better. Some things had broken beyond repair. Picture frames would need to be replaced. Art on the walls had to be tossed. Her television was a total loss.

Wilder sat for a moment on the floor, taking a break. Her couch had been slashed to bits.

"Who could do this?"

October didn't respond. She knew exactly who. But she also knew Wilder probably wasn't ready to hear it from her.

By ten, they'd just started on the kitchen, and she was beginning to feel the exhaustion in her bones. Wilder swept plates into the garbage while she worked.

She carefully stacked photos of her and her dad on one side of the table, making a mental note to order new frames for them.

"This is going well I think. We're making good progress," he offered.

She looked around. She supposed that was true. The floors were clear again, which did make her feel better. But her open shelving in the kitchen was empty. Nothing remained of the dishes her dad got her when she moved out. She picked a shard out of the garbage bag Wilder had leaned against the good table leg. They had pink flowers on them.

A tear sprang to her eyes as she looked at them. "My dad

said guys wouldn't like this pattern when he bought these for me. It was one of the only times he'd ever implied I might want to consider having a man in my life." She looked at Wilder, and let the tear spill over. "He was good like that. He understood. Maybe better than anyone, after mom left."

"Did he get those for you?" Wilder said, and she nodded, hoping a long drink from her Sprite would dislodge the knot that had formed in her throat. "Well, I'm sure the food tasted the same off of them."

October snorted. "What on Earth does that mean?"

"It was the most polite thing I could think of," Wilder admitted.

"Don't judge my beautiful plates based on shards."

He avoided all eye contact with her. "Right. Absolutely. I'm sorry."

"Say it like you mean it, or I'm calling ACME Apology Service."

"Oh dear. What would happen to me then? Is the coyote going to show up with some TNT?"

She couldn't take it anymore. She laughed. And once she'd started she couldn't stop. And her tears over her broken plates turned to tears of laughter. Wilder couldn't help but join in and before long, they were both unable to support themselves, doubled over the table laughing.

Until Wilder cleared his throat and straightened. "All right. Enough foolishness."

She blinked at him, unable, or maybe unwilling to let go of her smile. "Is there ever enough foolishness?"

His expression softened as he looked at her. "Never."

CHAPTER 10

*T*hey made good progress that evening. Her apartment was almost livable. She'd need to replace almost everything, but the bed was made and free of debris, the bathroom was cleared so she could use it, and everything was picked up so she could at least move around.

October thanked him about a hundred times for his help. Wilder finally lost count, and maybe stopped listening. He hadn't minded. In fact, he liked having another excuse to spend time with her. Something about her made him feel lighter. It was a sensation he hadn't experienced in decades. And he found himself drawn to it. Every time he went back to his house, that familiar sense of dread settled on his shoulders, almost like a blanket being draped over him. He hadn't even realized it until he was free of it. He found he didn't even want to go home.

So the next day, he went to his mom's. She had a couple of televisions, a pretty nice computer he could get up and running for October, and dishes. He was sure there would be more October could use, he just had to look.

With a renewed sense of purpose he walked into his

mom's house ready to work. He packed up her dishes first, and shook his head as the stupid cats watched him from their perch. "You're not going to October's house, so forget it."

His mom's television was bigger than October's had been, and heavier for that matter, but he didn't think she would mind that.

Then he set to her computer, backing up her files to the cloud to sort through later, with the idea of wiping it when he was finished. She didn't have much on there. Mostly photos from her trips with her friends, and their annual mother-son trips together. He got a little lost down memory lane, and decided maybe this wasn't the time to wipe her computer. If October didn't buy one for herself, he could always offer it to her later.

Then he ventured up to the attic to see if there was anything up there that might be useful. He thought she had some empty picture frames up there, and he knew October was upset about those photographs of her dad out of their frames.

He pulled the chain on the light bulb and bathed the small space in a yellow glow. There were boxes stacked on one side. An old rocking chair sat unused in the corner. Was that in his room at one point? He couldn't remember. A beautiful full length antique mirror sat next to it in its own dark wooden stand. He wondered if October would want something like that. It used to be in his mom's room. But she hadn't needed it when she bought the house. Something moved behind him in the reflection and he turned, but nothing was there.

He shook his head, feeling spooked. But something caught his eye. Sticking out of the top box was a picture frame. "Jackpot," he declared to the empty attic.

The box lifted easier than he thought it should, and he set it in front of him. But when he opened it up, he wasn't prepared for what he found. The picture frame held his prom picture. He was wearing a black tux with a pink corsage to match Abby's dress. And Abby. He crumpled next to the box holding the picture. Her hair was cut like Rachel Green's, and her pink spaghetti strap dress sparkled under the purple lights shining on them. She'd died two weeks later.

When had he started to shake? He put the picture down and took a deep breath. He hadn't looked at a picture of her since…well since the incident. His mom said it was an accident, the overdose. He was just trying to get some sleep. And he was. But he didn't want to wake up. He'd never said that out loud to her. He didn't want to break her heart. And he was glad she'd saved him. He wasn't then of course, but after some therapy he'd been able to find that gratitude for her. Now she was gone, and he was left with her things. Why did she have this?

It was a nice picture. He chanced another glance at it. They were so young. When he couldn't look at her anymore, he turned his attention back to the box. There were newspaper articles next, with headlines he didn't need to read to know what they said.

17-year-old kills girlfriend in crash
Senior at DHS not charged after deadly crash
Memorial for Abby Walters draws crowd

The picture for that one was hauntingly beautiful. One of Abby's best friends held a candle, while a sea of candles glimmered behind her.

"Why?" He breathed as he dug deeper into the box. He uncovered an envelope with Abby's parents' address on it marked return to sender. It hadn't appeared to have ever been opened, and Wilder couldn't bring himself to do it right then.

When he uncovered the first letter, he had no idea what he was getting into. It was made out to him.

Dear Wilder Davis,

You are a monster that deserves to rot in hell for what you did to that beautiful girl. I hope you get what's coming to you.

It wasn't even signed. He couldn't believe it. Someone had taken time out of their day to write that? His mom had never showed him, and he'd never known to look. But why had she kept it?

There were twenty other letters, all with the same sentiment, all unsigned. He threw them into the box, along with the articles and the picture and carried the box downstairs. But what then? What was he going to do with it? He couldn't take it home. But he couldn't leave it there either. And he couldn't bring himself to throw away pictures of her.

He took the box to his truck and climbed in. It had gotten dark sometime while he was in there, but he didn't bother to look and see what time it was as he drove automatically to Manning Funeral home.

"WILDER, WHAT'S WRONG?" October asked over the doorbell camera.

"I…" he couldn't finish the sentence. Why had he come? How in the world could he possibly tell her what was wrong? He hadn't told anyone about Abby since they'd left home. And now that his mother was dead, there was no one near him that knew. No one to share that burden with him.

"Wilder, I'm at home working on the mess. It goes a little slower without you." She chuckled but realized the depth of his distress and cut to the chase. "Can you come here, or do you want me to go there?"

"Okay," he said as he turned and sat on the front stoop of the funeral home.

"I'm on my way," she called to him, apparently assuming he wasn't fit to go anywhere.

He sat there in the cold for about twenty minutes. She was out of breath and carrying Queso in her arms when she arrived. She was wearing loose grey pajama pants and a dark grey knitted cardigan she wrapped both her and Queso in tightly, as if they'd been ready for bed when he rang the bell.

"Wilder. What's happened?"

The box sat in his lap and he looked up at her, bewildered. What had happened? His mother had opened a door to the past he'd hoped never to peek behind again, that's what.

October looked him over, and turned to the door, unlocking it. "Well, come on inside. It's cold out here."

He stood and followed her in, but loitered in the hall, not sure where he should go next. She started toward the upstairs apartment and thought better of it. "Wait for me in the office, would you? I want to check something upstairs."

Unable to think beyond the box in his arms, he nodded and obediently sat on the couch in her office. She appeared a few minutes later and sat down at the chair next to the couch, just as she had when they'd first met. The box was on the coffee table.

"What's this?" She gestured toward the box.

He'd come because he didn't know where else to go. But now that he was there, he didn't know what to do. Words failed him.

She looked next to Wilder, but he looked at the box.

"May I?" She asked.

If she did, she would know. She would know what he'd done. Who he was really. Did he want that? The thought scared him, and he looked at her, but he didn't see fear in her clear blue eyes. He saw concern, and kindness, and not a speck of judgement. So, he reluctantly nodded.

Carefully she opened the box and discovered the framed picture on top. "Is this you?" She asked with a smile. "Well aren't you handsome? And how thoughtful you were to match your corsage to your date's dress."

He looked out the window. It was too dark to see much of anything. But he imagined the leaves being tossed around like they had the first time he was in that seat. Watching the cars go by, and the leaves twirling in their wake. Not too many cars went by that late at night.

"I was looking for things for your place." His voice didn't sound like his own. It was deep and raw, like his emotions.

"Oh, at your mom's?" She asked.

Instead of responding, he looked out the window.

"Well, this is a great picture of you. And A…" She stopped short. "I mean, who's this girl with you?"

"That's Abby," he filled in.

"Well, she's lovely. She looks like a great girl."

"She was."

Blessedly, October didn't ask any more questions. She dug through the box. She found the newspaper articles first. She took longer reading them than Wilder had. He'd seen them when they were printed all those years ago. He didn't need to rehash it.

Whatever she thought, she kept it to herself as she uncovered the sealed envelope marked return to sender. She held it up to Wilder and he shrugged, so she set it aside and moved on to the bundle of letters.

Her hand went to her mouth at some point as she read, her hair cascading down her face. Wilder liked it like that. It made her look more relaxed. But he couldn't find the energy to tell her that out loud.

"Wilder," she breathed when she was done, and the box was empty. "I'm so sorry."

His eyes went to hers. She meant it. She didn't think he was a murderer. She felt bad for him, not Abby.

"Sorry for what? You don't feel sorry for the villain, October." It came out sharp and bitter, and he turned away from it, giving his back to October as he turned to face the dark window even more.

Her voice was soft, absorbing the barb he'd shot at her as if it hadn't even phased her. "Every story has a villain, Wilder. I play the villain in many stories in fact." When he didn't respond, she went on. "I'm the one who buries your loved ones. Or burns them. I'm the one who closes that chapter, whether you're ready or not. And I charge you money to do it."

When she said it like that, it sounded nothing like what she'd done for him. It sounded downright cruel. His shoulders relaxed in spite of himself.

"Everyone is the villain in someone's story. Not everyone's tale is as tragic as yours though," she offered.

"That's who you are for Abby's family I'm sure. That's who they need you to be. But you don't have to make that who you are for everyone else. Do you understand?"

He looked at her and didn't try to hide the tears that were building in his eyes.

"You aren't who they say you are."

"Yes I am, October. I killed her."

"Did you do it on purpose? Did you drive your car into that tree specifically to harm her?" She challenged.

Wilder shook his head no.

"Remember when my drink spilled, the day you brought dinner?" He nodded. "That was an accident. Does it define me?"

"That was weird. You weren't even near it."

October frowned. "Not my point."

"And spilling a drink is not the same as killing someone in a car crash."

"A car *accident*, Wilder. It was an accident. And I agree, something like that is very difficult to move on from. Maybe

93

you never will. And that's okay. But what's not okay, is letting it define your life in a negative way."

"What do you mean?"

"How has this impacted you since? You were what? Seventeen I think one of the articles said?" Wilder nodded. "And how has it shaped your life?"

He didn't want to tell her. Nothing about it had been good. Not the incident with the sleeping pills, the hospitals afterward, the psychiatric care, the fact that he hadn't dated anyone since.

"How do you think it shaped my life, October? What kind of question is that?"

Again, she seemed to absorb his venom. She sat calmly, her face remaining the picture of compassion as she hooked a stray bit of her wavy black hair behind her ear. "Do you ever read those human-interest stories on the internet? Or watch the videos? The ones where some couple's kid died of cancer or a heart condition?" Wilder kept his gaze fixed on the window, but she went on anyway. "The ones who rail at their fates, those aren't the ones who make the news are they? Although, I suspect they're more normal to be honest. The ones who make it to the news are the ones who turn their tragedy into something good. They start a charity. Or propose new legislation. Or clean up a park where their kid liked to play. Or start a pet rescue. Or a million other positive things that bring good out of such absolute, life shattering pain."

He glared at her. "What's your point?"

"I believe your pain has tried to shatter your life, hasn't it?" He didn't answer that either. "It can't do that by itself. You have to let it."

"You sound like a therapist. Albeit a better therapist than anyone I've ever paid good money to see."

"I'm going to take that as a compliment."

She started packing everything back into the box, when she stopped at the sealed envelope. She turned it over in her hands a few times before she asked, "Would you like to open this?"

"Not really."

"Okay." She laid it on top and closed the box up before sitting back in her chair. Queso hopped up on the couch and settled in beside Wilder. Absently, Wilder reached down to pet him, and he purred loudly, which calmed his nerves more than he expected.

"Why do you think your mom kept this stuff?"

"To torture me with it after she died?" He asked.

"Was your mom mean like that to you? She sure didn't treat me like that, but I know some mothers are different people to their kids than they are to outsiders." She was trying to give him the benefit of the doubt, even if he didn't deserve it.

"No," he said quietly.

"Good. I would've hated to think I'd been friends with someone duplicitous."

"Duplicitous. Good word," Wilder said.

"So, if she wasn't a horrible person, why do you think she kept this?"

"I don't know."

"Maybe she had a different reason for each thing. Maybe she liked that picture of you at prom. Maybe she kept the letters because she was worried about having to file a lawsuit against Abby's family for threatening you that way."

"You don't know those letters were from her folks," he defended.

She bit her tongue. "Who else would've written them?"

"The whole town hated me. They all thought I was a murderer. And I was."

"Okay. So today you want to be the villain. That's fine. As

the villain, what do you want to do with this box? Hold onto it forever because you believe you deserve that torture? Most villains are out for their own good. So, what would be good for you?"

The answer came to him so quickly, he didn't even think before it was out of his mouth. "To get rid of it. To never have to look at it again."

"Great. Would you like me to help you do that?"

"How?"

She shrugged. "There are a few options. We can bury it in the graveyard if you want. I could even order a headstone for it. I order so much from those guys I'm sure they'd give me a discount. Or I can cremate the box and dispose of the ashes. Or I can just store it in the basement for now, until you decide what you want to do."

"I don't...All of that feels extreme."

"You are the villain today, right? What would the villain do?"

"Burn it." He didn't want to think about whether or not he should be alarmed at how quickly that response came to him.

"Fine. I can go down to the basement and fire up the incinerator right now if you like. It takes a little bit for it to get hot. Or, like I said, I can store it and you can sleep on the decision for a day or two."

"What would be the benefit of that?" He asked, genuinely wanting an answer.

"It would give you a chance to change your mind. Free you from the possibility of regret."

He shook his head. "This has been hanging over me for nearly twenty years." He felt himself relax as a feeling of clarity came over him. "I don't want that anymore."

"Fine. I'll be right back then." She stood up and left him alone.

He thought he would feel anxious, but he didn't. He opened the box and took out the sealed envelope. If he was going to burn it anyway, he kinda wanted to know what was inside. The envelope was thick, and had cost his mom over five dollars to send, only to have it returned to her in the end. Carefully he tore the envelope open and pictures spilled out. Probably about thirty of them. All were of Abby, or had Abby in them. Some singles of her from Prom night. Some he'd remembered taking himself. Some from their dates, or time with his mom. There was a note in his mother's handwriting.

Dear Joan and Jeff,

I found these pictures of your beautiful girl, and thought you might want them. They seem to just bring Wilder pain, and I couldn't bear to throw them out. I hope they can make you smile someday.

Sincerely,

Aurora Davis

October walked in at that moment and caught him reading the note. "Unbelievable."

"What?" She asked.

"My mom tried to send old pictures of Abby to her folks. And they didn't even open them. They just sent them back. She tried to do right by them. And look what they missed out on by holding on to that anger."

"Indeed." She eyed him, and he threw up his hands and flounced back into the couch.

"Oh fine, now you're going to hit me with my own words of wisdom?"

"I just said, indeed." But she clearly couldn't help the self-righteous grin spreading across her face.

"All right. Give me the prom picture. And the other pictures. Burn the rest."

"Less and less the villain all the time," October pointed

out. "Do you want the box? Or do you want me to put the pictures in something else for you?"

"Something else."

"Good choice."

"You would've said that no matter what I picked."

"True," she said as she searched for a bag to give him. She came up with a plain brown takeout bag she hadn't tossed out yet. "How's this?"

"Perfect."

"Someday, you might be able to look at those without so much hurt."

"Not today," he said.

"Not today," she affirmed.

A picture caught his eye, and he picked it up. "Except..." He looked at it lovingly. "Gosh. I had forgotten all about this." It was a terrible picture. Blurry, and too bright. But they were laughing, that much was clear. It was an attempt at a selfie. "I had bought a couple of those disposable cameras? The ones you had to drop off to get developed, you know?" October nodded. "Took one with me everywhere we went. She was so beautiful." He couldn't help but smile at the image, or maybe it was the memory. "This day," he handed the photograph to October, and she smiled warmly down at it. "We'd taken a picnic into the mountains and laughed so hard Sprite came out our noses. That burns!"

October chuckled. "Yes, it does."

"I've been so focused on the tragedy, I forgot all about the good stuff. Why I loved her."

"Look at you finding the good already." She put on her best fake Freudian accent. "Vell, I declare you cured! Go in peace."

Wilder laughed, and it felt good. He felt good. "Thank you," he said quietly.

She reached for his hand, and he reached back for her. It

was soft, and warm, and he found he didn't want to let it go. "You're very welcome, Wilder. This is friendship, huh? You help me with one crisis, and I help you with another. You know, you don't need to outdo me the next time. You could just let me have my moment."

He laughed. "Oh my gosh. We have to go to your apartment. I have stuff for you."

"Stuff?"

"Yeah. My mom's tv, some dishes, although not nearly as garish as your old ones were."

She raised an eyebrow at him. "Tell me how you really feel."

He stood up and pulled her with him. "Come on."

"I can't leave with the incinerator on."

"Okay, well toss the box in and lets go."

"It's probably hot enough for a box of paper by now. Want to come with me?" She offered.

"Not even a little bit."

"Your loss."

He watched her walk away with all that bad in her hands, and looked down at all the good in his. "Not really, no."

CHAPTER 11

*W*ith the help of Mrs. Davis' things, she almost got her apartment back in order. Things were missing, and her heart still hurt from the damage, but it looked more like a home every day.

October couldn't help but notice Wilder was changing too. He was happier, more relaxed. She had no idea why Abby hadn't been there when he showed up with the box of her things that night. But she'd stayed away. Mrs. Davis said she rarely left his house anymore. And he didn't seem to like being there. The night before Halloween, they were working on things for the haunted house, and he asked if he could just sleep on her couch.

"You didn't bring a change of clothes, did you?"

He shook his head. "No. But I'm not that dirty. I can just shower in the morning and head to work, if it's not too much of an imposition. I took a half day so I could help you out here tomorrow afternoon."

"A sleepover? Like a real friend sleepover?" She didn't even try to hide her excitement.

Wilder looked at her like she had just told him she'd been

abducted by aliens as a kid, and she was too weird for them to keep so they sent her back. "Yes?" He asked cautiously.

"I've never had a sleepover before."

"Seriously? You're what? Thirty-five?"

She wrinkled her nose. "Isn't it rude to ask a girl her age?"

He shrugged. "Friends should know."

"Fine. Yes. I'm thirty-five." For one more day at least. She loved Halloween, but not because it was her birthday. No one had made a fuss about her birthday since her dad died. While he always told her Happy Birthday, her dad seemed sad he couldn't do anything for her, so she just tried to ignore it and focus on Halloween.

"Great. Me too."

"Funnily enough, I'd figured that out."

He stuck out his bottom lip. "Well, that's not fair. You know more about me than I do about you?"

"Not anymore. I've just told you how old I am."

"Fair enough. What other secrets are you hiding, you wily minx?" He asked.

She winked at him. "Wouldn't you like to know?"

"I would, yes. That's why I asked." She tossed a brand-new couch pillow at him, a purple one with haunted mansion graphics on it, and an all-out pillow fight ensued. It ended in giggles, with both of them lying on their backs on the floor.

"Yes. I think a sleepover would be lovely, Wilder Davis."

"Excellent. Thank you for your hospitality, October Manning."

They went to bed late that night, after staying up to put the finishing touches on a huge paper-mache zombie she was planning to put near the entrance. She'd brought the tents and other décor from her storage unit to her apartment over the course of the week, and she'd never felt so ready for the big day. She'd scheduled nothing, so she could spend the entire day setting up. She wasn't usually so compassionless, but most people didn't want a funeral on Halloween anyway. They said it felt weird, and that worked out just fine for her.

"Night, Wilder Davis," she called as she stood in the doorway of her bedroom.

"Goodnight, October Manning."

She moved to shut the door when he called to her. "Hey, October?"

"Yeah?"

"Do you have Ghostbusters on speed dial?"

She tilted her head, trying to puzzle out where he was going. He didn't know about her ghosts, did he? "Why?"

"In case the ghost that sacked your place comes back. The police said it was almost like a ghost did it, didn't they?"

Relief washed over her as she realized he was teasing her. "Goodnight, *mister* Davis."

"Hey October."

"Oh my God, *what?*"

"Thanks for letting me stay."

She smiled. "Any time, Wilder. Unless you make me stand in this doorway for another moment talking to you. Then you'll have to go."

"Okay princess. Go get your beauty rest."

She shut the door, smiling ear to ear. She went to bed thinking about Abby and Wilder, and how he seemed ready to heal. She wondered if that was the key to helping the ghost move on. Then her mind wandered to Wilder. Yes, he teased her a lot. But it didn't bother her. It made her laugh. She liked it. She also liked how he looked. His scraggly beard and sparkling green eyes that usually did a terrible job hiding whatever mischief he was up to. And his smell. That earthy, grassy, outdoors smell that felt like home.

She sat up in bed. She liked him. She'd had her fair share of crushes. Who didn't? Her latest was Jason Momoa. She'd loved him in *Game of Thrones*, and saw a clip of him pop into her feed on Graham Norton and was done for. But none of her most recent crushes were people she knew. Last time that happened was in high school. And it didn't end well. He'd thought it was funny to lead her on and then leave her waiting for a kiss on the bleachers with a bunch of his friends watching. They'd taken pictures of her sitting there alone, and written "NEVER BEEN KISSED" over her. Then they'd taped them to her locker.

She sank back down under the covers, creating a cocoon that made her feel safe. She couldn't have a crush on him. He wasn't ready to date. Not with Abby in the picture. She'd have to get it under control, and just appreciate him as a friend. Lord knew she'd never had too many of those. And far be it for her to chase off the first good friend she'd had with a misplaced crush.

Taking a deep breath, she rolled over, resolved to get some sleep before the big day tomorrow. Thirty-six was promising to be an interesting year, and she wanted to start it right, dog-gone-it. Not like some dewy-eyed schoolgirl who didn't know how to act.

In the morning, she found Wilder making coffee. "I ordered donuts. They'll be here in five minutes."

She nodded approvingly. "I really like this sleepover."

He beamed. "I aim to please."

"Oh really? Here I thought you aimed to tease." She couldn't help her grin and he gave her a thumbs up.

"Well played. You're learning."

After breakfast he left with promises to come back as soon as he could.

"Don't rush, and for the love of God, don't stress. I appreciate everything you've already done. This'll be great!"

"I can't wait to see it in action!" He was so enthusiastic

about it, she knew he meant it, and that didn't help her keep her new feelings of affection for him under wraps.

BY THE TIME he came back with lunch in hand, she'd made excellent progress setting up out front. She had tents and walls made from pieces of crinkled sheet metal creating a bit of a maze. It looked a little like a shanty town in the daylight, but she knew it would be great once it got dark. She was working on setting up the decorations inside the first tent when he poked his head in.

"Boo," he said.

"What?" She answered automatically.

"What?"

She stood up and brushed her pants off. "Sorry. That's what my dad used to call me. Boo."

"Cute," he said holding out a white bag to her. "I was just trying to startle you."

"How was work?" She asked as she unpacked the burger and fries he'd picked up on the way over.

"Good. Nothing exciting. Someday, I'd like to get back out in the field. But it seems like there's always so much paperwork to do. I never have time."

"Did you ever think about hiring a business manager?" She asked.

"Did you ever think about hiring some help at your place?"

She eyed him. "Had that little bullet all loaded into the gun, eh?"

He shrugged. "Nikki, the girl who works in the office would be perfect. She did beautifully handling things while I was out when Mom died. I just have to hand her the reigns. And I'm not sure I'm ready."

"I get that," she agreed. "Tell you what. As soon as you

make her the manager, I'll start looking for some help at the funeral home."

"Deal." The way he said it made her afraid he might actually do it, and then she'd have to hire someone, and hide her ghosts even more. Nope, that wouldn't work.

"You're sweating," he pointed out.

"Yeah, well. It's stuffy in this tent."

"It definitely isn't stuffy." He chuckled. "Don't worry. I'm not going to make Nikki my manager."

"Okay good. Because I could not think of how to weasel out of that one."

He threw a French fry at her, and she caught it. "Don't waste good food," she said as she popped it into her mouth.

He raised the next fry to her as if he was toasting with it, and they ate in companionable silence.

BY EVENING the house was ready. Her dad showed up at the usual time, and Wilder happened to be upstairs going to the bathroom when he came. He brought Mrs. Davis too, who still hadn't mastered the art of moving things, but thought it would be fun to watch.

Every year before, her dad had done the same, just watched. But this year, he thought it would be fun to spook the kids a little more. A tap on the shoulder. Tip something over. Pull back a curtain. Standard ghost stuff. But October couldn't deny how fun it would be to have him actually helping her this year.

She clapped when she saw him. "Dad. This is gonna be so great."

"You are bouncing," he pointed out.

"And why aren't you?"

He grinned. "You're right. This'll be a blast."

"Wilder's here, so I can't talk to you once he comes down."

"Oh," Mrs. Davis exclaimed. "What's he doing here? I thought he might hand out candy at my house. The kids will miss me."

"He told me earlier he got candy and left it in a bowl at the end of your walkway so kids would know it was there. He left a note too, saying how much you appreciated them," October explained.

Mrs. Davis brought a hand to her shirt collar and grabbed it. "Well. That was thoughtful."

Her dad put his arm around her. "Yes, it was. He's a fine boy."

Wilder rejoined her as it was getting dark, and a few minutes later, their first group came through her new and improved haunted house.

Her dad left them alone in the first tent, but started tormenting them in the second one. And by the last one, when he actually touched the mom on the shoulder, they were really spooked. They screamed and laughed and really enjoyed themselves.

"That was amazing," the mom told October. "I don't know how you do it every year, but it's always a blast. Thank you for doing it again."

"I wouldn't miss it," she said as she filled the kids' buckets with full sized candy bars.

Her dad kept it tame for the littler kids, and downright scared the teenagers. October couldn't tell who was having more fun, him or Wilder, who was stationed near the end dressed as a zombie and poised to jump out at unsuspecting trick or treaters.

Near the end of the night, Officer Stephens, dressed in plain clothes, showed up with her two kids. "How are you?"

She asked October, who was dressed as a vampire, complete with blood dripping from her lip.

"Good. Got the apartment back in shape thanks to Wilder there." As she gestured toward him, he was running from a five-year-old who was also dressed as a zombie. Her heart nearly exploded at the sight.

"Well, that was nice of him. Boyfriend?"

"No. Friend."

The officer watched October with a skeptical expression, but kept whatever she was thinking to herself. "Well, I'd say the evening was a success. No sign of your intruder I take it?"

"Nope." It wasn't a lie, per se. She really hadn't seen Abby all week, but she also knew the ghost wasn't gone for good either. Not yet anyway.

As the officer walked away, she caught a glimpse of a girl leaning against a tree two houses down. But when October blinked, the girl was gone. She didn't think anything of it. There were a lot of kids milling around after all. Abby wouldn't be so bold as to cause a scene in such a crowd. Would she?

October was having too much fun to worry about it.

THE LAST TRICK or treater left around ten and October was exhausted. "Can we clean up tomorrow?" Wilder asked.

"Absolutely," October said as she took out her fake fangs and moved her lips around, trying to regain proper feeling in them.

"Want to go to that party I was telling you about?"

"Oh, I'm so sorry. I forgot all about it. Is it too late?" October asked hopefully.

"Knowing Colin, it's just getting started."

October rolled her eyes. That kind of guy. A partier who

doesn't know when to quit. She narrowed her eyes. "How long do we have to stay?"

He laughed. "Driving a hard bargain, I see. An hour? Maybe two if you're having fun?"

"An hour," she agreed. "Do you want me to drive separately, so you don't have to leave early for me?"

"No. You'll give me an excuse to get out," he admitted.

"Why are we going if you don't even want to?"

"I told you. My friends finally invited me to something, so I need to go. Show them I'm a functional human again."

"Functional means partying until tomorrow apparently?"

"That might be some people's definition."

She shook her head. "I am definitely not functional then."

"Noted."

They stayed in costume and headed to Colin's house, who lived about twenty minutes away, about halfway between their small town and the city. Apparently, Colin worked in the city as a "penny pusher," or so Wilder told her on the way there. They'd met in college in their finance class. Colin majored in finance, and Wilder minored in business.

"Colin's a little...well you'll see. But he was fun, and he never asked questions. I liked that about him," Wilder explained.

"Asked questions?"

Wilder shrugged. "I don't know. Like why I was quiet. Or didn't want to hang out. He never really gave me an option not to hang out now that I think about it. He'd just show up at my place and we'd go. He was good for me."

"Was?"

Wilder nodded.

"It's okay to outgrow friends."

"I know. I just always thought he would grow up with me. But he never really did."

"Hence the midnight party for a bunch of thirty-somethings. How many people do you think will actually be there?"

"Quite a few. He hangs around with twenty-somethings."

"Cute," October said, not trying to hide her judgement.

"All right Judge Judy. Tom's in his twenties ya know."

"Tom is an old soul," she argued.

"Maybe. He's just a good kid I think." October heard the affection in Wilder's voice and hoped he'd start hanging around with Tom more, and Colin less.

There were so many cars lining the street, they had to park two blocks away. As they walked the distance to Colin's house, she scolded herself. She hadn't even met Colin and she'd judged him. She hated it when people did that to her, and she felt ashamed.

She reached out and touched Wilder's arm, stopping him. "I'm sorry," she offered.

"What for? Don't tell me we got all the way out here and you want to go home already. You promised me an hour," he whined.

"I'm sorry for passing judgement on Colin before I met him."

Wilder laughed, and when he didn't stop right away, she folded her arms over her chest, thinking he was laughing at her.

"What is so funny?" She demanded.

"You didn't judge him. I warned you about him. If anyone should apologize, it should be me. I should let you form your own opinions. I was just trying to protect you. I know you think people are creeped out by you. But you're just as likely to be creeped out by him. He can be a little…forward."

"Forward meaning…inappropriate?"

"That seems harsh, but probably. Yes. I've heard him called a slime ball more than once."

"Great." October regretted more and more agreeing to this party.

"Will Tom be here?" She asked as they walked through the door and were accosted by *Monster Mash* playing about three settings too loudly.

Wilder shook his head no. "He and Colin don't know each other," he shouted.

They wound through the crowd of dancing bodies through the living room, where people were sitting and talking, although October had no idea how they could hear each other. Wilder made his way to the kitchen, which was nicely upgraded. In fact, the whole house was at least one decimal place over from where October lived. Maybe two. The nicest finishes, minimalistic décor, and modern art adorned the walls telling October that Colin had done quite well for himself.

"Wilder!" A clean-shaven blond man yelled from across the kitchen. He held a red Solo cup up in toast to him and Wilder waved back.

They pushed their way across the crowd to meet up with him. Colin was dressed as a farmer, complete with overalls, and a straw hat. "Well, who's this beautiful little creature of the night?" He looked her up and down, making her glad her vampire costume wasn't revealing at all.

"This is October Manning. She runs the funeral home back home," he said automatically, making October wonder if he'd rehearsed it.

"An undertaker? Really Wilder? Did she do your mom's funeral?" He started to laugh and clapped him on the back. "Is *that* how you met? You're dating the undertaker?"

Wilder looked apologetically at October and she spoke up. "Wilder has excellent taste." She did her best to attempt a smoldering look, and Colin snorted.

"Sure. If you like it a little dead and cold between the

sheets," he guffawed at his own joke as he elbowed Wilder, expecting him to laugh along.

"Colin. You couldn't handle her, even if she wanted you to," Wilder shot back.

Colin straightened and swallowed his laughter. "She'd want to."

"You just keep thinking that." October patted him on the arm and made her way toward a sliding glass door that led outside. She needed to breathe. What had come over her? She'd never been so forward or confident in her life.

Wilder followed her out, and so did Colin, much to her chagrin. "Wait, guys. Drinks, do you want a drink?" He called after them.

"Sure," she shouted over her shoulder before disappearing onto the patio. It was a beautiful space. A well-lit pool with a waterfall cascading down from the hot tub. Tiki torches added to the ambiance, even though it was fall in New England. She noticed a few people gathered around a fire roasting marshmallows, and headed over there with Wilder in tow.

He grabbed her elbow. "Well, I like confident October very much." His breath on her ear gave her goosebumps.

"Not sure I like confident Colin."

"He grows on you. I'd be offended if he didn't try to come on to you. It's how he says hi," Wilder defended.

"Oh, now you're making excuses?"

"Hey guys," Colin called as he held up two cans. Wilder waved.

"Well. He is my oldest friend."

"Fine. I'll play nice if he will," she said under her breath as Colin walked over.

"He definitely won't. I choose to find it charming."

"I make no such choice," she stood firm.

"About what?" Colin asked as he jogged up to them and handed them two beers.

October didn't drink beer, but she took it politely anyway. Wilder took his, with a thanks and grinned at her.

"About finding you charming," she answered honestly as she took a seat near the fire. It was quieter out there, and although it was cool, the fire made it pleasant.

Wilder pulled up a chair close to her, and Colin sat next to him. He grabbed a plate of marshmallows and roasters, and passed them down.

She took hers gratefully and started to roast. "Listen, I'm sorry if my jokes offended you. They were just jokes. I'm in finance. I'm sure you could come up with something nasty to say about how I'm just a slimy Wall Street bottom feeder."

Her marshmallow browned nicely, and she smiled at it. "Seems I don't need to."

"Wow, Colin. You're growing. I've never heard you apologize for anything."

"Might be a sign of the apocalypse," Colin joked. "Better prepare yourself."

For the next hour, he upheld the cease fire, and managed to ask safe questions like what the best show she'd watched on Netflix lately was. *Wednesday,* obviously.

"A bit on the nose, eh?" He said, then held up his hands. "Sorry. I agreed not to make undertaker jokes."

"You have to admit it was a great show," October asserted.

"If that kind of dark humor is your jam," he offered vaguely.

She decided not to respond, remembering to keep the conversation civil. She had three s'mores while they sat there, and two other girls strolled up to join them. They were bubbly, and young. They truly did bring out Colin's charm, as Wilder called it. And she could see why they fawned over him. He had money, wasn't bad to look at, and was free with compliments, if in a backhanded sort of way sometimes. She couldn't say she liked him. But she could certainly see why other people put up with him. And if she was going to be a good friend to Wilder, she should try to like his other friends.

After she finished her third s'more, she realized her face hurt from smiling. She was having fun. The girls seemed to like her. No one had made any further comments about her job or how weird it was. And she kept stealing glances at Wilder, who was looking at her every time she glanced over.

No ghosts haunted their evening. Just living, breathing people who seemed to enjoy her company. It was refreshing in a way she didn't know she needed.

Wilder stood and stretched. "Well Colin, I think we'll shove off."

October looked at her watch and couldn't believe it was eleven thirty. They'd stayed longer than she promised. And she hadn't minded most of it.

She stuck out her hand to Colin who batted it away and hugged her. "Thanks for having us, Colin," she said into his shoulder as he crushed her against him.

"Of course. Any friend of Wilder's is a friend of mine."

"Is that so? What about Kyle Brown?" Wilder countered.

"Oh, that prick? Don't get me started on him. Good riddance," Colin said as he shook hands with Wilder.

"Mmkay, I'll need to know more about your friend Kyle," she asked as they walked back to their car. Surprisingly, most of cars were still lining the road on both sides, and more had arrived after them, parked in front of two more homes. But, he'd turned the music down as it got later. He did have some consideration for others, or so it seemed.

Wilder chuckled, and the sound drew October closer. She brushed against his arm as they walked, making her skin tingle under her costume. "Colin was probably right about him, in the end. He was a bit of a whiner. Always complained about what we were doing, but came along anyway. He was in one of my landscaping classes. Briefly, we'd talked about partnering, and starting a landscaping company together. But Colin chased him off."

She sat in the passenger's seat and buckled her seat belt. "Chased him off?"

"You know how he was with you at first?"

She nodded.

"Like that. But a million times worse. He was relentless. And I have to admit, Kyle was an easy target, as whiney as he was." He shrugged. "Turns out, Colin was right. I heard about five years ago Kyle's business folded. He declared bankruptcy, and now he's working two jobs."

"That's horrible."

"Could've been me too."

"Do you really think so? Don't you think you would've made choices to prevent that?"

Wilder shrugged. "It's hard to say. Kyle would've complained about every decision I made. I might have just let him have the run."

"Well, I hope not. That would've been stupid."

"How do you know I'm not stupid?"

She looked over at him. The streetlights cast a dim yellow glow on him as they drove by. She couldn't see his eyes in the shadows, and his face was covered in makeup, but she still thought he was handsome. "Give me some credit. I don't hang around stupid people."

He laughed and looked over at her. "A woman of discerning taste."

"Don't you forget it."

They laughed and talked about the party the rest of the way home, and about how well the haunted house had gone off.

"I have no idea how you pulled some of that off. More than one person swore someone touched them in tents neither one of us were in. And a couple people said the tent walls were moving, like someone was running a hand along the outside. Pure magic." Wilder stopped at the end of her sidewalk, admiring their pop-up haunted house one more time in the darkness.

Her neighbor hadn't come out, but she never did. October didn't even know if she stayed home for Halloween.

She did see Abby standing on the sidewalk near her property line. Not close enough for October to really do anything, but she did find it interesting Abby was hanging around. She hadn't noticed her at Colin's. How long had she been watching them? And what did she want? Was she finally ready to talk? October tried to smile her way when Wilder was appraising their haunted house, and make her feel welcome, but she couldn't tell if she saw or not.

He turned to her and caught her looking down the sidewalk. "Don't you think it went well?"

"Oh, it went great. I couldn't have done it without you. Literally, no way I could've pulled this off. Thank you for all your help," she said as they walked up to the front stoop. "I gotta tell you, Wilder. This was the best birthday ever."

"I'm so glad. Wait...what?" The word echoed, and she cringed, glancing at her neighbor's porch light, which was currently off.

"Shh. It's almost midnight," she scolded.

"I'm sorry," he hissed. "Today is your *birthday*?"

"It is. And this may have even been better than the year my dad took me to Disney and let me ride the haunted mansion six times in a row. He didn't complain once. But don't tell him I said that."

"I..." he trailed off processing. "I won't. But October. Why didn't you tell me it was your birthday? I would've done something for you."

She looked into his brilliant green eyes, filled with gratitude and affection for him. "But you did. I just told you this was the best birthday ever. Even if your friend Colin is a little hard to like," she teased.

He looked down at her, taking both her hands in his, moving closer as he went. "Thank you for sharing the day with me, October."

"That's not how this works. I say thank you, and you say, don't you forget it. I'll be waiting for the paybacks in the form of Mission Bar-B-Que." She knew she should look away. His eyes were boring into her like he wanted to devour her right then and there.

"You taking that zombie costume a little seriously?" She asked. "You look like you want to take a bite out of my lip."

"Am I that transparent?" He was so close, his breath felt warm against her face.

Words failed her. "Mmm." Her skin was on fire, and she knew if she didn't have all that vampire makeup on, it would have shown. Was he going to—

Before she could finish her thought, their lips met.

CHAPTER 12

The world stopped. Her breath hitched and nothing existed except Wilder. He held her hands, and she squeezed his. He tasted like s'mores, and his lips were soft. His beard tickled her nose, but she didn't mind.

The pop felt distant, and the flash didn't seem important. Even the pain she felt wasn't as demanding as his lips against hers. But he pulled back reflexively and looked up, forcing her to pay attention to those things.

"You're bleeding," he said. But she couldn't process it. Why would he say that after their first kiss?

"Well, it was good for me too," she said.

"No. October, it's bad."

"Well, I'm sorry I don't have much experience with kissing. Sheesh."

He looked up. "The light fixture broke. You need to go to the ER. There's probably glass in your face."

"What?" The pain started becoming more demanding, pounding with her heartbeat.

She looked at Wilder, who seemed unscathed, and Abby was standing at his shoulder not touching him, but clearly protecting him from the falling glass. She had a venomous look on her face.

The ghost had hurt October. On purpose. What on Earth was she doing? She lifted a hand to her face, and it came away covered in blood. "I should go in and take care of this. Shoot." She looked at the bright red blood on her hand, suddenly overwhelmed with fear. "I'm sorry Wilder. I can't do this. You should go home."

"Wait, what?"

"I'm sorry, Wilder. Please. Just go."

"I will not. You're hurt. I'll take you to the hospital right now."

She watched as Abby grabbed his elbow and tried to pull him away. His face darkened when she did it, but he didn't say anything. He held his ground.

October shook her head. She couldn't do it. How far would Abby go to keep him in her clutches? Physical harm was beyond October's limit. Wilder was on his own. "I'm fine. I'll be fine. I wish you the best. I truly appreciate every-thing. This is just too much too fast. I just wanted a friend, ya know?" She held her fingertips to her lips, the ghost of the kiss lingering there. "You're grieving. You don't know what you want, and I don't need to get caught up in it. Just. Just go, Wilder. Please."

She turned and went inside, locking the door behind her.

"October. What…" he trailed off. She could hear him standing by the front door, trying to decide what to do. Blood dripped onto her costume as she counted in her head. One. Two. Three. Four…she got to twelve before she finally heard his footsteps retreat, and his truck start up.

Only then did she feel comfortable going to the kitchen for a paper towel. She walked to the bathroom to assess the damage, and it was worse than she thought. There were a hundred cuts in her face, all of them bleeding, and a few of them deep. How could a ghost do this?

She sighed, knowing she had to go to the hospital. She grabbed her keys and left. 12:05 the clock Wilder had brought over from his mom's read. At least she was starting a new day. Abby hadn't ruined her best birthday ever.

EIGHT STITCHES, over an hour of work with the tweezers, and two tubes of antibiotic cream later, she was heading back to the funeral home. It was three a.m. but she didn't care. Her dad would want to know about this. And Mrs. Davis for that matter.

They must have heard her coming, and met her in the lobby. The hospital staff cleaned the makeup off her face, but she was still wearing the rest of her vampire costume.

"What happened?" Mrs. Davis asked.

"You weren't done up like that when I left you," her dad said, trying to piece together her bandaged face with the theatrics she'd put on that night.

"Abby did it."

"Abby did what?" Her dad asked.

"She broke the light fixture over my head, and it shredded my face." Saying it out loud sent a shiver over October's entire body. A ghost had hurt her. "Needed eight stitches. But the doctor didn't think it would scar." She tried to take consolation from that, but she couldn't. A ghost had hurt her. It kept repeating in her head.

Her phone binged. It wasn't even a gif. *Are you okay? Did you go to the hospital.*

I'm fine. I did. So, stop worrying. Go back to your life.

He didn't respond, and she didn't understand how she could be relieved and crushed at the same time.

"Where's Wilder?" Mrs. Davis asked, not realizing what October had done.

"I sent him home." She looked at Mrs. Davis, begging her to leave it. "I can't do this, Mrs. Davis. I'm so sorry. I've never had a ghost hurt me before. This is beyond anything I'd ever imagined." Tears filled her eyes.

"What did you do?" Mrs. Davis wasn't angry or disappointed. She was confused.

"I told him to leave me alone. That I couldn't do it. I just wanted a friend. And he kissed me. And then the light broke, and this happened." October gestured to her bandaged face. "I look like the Phantom of the Opera."

"Can't carry a tune though," her dad joked.

Mrs. Davis glared at him, and he held up his hands. "Not ready to joke yet. That's fine," he offered.

She reached for October's hand, and passed through. October fought the urge to move away. Being touched by a ghost felt different now. Like it was something to be afraid of all of a sudden. She looked at her dad, desperate, but he didn't move. Almost as if he didn't want to touch her if it would frighten her.

Tears spilled over, and dampened her bandages. She started to swipe at them, but Mrs. Davis stopped her. "Oh. I wouldn't, honey."

October nodded. "I liked him, Mrs. Davis. I liked him a lot. And for the first time, he liked me too."

"Isn't that worth fighting for?" Mrs. Davis asked quietly.

October shrugged. "What do you think? Should it cost me my life?"

"No. Absolutely not," her dad interjected. "I have half a mind to beat some sense into that girl."

"How exactly? Last time we tried to talk to her, she disappeared. Didn't do a lick of good," Mrs. Davis said. "She's got such a hold on Wilder. Like he belongs to her.

And he doesn't even know it. What kind of relationship is that?"

"The only kind she's ever known."

October looked at Mrs. Davis, and her dad, who was standing behind her friend, hands on her shoulders. "I'm so sorry Mrs. Davis. I don't think there's anything else I can do. I think you should move on."

The ghost looked stricken, and her dad frowned. "What do you mean?" He asked.

"I mean I think it would be torturous of her to sit and watch her son be unhappy for the rest of his life, and she should move on." October slapped a hand over her mouth and cried out in pain when she did.

"Oh, October," Mrs. Davis said, standing up and going to her. She sat at her feet, and reached for her hands again, so October moved them to her lap. The ghost looked up at her with nothing but compassion in her eyes.

"I'm not going anywhere. I've done this to you. And whether or not you decide to help him again, I don't care." She stopped, reconsidering. "Well, I do care. I care very much about him, and if he's okay." Mrs. Davis shook her head. "My point is, this is my fault, and I'll hang around at least a little longer to make sure I've done everything I can to set it right."

"Like what?" October asked through her tears.

"Well. I don't know exactly. Maybe the day will shed some light on it."

"Or it'll show my clients just what a monster I am."

"Who do you have tomorrow?" Her dad asked.

"I have two appointments. No services," October answered.

"Might want to send them somewhere else," her dad suggested.

She'd only done that once before. When her dad died. She'd taken no one for over a week. She'd put a recording on the voicemail, and not even bothered to answer the phone. She'd sent everyone to homes outside of town.

She chewed the inside of her cheek. "I hate to leave someone in the lurch."

"But you'd rather meet up with them as the phantom of the opera, and deal with their ghosts that they bring in?"

That did it. The thought of another ghost overwhelmed her with such panic, she reached for her phone right then.

"You can't call a grieving family in the middle of the night," Mrs. Davis reasoned.

Hesitantly, she put her phone back down and nodded.

Her dad sat in the chair where Mrs. Davis had been. "We'll sort this out, Boo. I promise. Like gas, this too shall pass."

"Steve," Mrs. Davis scolded.

"What? I say that all the time. It will."

October chuckled through her tears, sending a spray of tears and snot through Mrs. Davis. "Oh my gosh, I'm so sorry."

It was Mrs. Davis' turn to laugh. "Didn't feel a thing."

Maybe they were right. Maybe it would be okay. Maybe she would get over it, and go back to the way her life was before. The thing was, she wasn't sure she wanted to. She liked having a friend. Someone she could talk to about almost anything. Someone she could give and take with. But Wilder wasn't just someone. He was Wilder.

As she sat at the kitchen table with the ghosts that were her family, she struggled to believe them. It would be okay. It would be okay. She repeated it over and over, trying to believe it. But as she looked at the concern etched into her dad's face, she wondered if it would ever be true.

CHAPTER 13

Wilder didn't sleep at all that night. He called in sick, and told Nikki to just take care of everything. Sign checks for him, make decisions, he didn't care. He couldn't think. She asked him what happened and if he was okay, and he didn't answer. He wasn't going to lie to her. He wasn't okay. At all. He couldn't put the pieces together. They'd had such a great night, and then something spooked her. He didn't think she was superstitious, but had the light breaking at the moment they kissed been some kind of sign for her? That they shouldn't be together? Who could tell with some women? Especially when they shut a guy out.

The thought made Wilder mad. He wasn't a mind reader. He was a grown man, too old for games. But October was different than anyone he'd ever known. She didn't mind his sense of humor, and even made him laugh more than he had in ages. He liked that about her. He felt relaxed around her in a way he'd forgotten was possible. He wasn't willing to let go of that without a fight.

He decided to go down to the funeral home. He'd talk to her in the light of day. Maybe that would change things.

She'd see how much she'd over reacted. But when he got there, there was a sign on the door.

Manning Funeral home is closed for the time being. For inquiries, please call Woodland Heights.

She'd left the phone number, along with an apology for any inconveniences the circumstances may have occured. She said she was okay. But was she? He started to worry, and drove over to her place.

But she didn't answer when he knocked. "October?" He called.

He hadn't answered her last text. So, he sat on the front step and texted her. "You alive?"

She didn't answer. He waited ten minutes and his hands started getting cold. As much as he hated using a phone for its original function, he dialed her number.

"You have reached October Manning," her voicemail answered. "Director of Manning Funeral Home. I am out of the office indefinitely. Please direct inquiries to Woodland Heights at—"

He hung up. Touching the screen to hang up was so unsatisfying. He wanted to slam the receiver down. To throw something. So, he picked up a rock and launched it. But as he watched it bounce across the street, he didn't feel better. She'd ghosted him. Simple as that. For what? For kissing her? What the heck.

She did say she just wanted a friend, and he'd crossed that line. But she'd wanted it. Hadn't she? Or had he just seen what he wanted to see?

After about a half hour, he got up and went back to his truck. But where could he go? The funeral home, and October had become his safe space. And maybe that was his mistake. He'd thought he could trust her. And she'd vanished.

. . .

THAT NIGHT, Colin texted. First time since he'd texted to invite Wilder to the party.

You up for a drink tonight?

Not even a little bit, Wilder thought. He had no desire to put on a happy face for his friend who didn't know how to deal with emotions.

Come on man, just you and me? Realized how long it had been since we hung out at the party. Wouldn't mind spending some time with ya.

He started typing and stopped, leaving the message on read for Colin. Then he got a cricket gif. Wilder couldn't help but laugh.

Fine. Name the time and place, Wilder typed. What could it hurt? He needed to blow off some steam anyway.

Colin texted a bar they'd been to a few times together, and asked Wilder to meet him there in an hour.

Wilder changed out of his t-shirt and basketball shorts, and into a blue button down and khaki shorts. October could be without him, he could be without her, he told himself as he grabbed his keys and marched out the door.

He felt a tug, but couldn't place it. He stopped and looked back, thinking he'd forgotten something. Keys, wallet, phone. Inventory checked out good, so he shrugged off the feeling and left. The lights flickered as he locked the door behind him and he shook his head. "Dang power company can't keep the power grid stable to this house."

He drove aggressively to the bar, letting his anger replace any of his other emotions. It was easier to deal with.

The parking lot at Harpers wasn't too full at eight, and Wilder was surprised Colin had wanted to meet so early. He must have had a morning meeting the next day.

When he went through the old, heavy, wooden door, the bar was just as he remembered it, even though he couldn't place when he'd last been inside. He preferred dinner with

Colin, and often talked him into that. But it hadn't occurred to him that day to push back. He was too lost in his own thoughts.

Colin sat in the back corner of the dark bar. A song Wilder didn't recognize played on the old jukebox, and he stopped at the bar to order a beer before making his way toward his friend.

"What's up? You look like death warmed over," Colin asked.

"Thanks man. What's up?" He deflected.

"Nothing. Landed a huge deal today. Wanted to celebrate."

"That's great. But shouldn't you be doing that with your work buddies?"

Colin snorted. "Like that bunch of yuppies would go for a dive like this?"

Wilder looked around, a thick haze of cigarette smoke hung in the air, and he fought the urge to cough, suddenly remembering even more why he didn't care for Harper's.

"You don't even smoke. Why do you like this place?" Wilder asked.

"Been coming here since before I was legal. They never asked questions."

Sounded about right.

"So, what are you gonna do with the big fat raise I assume you're getting?" Wilder asked, trying to keep the conversation on Colin.

"Not sure yet. Won't have a lot of time for travel. Got the house how I like it. Maybe buy another car."

"You don't really drive the ones you have," Wilder pointed out.

"Says you. I drove the Vette here."

"Maybe you'll have to take me for a ride," Wilder suggested.

"Why do you think I asked you here? There's a great back road not far. Nice and straight. Bet we can get it over a hundred in less than six seconds."

Wilder raised his glass to that. "You're on."

Colin eyed him as he drained his beer. "What's on your mind, Wilder?"

He didn't want to talk about it. "Nothing. Just some stuff with Mom's estate." He knew that would stop the questions.

"Oh good." Colin sipped his own beer while Wilder ordered another. "I thought maybe you'd gotten wrapped up about that creepy undertaker."

Wilder shot him a look. "She wasn't creepy."

"Anyone who wants to spend time with dead people is creepy, Wilder."

"It wasn't like that. She didn't get her jollies from it," Wilder argued.

"How do you know? Did she tell you what she was into?" Colin raised an eyebrow and leaned in closer. "I bet it was weird."

"She helped people in a way you'll never understand. She helped me," Wilder admitted.

Colin elbowed him. "Oh yeah. With what?"

"Not like that. Can we change the subject please?"

"Sensitive topic?" Colin asked.

"No. It's just. She said you'd be like this."

Colin scowled. "Oh, she thinks she knows me, does she? What did she say?"

"That she can't have friends because everyone judges her. Everyone thinks she's creepy."

"Well, if the shoe fits, Wilder. She's an undertaker. Of course she's creepy. Look at your mother. She taught elementary school her whole life. She liked kids, and made a mean queso dip. Man, I could go for some of that right now."

"Right. So, my mom is gone, and all you miss is her queso.

127

Noted." Wilder finished his second beer and started to wonder why he came. Maybe he was right about October. Maybe she was a little weird. But Wilder liked it. She was honest, and didn't put on airs. And she sure was right about Colin. Wilder had enough, and stood to leave.

"Hey now, that's not what I meant at all." Collin looked up in surrender, the closest he would come to an apology, Wilder knew. "I shouldn't have mentioned your mom."

"Because you don't know how to talk about grief. I know that about you. Listen, I'm sorry, man. I shouldn't have come. I'm not in the right mood for you."

"What the hell does that mean?" Colin asked, clearly offended.

"It means whatever you think it means, Colin. Like it or not though, October was a better friend than you." Wilder threw down some money to cover his drinks and stormed out.

"What about the ride?" Colin called after him, but he kept walking.

She was right. About Colin. About what people thought of her. He'd told her she was being paranoid. Was she right about him? About them? Was it too much? The thought broke his heart even more, and he longed to go back to just being angry.

CHAPTER 14

*S*he gave herself almost a week. By then her face had healed a bit. She no longer needed to bandage it, and just had a few strips of tape over the stitches. In a few days she'd be able to have them removed.

When she did agree to open back up, she only agreed to one client. Mr. Miller. He was very well loved by his family, and she hoped he would be kind to her.

"Hey there, Scarface. What happened to you?" He asked after sneaking up behind her.

He was an older man, a few tufts of white hair left on his head, and the kind of expression that made it hard to stay mad at him.

October turned around, ready to lay into him, and saw the kindness in his eyes, and her anger melted away. But it wasn't replaced with fear like she thought it would be. What was left, felt like…companionship. A familiar feeling she had around the ghosts, but she thought Abby had destroyed that.

"A ghost did this to me. A friend of yours, maybe?" She accused.

She'd gotten him. His kind expression turned confused as

he tried to comprehend what she'd said. He reached out for her face, and she flinched back. His frown deepened and he dropped his hand. "How?" He demanded.

"She's been here a very long time. If I were you, I wouldn't follow in her footsteps. It's a path of loneliness and anger."

"What can I do? You know, I used to be a salesman. I can be very persuasive."

October smiled. Of course he was a man of action. Why wouldn't he be a natural knight in shining armor?

She shook her head. "Nothing. There's nothing anyone can do. I was trying to help her when this happened."

"Well, that's a stretch, isn't it?" Her dad asked, as he walked up behind her and held out his hand to Mr. Miller. "Steve," he said as they shook hands.

"Arthur," Mr. Miller said. "And who's this lovely lady?" He took Mrs. Davis' hand and kissed the back of it.

"Aurora Davis," her dad offered warily, making October smile. Was he getting possessive of Mrs. Davis?

"Nice to meet you, Arthur," Mrs. Davis said. "I hope you enjoy your time with us."

"You guys stay?" He asked.

"I'm October's father. I used to own this place. I hang around and help her run things, manage the ghosts. You're our first since the…incident." Her dad glanced at her face and looked quickly away.

"How could a ghost do that?" He asked again. "I can't do anything. Except apparently shake hands with you."

"We're learning. Emotions are powerful, and a young, sixteen-year-old ghost who's been sixteen for nearly twenty years has a lot of emotions," Mrs. Davis explained.

"What did she do? Claw you to death like a feral cat?" Arthur asked.

"No. She broke a light fixture over my head, while protecting the man she loves from harm."

"Boo here was making out with him," her dad added.

Arthur raised an eyebrow. "Oh really. Now there's something I'd like to hear more about."

October shook her head and laughed. "I think you're going to be a bit of a handful, Mr. Miller."

"Arthur, please," he insisted.

"Arthur," she conceded.

"I'd like to help if I can," Arthur insisted.

"We appreciate that, Arthur." Mrs. Davis said. "We just don't know what to do right now. We're just giving her space and time to heal."

"Who her? The ghost? Seems to me she doesn't need any space. A sixteen-year-old you say? Sounds like she needs a swift kick in the pants," Arthur said.

Her dad smiled. "I like this guy."

"October," Mrs. Davis explained. "You're her first since the attack."

"I see. And my startling you probably didn't help matters, eh?" He rubbed the back of his neck sheepishly.

October laughed. "It's fine, Arthur. I need to loosen up."

"Honey," he said in the most grandfatherly way, and her heart nearly exploded for him. She'd never had a grandfather and suddenly she understood what she'd been missing. "You need to be exactly how you are. Nothing more, nothing less."

Tears sprang to her eyes, and she walked toward him, reaching out. Surprised, he reached back for her. But he passed through her. She stood there, in the cool fog of his embrace, choosing to take comfort from it. Until she felt a hand on her shoulder, and turned. Her dad was there with open arms and she fell into them, sobbing.

"Dad," she breathed.

Arthur cleared his throat. "Should we let them have a moment?" He asked Mrs. Davis, keeping his voice low.

"Not on your life." She looked over at him. "Or death, as the case may be."

He chuckled and stood awkwardly with Mrs. Davis.

"This will be ok, right?" October asked them.

"This will be okay," they all said in unison. And she wanted desperately to believe them.

LATER THAT DAY, she met Arthur's family, who proved to be as much of a hoot as he was, and just what she needed to remind her why she did what she did. Everything came to a head when they presented the outfit they wanted Arthur to wear.

It was more informal than what most families presented. A blue sweatshirt, and pants. A simple outfit for a simple man. "I don't need anything frilly," he commented with approval.

One of his daughters, Alex, giggled as she handed the package over. "Ally, tell her what you said."

"I absolutely will not," Ally protested.

Alex's eyes sparkled the same way Arthur's did and he laughed. "This ought to be good," he said.

October ignored him, but wanted to smile right along with them both. His wife shook her head, but didn't try to hide her smile. His third daughter, Amanda laughed out loud before explaining the story.

"Ally's been busy with work, so mom, Alex and I had to make some decisions without her."

"Of course," October sympathized.

But Amanda didn't need it. She was smiling even bigger as she got to the good part. "We told her what we'd picked out for dad to wear, and she said, I kid you not, 'Oh, that'll be perfect. It'll match his eyes so well.' " With that, Amanda burst out laughing.

October paused. Arthur did have beautiful blue eyes. But...they wouldn't be open on his body. Ally folded her arms over her chest in protest, but October caught the hint of a smile pulling at her mouth.

"Well. I could start a new trend among funeral homes," October ventured. "Eyes open viewings? What do you think?"

Arthur burst out laughing and tried to clap her on the shoulder, but his hand passed through. He didn't notice and kept right on laughing along with his family. All four of them had happy tears streaming down their faces, and October soaked it up. This is why she did what she did. The ghosts were great. But it was the families that mattered.

When his family left, she turned to Arthur. "Thank you."

"For what, honey?" He asked.

"You asked me if you could help. And this was exactly what I needed."

"My crazy family? Can you believe Ally said that?"

October chuckled. "I've heard a lot of things, but eyes open viewings is new, even for me."

"That was such a great comeback, by the way," Arthur said with warmth in his eyes, but October noticed he was fading. He smiled at her.

"They're going to be okay," he commented out loud as he watched his family get into their car, their laughter carrying across the parking lot. He turned to October, becoming more and more translucent all the time. He was moving on. "And so are you," he added.

"Thank you Arthur."

"Thank *you* October." With that, he disappeared.

Some ghosts she was ready to say goodbye to. Most of them she was happy for, like Mrs. Catrakas. But Arthur had tugged at her heart, and she found herself sad he was gone, and eternally grateful for the reminder that she loved her job.

WHEN SHE GOT HOME that night, she found Wilder sitting on her front stoop, and Abby standing near him. He'd repaired the light fixture.

October stopped short, and wouldn't come any closer. Abby stood with her arms folded over her chest in defiance, leaning against the tree in her front yard, while Mrs. Davis sat next to Wilder.

"October. You're safe," Mrs. Davis tried, but there was no way she was going to believe that. "I won't let her hurt you."

"What are you doing here?" October asked, but didn't direct it at Wilder, hoping Abby would answer.

She just smiled deviously at October, knowing she'd won.

Wilder stood and moved to go toward her, but she instinctively took a step back as Abby moved one step closer, so Wilder stopped. He looked over at the tree, following her gaze. "Something making you nervous?"

"You are," October said to Abby, and her smile widened.

"Abby, please," Mrs. Davis begged. "Stop this. Wilder is living. You have to let him go. He could be happy."

The young ghost turned her glare on Mrs. Davis. "You don't understand."

"Help me to, then," Mrs. Davis begged.

"You're a lost cause. You'll move on and leave him. I'm the one who stays. I'm the one who really loves him. Not you, and certainly not *her*," Abby spat. Her voice was young and vindictive, and it surprised October.

"Um, October?" Wilder asked cautiously, oblivious to the ghostly conversation.

She finally turned her attention to him, and it hurt to look at him.

"Your face looks…" he hesitated, searching for the right word.

"It looks like a face that got shredded by a broken light fixture." She gestured toward the repair. "Thanks for that."

He shrugged. "Least I could do."

He didn't try to come closer, and she didn't move toward him. She felt a little trapped. Could Mrs. Davis stop Abby if she wanted to do something? She could only hope.

"Listen, October. This is silly. It was just an accident, not some sign we shouldn't be together," Wilder offered. Then he seemed to hear himself. "Not that you're silly. Or what you believe is silly. I didn't mean that. Let me start again."

She ached to go to him. To be in his arms. To take comfort from his solid body, and his beating heart. But Abby's eyes on her kept her feet rooted to the ground.

"You honestly think you're making him happy? Are you making yourself happy?" Mrs. Davis asked.

"Happiness? I lost all hope of that eighteen years ago. We were going to have such a magical life together. Now, this. This is what we get. And *she's* trying to interfere." The bitterness in Abby's voice made October take a step back.

"October," Wilder said as he glanced back to the tree. "Come back to me. Stay here with me. Please." His voice waivered as he begged her.

She longed to say yes. But Abby kept her firmly in place. "Wilder. I can't. You need to move on. To let go. Of Abby. Of your mom. Of me. Start fresh, okay?"

"Abby? What does she have to do with this?" His anger flared in a flash, and October regretted mentioning her at all.

"Let me get this straight. I told you about my past, and you're running because of it? You think I can't handle a relationship because I'm not over my girlfriend from twenty years ago?" His voice echoed in the street.

"Eighteen," Abby corrected.

"October, tell him about us. It's the only way," Mrs. Davis pleaded.

Abby's expression faltered. "You wouldn't dare. He'll just think you're a psycho."

Her panic almost loosened October's tongue. What did she have to lose after all? They were over anyway. If she told him, maybe Abby would leave, and he could be happy. Just as she was about to get it out, he lost his patience with her silence.

"You really don't have anything to say for yourself?" Wilder demanded.

She frowned. He wasn't ready to hear what she had to say. And maybe he never would be. "I'm sorry Wilder. This is how it has to be," she responded quietly.

"Maybe you were right. You are too creepy for me." He stomped down her walkway and off in the opposite direction. Abby smiled deviously, knowing she'd won.

Mrs. Davis stopped in front of her. "I'm sorry. Don't give up. Please," she begged before following her son and his ghost down the sidewalk and into his truck.

They all left her standing there alone in the night. Alone. Just as she'd been as long as she could remember. And just as she'd be forever.

CHAPTER 15

It was two weeks until Thanksgiving, and October was scrolling Instagram at home. True, she didn't have any friends or family to follow, but she did follow local businesses to see what was going on in town, and authors to see what they were writing. She also followed several cat accounts, because they were just fun.

She was living her life. Alone. The ghosts tried. Even Mr. Miller tried to talk to Abby, but she scared him off with some sort of "flash in her eyes," or so Mr. Miller said.

"That girl's no ghost. She's a demon," he declared before wishing October the best. "I'm sorry I couldn't help you more."

"Mr. Miller, you helped me plenty. You reminded me why I do this. And, that I still can do this. If not for all the ghosts. Most of them."

That's when he declared Abby wasn't a ghost, thus freeing October from any obligation to her. Declared a priest would be better suited to deal with her.

Mrs. Davis was her friend as always, which almost made October feel worse. She never pressured October to go help

Wilder again, and never voiced an opinion about how she should be acting. She was just there. Just like her dad. Supportive and loving. A true friend.

Except for the fact that she was a ghost now.

October missed Wilder terribly. She missed how he seemed to understand her, their last encounter notwithstanding. That was just as much her fault as his she guessed. She hadn't given him all the information, had she? But she couldn't now. She'd missed her opportunity. Or had it stolen by a teenaged ghost. It didn't matter.

What mattered was she was home alone on a Thursday night scrolling Instagram with Queso purring softly in her lap.

That's when something unusual popped into her feed. It was an ad for a friendship speed dating style meet up Friday night in the city. October had never done anything like that, but she'd seen speed dating in movies. The post specifically stated it was for friendships.

"Looking for a friend?" the ad asked. "Come to our meetup at The Book Nook Friday night. Groups divided into men and women. All ages welcome. Only rule is to be kind."

October clicked on the post, intrigued. Could she be so bold? No probably not, but reading more couldn't hurt. The caption had all the information she needed to find the shop, and sign up if she wanted.

"Or, just show up and try a few friends out," the caption suggested.

She clicked on the link, thinking. Or spiraling. Whichever. Could she do something like that? Every time she'd tried to make a friend, it had ended in disaster, including Wilder. What did they all have in common? Her secret. She'd kept her secret since she told her best friend when she was little about her ghosts. She'd never told anyone else since Rosie. Rosie had cried, and told her mom, who wouldn't let her hang around anymore. She wouldn't let her come over anyway. Any time October wanted to see her, she had to go to Rosie's house. The undertaker's home wasn't appropriate. Even though they weren't living at the funeral home at the time, and she knew it. October had no idea what Mrs. Fields thought went on at her house, but she didn't think Jenga and dinner was all that inappropriate.

She hovered over the sign-up button. If she signed up, she was committed to the event tomorrow. She checked her calendar, even though she knew there was nothing Friday night. She was still keeping herself more open than normal. Two ghosts a week felt like all she could handle at the moment, and she didn't need the money. After working so hard for so long, she had plenty saved up. If she lived frugally, she could probably sell the business and retire right then.

She daydreamed as she hovered over the button. What would she do if she retired? Would the ghosts find her, or would they leave her alone? The thought was both terrifying, and relieving. She knew her dad wouldn't go. But maybe he would if she sold the business.

She shook her head. Nope. Not ready for that. But was she ready for this? She clicked on the button. Just because she clicked on it, didn't mean she had to do it. It opened a form asking for some contact information. That's it. That's all it wanted.

"Why sign up?" The form asked. "Because we like to know how many people might come. And if you sign up, you don't have to walk around. You can be the one who sits, and people come to you. How great is that for us lazy people?"

October snickered. It did sound nice to have people come to her, instead of having to be the bold one, going to others, and moving on if it wasn't a good fit. Alternatively, she was trapped there if someone was awful. Or was she? It's not like she'd be chained to the chair.

She typed in her first name. She still wasn't committed just by typing information in. Not until she hit that submit button at least.

Last name, email, and phone number were all that were left. The form said they'd be creating unique QR codes for your table, so if someone wanted to keep the conversation going, they could get in touch with you. It seemed like it was all very well thought out.

"Why don't we ask for a bio?" The form asked. "Because we think it's important for you to tell your new friends what you want face to face. That way no one makes a judgement about you before they can meet you. It keeps the playing field level, and everyone strangers when they meet."

October liked that. Frankly, she liked everything about it. Except for the whole trying to make friends bit. That part made her want to suck all the oxygen out of the room one short gasp at a time. But no matter. Just, don't focus on that, she told herself as she clicked the submit button.

FRIDAY MORNING, she was doing paperwork at the funeral home when her dad popped his head into her office. "So, whatcha gonna do tonight? Want Aurora and I to come over? We could watch a movie together or something. Aurora asked just not one of your horror movies please. They don't sit well with her. Which I told her was very ironic, all things considered," her dad rambled.

October signed the bottom of the last form on her desk. "Oh, thanks Dad but I actually have plans tonight."

"You do?" He asked gleefully. "With who? Did you make up with Wilder?"

"No," she said flatly, taking the wind out of her dad's sails. "I signed up for a friendship speed dating thing."

"Speed dating? Boo, that doesn't seem like something you'll enjoy." Her dad was nothing if not honest.

"It's to find a friend dad. I'm not looking for a husband." It didn't sound any better, even when she said it out loud.

"Is that a thing?" He asked.

"Apparently. I thought it sounded like fun." In a put myself in a pot of water and turn the heat on high sort of way, she neglected to say.

Her dad raised an eyebrow like he could hear her thoughts.

She checked the room quickly for Mrs. Davis and lowered her voice. "I miss Wilder, Dad. And I'm not making any friends this way. I just thought I might try something new. If it flops, so what. Not like I can get any more alone."

He nodded, as if he agreed with her last statement then caught himself. "Boo, you're not—"

She cut him off. "Save it."

"Fine. Want one of us to go with you? Maybe Aurora, since she probably wouldn't make jokes about the other people in your ear?"

October laughed out loud at the thought. "Oh my God, that would be a disaster. No. Neither of you are invited. The point is to do something among the living, Dad." Then she heard herself and backpedaled. "Not that I don't love and appreciate you and want to spend time with you."

But it was too late. She left an opening, and her dad seized it with both hands. He turned away, feigning injury as he clutched his chest. "No, no, that's fine. All fledglings leave the nest eventually."

"Dad." October was not amused.

He held up a hand. "I'll be fine. Don't you worry about old dad. You go have fun. Without me."

"You didn't even want to go. You said Mrs. Davis should come."

"Fair point," he said with a straight face, then cleared his throat and went back to his whiny voice. "I'm sure Aurora and I will find something to do without you," he went on.

October eyed him. The two ghosts had been spending a lot of time together. But who else were they going to hang around? "Mmm," she said, not wanting to put any effort into that thought.

He turned around, his expression warm. "Have fun, Boo. You deserve a friend. Just promise me one thing?"

The earnest way he spoke caught something in her throat and she swallowed. "What?"

"Tell whoever you like the truth. See what they say. What could it hurt?"

Her breath caught. Tell them the truth. "What truth dad? What do you mean by that exactly?"

"Tell them about us. Your ghosts. See if you're right. Because..." He hesitated and shrugged. "What if you're not?"

"I'm right dad. I've seen it."

"Have you though? Have you come out and actually told anyone since Rosie?"

"No. I don't have to. Everyone thinks I'm a weirdo already, being the undertaker."

"That cross you bear is getting a little old, honey."

"Hey, that was uncalled for," she shot back. How did this turn into an attack?

"Maybe," her dad admitted. "But maybe not. All I'm saying is, if you want a true friend, they need to know the true you. That's all."

"Maybe I don't want a true friend. Maybe I just want a friend."

"With the hope of what? Keeping them at arm's length forever? Seems like a lot of work to me. Might as well just keep being alone so you can do what you want, when you want." He looked at her. "Are you prepared for the work it takes to pretend to be someone else just to get a stranger to approve of you?"

"I don't know, Dad. I just…" She just what? She thought she wanted a friend. Someone who understood. Like Wilder. But he didn't understand, did he? Because he couldn't. She hadn't told him everything. She looked up at him, and saw that his eyes were full of love and not a trace of judgement.

"It was just a suggestion, sweetie. Of course. I know this is hard for you, and I'm proud you're taking a step."

She nodded once. "Thanks Dad. I'll keep it in mind."

He smiled like she'd just told him she was making his favorite dinner, and he could actually eat it, and then schooled his face into seriousness. "Great. That's all I ask. Have fun." He blew her a kiss, and left her alone to wrap things up for the day.

THAT NIGHT, she'd picked a long patterned flowy green skirt and matching green sweater. She'd worn her hair down since she wasn't at work and it wasn't in the way. The Book Nook wasn't hard to find, just a short one-block walk from the station. October hated parking in the city, and decided the train was her best option.

The store was set up with small, two person tables scattered around with arrows on the ground, giving the feeling of a path to travel. She wasn't the first one there, thankfully, and everyone already seated looked just as nervous as she felt.

"Okay everyone. The event will start shortly. Ready?" The shop owner asked. She was maybe in her fifties, too young to have her glasses on a chain like she did. Or at least that's what October thought, but maybe she was going for that librarian feel, being a bookstore owner. October had to admit, it was a disarming look. Her short, curly hair was greying on the sides, but only added to her studious vibe.

October couldn't help but smile at the woman as she opened the double doors with a flourish and people streamed in around her. She welcomed each of them with a handshake and a warm smile, taking the time to spend a moment with all her guests, setting each of them at ease.

The first woman who sat down across from October was giggly. Marcy she said her name was. She had blonde hair in a high ponytail and was working as a store manager at Hallmark. October learned quickly she did not like her job, and dreamed of moving south to be a professional surfer. By the time she stopped talking, the bell dinged for her to change places, and October hadn't said a word. She smiled apologetically and got up. October just shrugged and greeted the next woman.

Avery was dressed in all black, complete with black lipstick and said her therapist forced her to come because she thought social interaction would be good for her. Then, she stopped talking.

"Oh. How's therapy going?" October asked.

Avery glared at her. "How do you think?" She folded her arms over her chest and turned her body sideways in the chair, away from October.

It was the longest five minutes ever. October tried a few more times to engage, and finally asked her, "Avery. It's probably not my place, but why come at all if you weren't going to put any effort into it? Because your therapist 'forced' you? You're a grown woman. You're not even proving your point that it didn't work if you don't try. The last woman I met didn't even let me talk. This room could be full of duds and you wouldn't even know because you're not trying. But you can't go back to your therapist and say you were right until you know."

Avery turned slightly towards her and dropped her arms to her sides. "I…" The bell rang and she moved on.

I'm trying, right? She thought to herself as she watched the next woman sit down. A woman in her forties with two kids and no time for friends.

"So, why did you come here?"

"To make friends," she answered shortly, like October was one of her kids who wasn't listening to her.

"But, if you don't have time, what are you going to do if you find someone you connect with?" She asked, genuinely curious.

The woman sighed loudly. "Well I don't know, Miss Know-It-All. I'll figure it out."

Feeling scolded, October didn't ask any more questions, and when the bell rang, the woman didn't even say goodbye.

The next three people who sat down – two more women and a man – weren't any better. One was a fitness instructor, looking to push her club. The guy only wanted to talk about Star Wars, and while October had enjoyed the film, it didn't define her the way it did him. And the last woman was a hippie born seven decades too late, and asked October if she was enlightened.

None of them asked for her contact information, and she hadn't asked for any of theirs either. She was starting to think the idea had been a colossal mistake when a forest sprite sat down in front of her. That was the only way to describe her. She was small, with short pink and purple hair. She was wearing combat boots, jeans, and a bright blouse that complimented her green eyes nicely. She smiled broadly when she sat down.

"Wow, this is an interesting case study on humanity, isn't it?" She asked as she settled in, holding a Styrofoam coffee cup in both hands as she leaned on the table, taking up more than half the space such a small person should need.

October chuckled. "Indeed it is."

"Gotten any contacts?"

"No. You?"

She shook her head. "I've given out plenty though. My name is Joey." She put her card on the table in front of October.

"Were we supposed to bring cards?" October asked. She certainly didn't want to hand out Manning Funeral Home cards at a friendship speed dating event. That would go over about as well as a vegan, gluten free dish at a southern church potluck.

Joey shrugged. "I'm having an opening in a few weeks. Thought it would be a good way to spread the word."

"Opening?" October looked at her card. Joey Potter. Artist. But not a potter. Then it had her contact information.

"Yeah. I'm pretty excited about it. You should come. I have about seven pieces for sale. Eight if I can finish the last one in time."

October found herself nodding. She loved her energy.

Joey smiled. "What do you do?"

October swallowed. Here went nothing. "I'm an undertaker."

"No way. Really?"

October nodded. "And I see ghosts."

"Shut up. Seriously? That's awesome. Are there ghosts here now?" A few people looked Joey's way and October leaned in, trying to clue Joey in to settle down.

"Probably. None that want to be seen at the moment. The two that hang around the most are my dad, who died about ten years ago. And a recent client. The mother of a friend I just broke up with."

Joey looked at her wide-eyed. "Do I want to know?"

"Probably not on the first date."

Joey laughed. "We're not dating."

"What is it called when you make a new friend and want to do things with them?"

Joey shrugged and took a sip of her coffee. "Not dating."

"Fair enough," October conceded.

"What happened to your face?"

October didn't even consider not telling her the truth. She'd already told her about her ghosts. "A ghost attacked me."

Joey nearly spit her coffee all over, but thankfully restrained.

"Which one? Your dad? Or the other one? I didn't peg you for the abusive father type. And then to be haunted by him." Joey's expression turned sympathetic.

October waved her hands. "No no. It wasn't my dad. It's the ex-girlfriend of the friend I just broke up with. She's kinda the reason we broke up."

Joey sat forward and raised an eyebrow. "Okay, I'm definitely going to need to hear more about this soap opera drama." She dug her phone out of her pocket and checked the QR code glued to the table. "Got it. You're the most interesting person here I think. And I'd like to get to know you better."

October stared at her. Joey was smiling. She was being honest. October couldn't see a single trace of teasing, or cruelty in the words. "You believe me?"

Joey shrugged. "Why wouldn't I? Are you lying to me?" Her expression said she didn't think October was lying at all.

"No. I just...I've never met anyone who just accepted it. I stopped telling people." October had never been so honest so quickly with another living person. Not even Rosie. It had taken months to get up the courage to tell her, and then Rosie had acted like October was cursed by the devil.

Joey watched her carefully, calculating what to ask next. "When was the last time you flat out told someone?"

"I was in second grade. Rosie was my best friend. Her mom decided I was some kind of demon or something I don't know. The kids in school spread a rumor after that and it followed me until graduation."

"Sheesh. That's worse than getting stuffed in a locker in your underwear because you were snatched out of the locker room when you were changing."

October's eyes widened. "Did that happen to you?"

She shook her head no and October let a breath out she didn't know she'd been holding. "No. But that would be horrible right?" October couldn't help but laugh. Joey was a piece of work.

"No, my childhood was unabashedly normal I'm afraid. But I find it hard to make friends now that I'm not forced into close proximity with the same group of people every dang day. The other artists where I rent space to work aren't there when I'm there. Apparently they're all weirdo night owls who sleep all day." She shrugged. "I work the night shift at a bar, so I can't be there when everyone else is."

"Maybe they have day jobs?" October offered.

Joey rolled her eyes. "That is so normal." That's when the bell rang and Joey slumped, pouting. "Dang it," she said. "My first fun conversation and it's over. I promise not to meet someone I like better than you." She stood up and held out her pinky.

October wrapped her own pinky around it. "I promise not to meet someone more interesting than you."

Joey beamed. "Even better. I'll text you later." Her tone made it sound like a threat, and October chuckled as she watched her new friend move on.

It hadn't been hard to keep her promise. No one measured up to her forest sprite. There was an accountant with no personality that October kind of felt bad for, and was relieved when she didn't ask for her contact information. She would have given it if she'd asked. She wasn't heartless. But she nearly fell asleep listening to her talk about tax season in such a monotone voice.

When the event was over, she didn't catch sight of Joey, so she headed back to the station wondering if she really had been a sprite that disappeared back into the forest. A figment of her imagination maybe? Was it that outside of the realm of possibilities? She did see ghosts after all.

But then she got a text on the train ride home.

Omg. There's a guy on the subway smacking his gum and I can't.

It was Joey. She was real.

October found a gif of a camel chewing and sent it back.

Perfect. Joey typed back. *Do you think I could come visit you? I'd like to meet your dad.*

October stared at her phone. *That sounds awfully date-ish.*

LOL. IT DOES. I swear we're not dating.

You're welcome to come visit any time, October typed back, genuinely meaning it. *But you know you won't be able to see him or hear him.*

But he can see me? Joey asked.

Yup.

Good enough for me. How's Thursday? I'm off that night. Gotta be back by Friday night for work though.

Sounds great! October typed. She had a friend. One that wanted to meet her dad. She'd never had anyone like that. She sat back in her seat on the train and tried to absorb it, but couldn't. She had a true friend. One who knew her deepest, darkest secret and didn't care.

She was wrong. And she loved it.

CHAPTER 16

Saturday night, October's dad and Mrs. Davis came over for dinner. October only cooked enough food for her, since her guests never ate.

Once they sat down at the table, and Queso was settled into Mrs. Davis' lap, the grilling started.

"So, tell us about last night," Mrs. Davis asked excitedly.

"What do you want to know?" October teased as she dug into her dinner, and the two ghosts sat politely with their glasses of wine they couldn't touch.

"Well, how did it go? Did you meet anyone interesting?" Mrs. Davis inquired.

"Mostly I want to know about the weirdos who were there," her dad chimed in.

"Me, Dad. I was the weirdo who was there." October didn't have to look up to hear Mrs. Davis elbow her dad.

"No you weren't, dear," Mrs. Davis assured her. "I'm sure you were delightful, with just the right amount of quirk."

October smiled. She'd never heard herself described quite that way, and it felt...perfect. "There were some duds. A lot of duds actually."

"Oh. Well, I'm sorry honey. I'm proud of you for trying," her dad interjected a little too quickly.

She looked at Mrs. Davis, who was still clinging to some hope that the evening had been a success. The poor woman was practically on the edge of her seat.

"There was one," she teased.

"Yes?" Mrs. Davis leaned forward.

Her dad chuckled. "Be cool."

"Oh you," she swatted him, but October noticed he still smiled. They were acting like an old married couple. "Tell us about them. Guy or girl?" She asked anxiously.

Suddenly, October thought she understood some of Mrs. Davis' unease. She wanted to know if Wilder was being replaced. Was he? "Mrs. Davis. Wilder is very special to me. No one will take his place in my heart."

She seemed startled, but relaxed in spite of herself. "Of course not. That's not. I mean. Oh, just tell us about your new friend. It's not nice to torture the dead."

October laughed. "Well, she wants to meet you, dad. She's coming Thursday."

He watched her carefully, as if the words didn't quite sink in. "You told her. About me."

"I did."

"How did she react?" Mrs. Davis asked.

"Like I told her I had a mole. She embraced it, and moved on. It was bizarre, and refreshing, and exciting, and all the things." October realized she was talking kind of fast, but she couldn't help it. She was happy. Happier than she'd been since Wilder had taken a shining to her.

"Well," Mrs. Davis sat back and swallowed her emotions. "Isn't that something."

"Did you tell her what you do?" Her dad asked, his tone even, like he was still processing.

"I did. She wasn't bothered. She's an artist and is having

151

an opening in a few weeks. I need to look up what that means. I think her stuff's going to be in a gallery for sale or something. I'm going to try and go."

"That sounds wonderful. Maybe we'd like to go too," Mrs. Davis offered, caught up in the excitement.

Her dad patted Mrs. Davis' hand. "That defeats the purpose of letting her have her own friends, Aurora. Let her have her time."

Mrs. Davis deflated a bit. "Oh. I guess you're right." But she brightened quickly. "Tell us all about her."

October spent the next hour talking about Joey, and her abrupt sense of humor, how she looked like a forest sprite.

"She's really excited about coming for a visit," October said as she cleaned up the dishes and dumped out the wine glasses she'd poured for her guests.

"How do you expect that to go?" Her dad watched her with a bit of wariness. "Do you think she's just interested in you because you're a freak show?"

"Steve," Mrs. Davis chastised severely before turning to October. "Honey, you are *not* a freak show."

Her dad looked seriously at October. "Boo. You know what I mean."

"I do dad. And honestly, I wouldn't have agreed to let her come if I thought that's what she wanted. She just seems interested."

He concentrated, and handed her a glass from the counter. "I hope you're right."

October was impressed by his progress, and smiled at him. "I'm not worried, Dad."

That night, she warned Joey about her dad, and asked her if she wanted to reconsider.

Oooh, overprotective Dad ghost? Nice. Not sure my dad cares that much about me, and he's still alive.

October paused. That was a new little nugget. *What makes you say that?*

He ran off with his secretary when I was 12. I get a card near my birthday every year. That's about it. I sent an invitation to the opening to the return address from my last card, but I doubt he'll show.

What was the right thing to say here? Should she be mad at him? Tell her she didn't need him? Or be encouraging, and say she hopes he shows up?

Do you want him to? She asked, hoping she'd know how to respond with more information.

October watched the triple dots for a few moments. Longer than it usually took Joey to answer.

I'm not sure, actually.

Well that didn't help. *Well, I'd like to come, if that's okay.*

She got a string of exclamation points and emojis in response. *Yay! And you don't even have to buy anything.*

Ha! Good. You're too expensive for me.

Don't you forget it.

They chatted back and forth until October was too tired to keep texting. They talked about books and movies, and all the things that made them, them. She stayed away from talking about Wilder, and Joey didn't ask, thankfully. Even though she'd told Joey her secret, she wasn't sure she was ready to talk about Wilder, and somehow Joey knew that.

BY THURSDAY, October was so excited. She'd cleared her schedule for the afternoon and Friday morning. It had been nearly a week since she'd last seen Wilder, and the time had flown. She found herself wondering if Wilder was doing as well. But that wasn't any of her business. She was too creepy for him after all.

At lunch time, she wrapped up her work and left for the train station to pick up Joey. They had lunch at her favorite sushi place, which Joey approved of. October was worried it would be better in the city, but Joey said it was too expensive there. Everything was. And she insisted October's place was just as good.

"I like how liberal they are with cream cheese," she commented.

October helped Joey carry her small suitcase into her place, and was greeted by Queso and Mrs. Davis who was pacing the room.

"Hi," October said awkwardly. "What are you doing here?"

Joey looked around. "Doesn't your cat live here?" she asked as she bent to pet him, and he ate it up purring like he'd never been paid attention to before.

"Yeah. Sorry. That's Queso. Mrs. Davis is here."

"The mom of your ex-friend?" She asked.

Mrs. Davis' face was stricken, as if something had happened. But she wasn't ready to talk about it yet. "You told her about me too?"

"I did. Seems you've become part of my life too."

Mrs. Davis nodded and went back to pacing.

"Do the ghosts often hang out at your house when you aren't here?" Joey asked.

"No."

Joey nodded. "Probably best. Might be hard to have some privacy."

"I'm just going to show Joey where to put her things," October offered. But Mrs. Davis just waved her off.

"I'm sorry. She isn't usually so...rude." October's mind was spinning. Was it her dad? They were meant to see him at the funeral home later that day. Whatever Mrs. Davis wanted was too important to wait for that apparently.

"What's wrong?" Joey asked as she led her to the back of the apartment where October's room and bathroom were.

"I'm not sure yet."

She set her suitcase on the bench at the end of October's bed. "This is really nice, October. I love it."

October smiled, relieved. Her apartment was clean, and pretty minimalistic since Abby had trashed everything. Even though Wilder had helped her replace a bunch of stuff, she still didn't have as much as she did a few months before.

Joey read her mind. "You didn't think I'd like it?"

"Well, it's a far cry from a hip city studio with big industrial sliding doors and exposed pipes."

"Is that where you think I live?" She asked. "Now, that does sound awesome. But it also sounds disgustingly expensive." She breezed by October to put her bathroom bag in the bathroom. "Oh my God this bathroom is huge." She called before gasping and running out of the room. She grabbed October's hands with both of hers. "You have a tub! Can I please take a bath tonight? I know we're meant to be spending time together, but oh my God you have a tub. Do you know how long it's been since I had a tub?"

"City life seems less glamorous than I imagined..."

"That's not an answer," Joey pointed out.

October laughed. "Of course you can take a bath. I did clean the tub before you came over."

"You knew?"

"No," October admitted. "I just cleaned everything."

"October?" Mrs. Davis called from the living room, where October could only assume she was still pacing.

"Oh yeah. My ghost."

Joey looked out the door with interest. "Should I wait here?"

"No. I mean, you can if you want. But Mrs. Davis is usually really nice and calm. I don't know what's going on."

"You worried?"

"Maybe? I hope my dad is okay."

Joey puzzled. "What could happen to a ghost?"

"I have no idea." October absently reached up and touched what was left of the scabs on her face from Abby.

"She won't hurt you right?"

"No." But Abby would. And if Mrs. Davis was trying to warn her about something…But why would Abby still be mad? She'd stayed away. Abby had won.

October walked down the hall, finding Mrs. Davis done pacing and standing in the middle of the room, looking resolved.

"It's Wilder," Mrs. Davis revealed.

"Wilder," October repeated.

"Your ex-friend," Joey asked. October nodded. "What about him?" Joey asked.

Mrs. Davis frowned suddenly realizing how she was behaving in front of October's new friend. "I'm so sorry," she realized. "I'm being rude. Tell her I'm sorry, won't you?"

"Joey, this is Mrs. Davis. She apologizes for ignoring you. Right? That's what you're apologizing for?" October asked.

Mrs. Davis nodded. "That, and hijacking your evening."

"How are you hijacking our evening? We're going to meet Dad, Mrs. Davis. That isn't up for negotiation," October insisted.

Mrs. Davis frowned, and Joey shivered. "Did it just get cold in here?"

October didn't respond. "Wilder made it clear he didn't want anything to do with me. What exactly do you hope I will accomplish at this point? His ghost of a girlfriend sent me to the ER less than two weeks ago. I know you're not pressuring me to put myself back in that situation. Because you're a caring woman who knows what I would be up against," October reminded the ghost.

The lights flickered, just barely and Joey looked around but didn't seem nervous. It wasn't anywhere near the display Abby put on. And it wasn't out of anger. It was distress.

"Wilder didn't know what he was saying. He needs you."

October shook her head. "No he doesn't. He needs to solve his own problems."

"How can he when he doesn't even know what they are? He has no idea Abby is hanging around him," Mrs. Davis shouted. That time the lights went out completely for a second. Anger was apparently much more powerful than distress.

Startled by what she'd done, she collapsed onto the couch and put her face in her hands. Joey seemed unsure and stayed where she was while October went and sat with the ghost. "Mrs. Davis. Tell me what the problem is."

"Wilder isn't himself. He's drinking more. Isolating. It's like it was right before…" she paused. "Right before things got really bad. He went to rehab for a bit. That helped. But there's no one there to tell him he needs it."

"What about Tim? He's there. He's a good kid."

"True. But he can't see me. He doesn't know how bad Wilder is," Mrs. Davis protested.

"Maybe. Maybe not. Men can be more perceptive than you think. And Tim is a great kid. Caring. Kind of like someone else I know," October tried to reassure her.

"Just think about it. Please?"

October didn't like how she was begging. "I have thought about it. There is no way forward between Wilder and I. Not while Abby lingers."

"And why would Abby ever move on with you out of the picture?" Mrs. Davis pushed.

"She won't. Unless Wilder decides he's done with her. And he came close. Maybe he'll get there in time."

"Not without you." Mrs. Davis stood, trying to will

October into cooperation. But she wasn't willing to endanger herself like that anymore.

Mrs. Davis went for the door, but before she got there, she turned. "Wilder would do it for you." Then she disappeared through the front door.

"Oh real nice. She lays a guilt trip on me and disappears."

"Okay, I need to know what happened. I didn't want to push you before you were ready but what on Earth happened? Why is she so mad? How did she make the lights flicker? Would she hurt you the way that Abby did?" Questions poured out of Joey until October lost track of them.

"You know Mrs. Davis is Wilder's mother. I met him because he sent her to my funeral home. He and I hit it off right away. Kinda like you and me to be honest. He wasn't judgmental, and he was so supportive. He brought me dinner, and helped me with my haunted house."

"Haunted house? Can I help next year? That sounds like fun!" Joey exclaimed.

"I wish you would! The project is getting out of hand."

"So what happened?"

"Abby. The sixteen-year-old girlfriend who died in a car accident when they were coming home from a date. Wilder was run out of his hometown. They called him a murderer. Abby still hangs around him, torturing him basically. And in her nearly twenty years as a ghost, she's learned some skills. How to hurt people for example," October gestured to her face.

"That sounds messy," Joey sympathized.

"It is. Or was, rather. I did like him. A lot actually."

Joey smiled sadly. "I can tell by the way you talk about him. Your eyes got all dreamy."

"They did not," October protested.

"Oh please. You're the definition of a dewy-eyed school-girl." Joey fought off the pillows October hurled at her before asking her next question. "So, he didn't like your ghosts and left? He chose Abby?" She didn't try to hide the disgust over making such a self-destructive choice.

"Not exactly."

"What does that mean?" She asked.

"I never got around to telling him about the ghosts."

"He doesn't know his sixteen-year-old dead girlfriend is making him miserable on purpose?" October didn't like how quickly the disgust shifted from Wilder to her, and said nothing. So Joey pressed her.

"October. Why doesn't he know?"

"Because. The night she hurt me, I pushed him away, thinking that was what was best. I was scared. I'd never been hurt by a ghost before, and I hope I never am again."

"Understandable. But after the dust settled, you didn't—"

October interrupted her. "He came back a few days later. Found him on my porch, and Abby was lingering in the distance, letting me know who he belonged to. He tried to figure out what happened. Make it right. But I backed up. Just as I was about to tell him the truth, he got mad and said I was creepy and stormed off."

Joey digested that longer than October liked. Had that singular incident really ruined two friendships? She'd thought honesty really was the best policy, but maybe she'd been wrong to share any of it with her forest sprite.

"You didn't go after him?" She asked quietly.

"He said I was creepy," October reminded her. That was justification enough, right? After everything that had happened, he knew what would hurt her most, and used it against her.

"I'm sure lots of people say that about you, October. You're an undertaker." The way Joey brushed the insult off made October bristle, but Joey didn't back down from it. "He fought for you, and when it was your turn, you ran?"

October didn't answer. She didn't need to. The truth was written all over her face, in tears and scabs.

Joey sighed. "Okay. This is messy, you're right. The question is, do you want to fix it?"

October felt completely helpless. "I don't think it matters what I want."

"Please. Don't turn into a sad sap on me. Of course it matters what you want. Do you want to fix it or not?"

"Yes."

"Well, there you go then. Fix it," Joey said firmly. As if that's all there was to it.

"But."

"No buts. Either you do or you don't. And you said you do." She acted like the discussion was closed. Like the jealous ghost, and all the obstacles in their way didn't matter.

"Yes buts Jo. I can't see a way to fix it peacefully. In every single scenario I play out, someone gets hurt. Even if I tell him the girlfriend he thinks he killed is haunting him and he believes me, he's going to be devastated. Who knows what she'll do. What if she hurts him?"

Joey took her hand and snapped her out of her spiral. She looked at October right in the eyes for several beats and said nothing, making sure October was there in that moment with her. "You control you. That's it. You are not responsible for his actions, or the ghosts for that matter."

"But—"

Joey shook her head. "No. Buts."

"Mrs. Davis. She wants me to…"

"No. Buts. October. You are *not* responsible for the ghosts."

"Then what's the point? Of any of it?"

Joey's expression softened into something that looked like amazement. "The point? The point is a miracle. You can see the other side. It's an absolute wonder."

"But, if I'm not responsible for it. For any of them, what's the point?"

"I didn't say you weren't responsible for your gift. I said you weren't responsible for them."

October huffed in frustration. "What's the difference?"

Joey smiled, not a bit deterred by October's outburst. "What you do with your gift is up to you. What they do with what you offer is on them. If you've tried to talk to Abby, and all she's done is lash out, that's on her. It's your choice to stay away from Wilder for the rest of your life. And if you can be at peace with that, great. But it doesn't seem like you are. Seems to me like you miss him. Like maybe you wanted him in your life. Like maybe you wanted him to be more than a friend."

October folded her arms over her chest and looked at Joey sidelong. "So, what if I did?" She was acting like a child, and she didn't even care. Everything was crumbling around her, and her new friend was pushing her in ways she wasn't prepared for. October wasn't sure how she felt about any of it.

"It's up to you to either get over those feelings, or do something about them." She said it so simply.

"You say it like there's nothing to it."

"Maybe there isn't. Maybe it's people that make it complicated, and it doesn't need to be." Then she burst out laughing, and it was such a contagious sound, October joined in, although not as heartily as Joey. "Just kidding. It'll be stupid hard. But, anything worth having, is worth working for, right?"

October let a single, sad chuckle escape. "My dad says that."

"He's a smart man." She looked at her watch, an old thing she picked up at a thrift shop with an army green fraying band, and the glass so scuffed October didn't know how she could tell the time at a glance. "Speaking of which, when do I get to meet him?"

"We can head over there now, if you like."

She stood up and hooked her arm through October's. As they walked arm in arm through the first snow of the season, October marveled at her new friend. She took everything in stride. October's wild claims, her emotions, all of it. Nothing made Joey rethink wanting to be part of October's life. She only hoped she could be that kind of friend for Joey in return.

The funeral home was quiet when they arrived. October gave Joey a brief tour of her office before leading her up to the apartment. She knocked once and her dad came to the door looking...disheveled.

"Hey Boo. I wasn't expecting you so soon," he commented as he tucked in his shirt. She puzzled at him. His shirt was never untucked. In fact, she didn't think he ever had to get dressed. He was a ghost. He just...was that way.

Mrs. Davis appeared behind him, her hair a mess, and her lipstick smeared. She looked uncomfortably at October and pushed past her without a word.

"I..."

"What's going on?" Joey asked.

"Dad. Are you and Mrs. Davis..." she couldn't get the thought out. She couldn't even get her head around the idea.

Her dad cleared his throat. "I don't know what you're talking about. And you're being rude. Who's this lovely lady?" He asked as he extended a hand to her. He helped her find him, and grabbed her hand.

Joey was surprised, and then smiled at the feeling. "Hi Mr. Manning." She turned to October. "It feels warm and cold at the same time, if that makes sense."

October nodded happily.

"Steve, please," her dad insisted.

"He wants you to call him Steve," October translated.

"Of course."

"Please, come in."

They spent the next hour talking and laughing, with October translating all of it. She thought she might get tired of being their go between, but she never did. It was so nice to share that part of her life with someone, finally. And have them accept it so completely. Could Wilder do the same? October didn't think so. Her forest sprite was unique in every sense of the word.

Joey revealed she'd never had much of a father figure, and wished she'd had a dad that cared as much as he did. And Steve told her he was sorry, and if he ever saw him on that side of the veil, he'd give him a hearty punch for her. That made her laugh. He told her he'd love to see her art sometime, and she said she'd love that. More than if her actual dad showed up.

Steve told her about how he started the funeral home, and how he loved working with October. He told more than enough embarrassing stories about her, including when their most recent practical jokester Mr. Miller scared the daylights out of her.

"Nope. I'm not telling her that," October refused.

"Telling me what? Come on. I want to know," Joey whined.

"Now you have to tell her." Her dad was way too satisfied for October's taste.

"The ghost that hung around for a little bit after this happened," October gestured to her face. "He was quite the prankster. And I was a little jumpy after what Abby did. He liked to sneak up behind me and startle me. Dad liked to do that too until he figured out he could move stuff. He was quite the hit at our haunted house this year, let me tell you."

"Oooh, I bet he was," Joey said.

"Get back to the story," her dad insisted.

"All right, relax ya old ghost." October turned back to Joey. "You'd think the dead would have more patience. Anyway, one day I was carrying my coffee back to my office when he followed me. He slipped into office without me noticing him and literally said boo. Like I'd never heard that one before."

"It worked," her dad said.

"Needless to say, I needed a change of outfit before my next appointment, and a new keyboard as it turned out."

Joey was laughing so hard she couldn't breathe. "Nice to know a sense of humor survives all realms."

"Mr. Miller at least had the decency to feel bad. He thought something so cliché would bore me. He was wrong."

"Clearly," Joey said through her giggles. "Why isn't he still around? I'd have liked to help him with his pranks."

"I bet you would," October looked at her friend with a new level of distrust. "He'd wanted to help with Abby but didn't know how. He tried to talk to her but she wouldn't listen. He said we needed to hire an exorcist. He apologized for not being able to help and moved on. He did help in his own way, though. He was the first ghost I'd seen since she attacked me. And he was the perfect one for the job. He wasn't stoic or standoffish. He wasn't too demanding. And he certainly didn't threaten me, even if he did make it so I started leaving a change of clothes here at Dad's just in case."

"You might want to consider taking those home, now that Mr. Miller has moved on," her Dad suggested.

"Oh, because you have so much need for the storage space?" October countered.

Joey hid her smile behind her mug of hot tea when her eye caught something outside. "Who's that?" She asked.

October went to the window. She didn't have any appointments that day and wasn't expecting anyone. She sighed so loudly it fogged the window.

Wilder Davis was outside shoveling the first snow of the season.

CHAPTER 17

*W*ilder hadn't meant to go to the funeral home. He'd meant to go to the bar. He needed a drink. Tim asked him to grab a bite to eat. That's what he should've done. And he hated himself for saying no. But Tim wouldn't want to be around him when he was in such a state.

He had no idea what had come over him. He felt worse than after Abby died. Over a girl he essentially just met. He figured it was the combination of the grief from his mom, letting go of Abby a little bit, and then losing October.

The things he said to her still haunted him. How could he have called her creepy? He knew what that would mean to her, and he'd done it anyway. He'd wanted her to feel how she was making him feel. Out of control, confused, and hurt. He'd done that and then some.

The snow wasn't really coming down that hard, and he didn't have that much to shovel. But it felt good to do it. Felt like clearing his head. He'd been in such a fog since she'd pushed him away. He'd been drinking too much. Working not enough. And spending too much time alone. He always felt worse when he was alone, and he couldn't put his finger on why. Like everything was his fault and he was meant to be alone forever. Like he didn't deserve happiness.

He pushed the thought away as he scraped the shovel against the pavement. She probably had a truck go through and do the job when the snow got deep, but he didn't care. It helped to work those muscles and focus on what needed to be done, instead of what was in his head.

To his surprise, a wild looking girl popped out of the funeral home. Had October hired help? He couldn't imagine she'd hire someone so…unprofessional looking.

Her hair was brightly colored and cropped short. She pulled what looked like an army jacket around her as she walked over to him.

"Wilder Davis." She didn't ask. It came out like a demand. Her voice wasn't as small as she was and it commanded his attention.

He stood up straight and leaned on the shovel handle. "Yes?"

"What are you doing here?"

"Picking my nose. What does it look like I'm doing?"

She cracked a smile, and Wilder found himself wanting her approval. Who was she?

"Does October know you're here?" They both asked at the same time. Then they both responded "Yes," in a tone that said of-course-she-does-who-do-you-think-you-are?

Joey smiled knowing she had him. "Fine. Did she ask you to be here?"

"Not exactly," Wilder admitted.

"So how does she know you're here? You don't strike me as the lying type, Wilder."

He liked that she didn't think he was a liar, but he didn't know why. Why did he need her approval? He tried to correct himself, but when he looked at the mischief in her eyes he couldn't. He was drawn to it. He wanted to know more about her, where she'd come from, and why she was there. So, he'd play her game.

"She saw me in the window, I'm sure."

"You assume she's here?"

He shrugged. "She's always here."

"Not anymore," Joey said with a level of confidence that made him think she really had hired help. Did that mean he had to make Nikki his manager? The thought made him break into a cold sweat.

"What's wrong?" She asked.

"If October hired you, I have to make some changes."

She screwed up her face as if his conclusion made no sense at all. "Why?"

"We had a deal. If she ever hired help, I had to give the business manager spot to my secretary. Not sure I'm ready to give up the reigns yet." Why was he telling that to a total stranger? He looked her over. She was so…unassuming. Disarming. He both liked and hated it about her. He needed his secrets, and he had no idea how he'd hold on to any of them with her around.

"I should go," he said abruptly. "Tell October…"

She waited for him to finish, and when he didn't, she prompted him. "Yes?" She watched him coyly, as if she knew exactly who he was, and liked her unfair advantage.

"Never mind." He turned to walk away, and she stopped him.

"Hey, why did you assume I work for her?"

"Because. Why else would you be here?"

"Maybe I'm a friend," she offered.

Wilder laughed, and it came out more derisively than he intended. "October doesn't have friends."

He watched the small woman bristle, and couldn't help but take a step back from her. "The reliable word of a man who thinks she's creepy but still comes over to shovel her drive. Not sure how to take you."

Wilder bristled right back. October clearly had divulged quite a bit about him, and had spent some time bashing him. "Well, clearly you've heard one side of the story. No sense in hearing mine."

"I know your side. She treated you unfairly and isn't sure how to fix it without hurting you in the process." It was so matter of fact, Wilder had no response. The woman was a piece of work.

"Who are you?" He finally asked.

"I'm October's friend. Joey."

"She never mentioned you before," Wilder posed the statement like he was trying to catch her in a lie. But he knew she wasn't lying. She knew too much.

"We met last week."

"You've gotten awfully friendly with her in a short time then," he accused.

"Is that such a bad thing?"

He thought for a moment. "No. I suppose not. She needs a friend right now." He hadn't meant to let his tone soften. He'd gone there to work out some frustrations without grabbing another beer. Not have some kind of therapy session with a weirdo at the funeral home.

Letting the anger and frustration go out of him, he was left with mostly sadness, and it felt heavy. He sat down on the curb and Joey joined him. "Sounds like you know quite a bit about me, and I know nothing about you."

Joey didn't respond. He looked out at the snow falling, and wanted to feel the magic of it, but all he felt was heavy. The weight of his life, of his choices, could never be as light as the snow falling, could it?

"I didn't want to break it off with her, ya know?" Had he said that out loud?

Joey didn't respond right away, so he hoped maybe not.

"So why did you say she was creepy?"

Defeated, he sighed heavily. "I didn't know what else to do. I was frustrated."

"The first part, I do not accept. That's a cop out and you know it. The second part I believe."

Wilder put his face in his hands. "She pushed me away, and I still don't know why."

"Did you ask her?"

"I tried to. I think I did." He thought for a moment. Had he asked her? He couldn't remember. He'd pushed her to give them another chance. He'd dismissed her superstitions for sure. Had he given her a safe place to exist, the way she had for him? He wasn't sure, and the feeling horrified him even more.

"Well, if you aren't sure, you can always remedy that," Joey suggested as she stood up. "It's too cold out here." She turned to Wilder and held out a hand.

He stood up and took it. "Nice to have met you, Wilder. I'm sure I'll be seeing you around."

Before he could respond, she disappeared into the funeral home, and locked the door behind her leaving Wilder baffled.

"You betrayed me!" October accused the moment Joey came back inside.

"I did not. Calm down ya drama queen," Joey said as she dug into a box of cookies that were sitting on the table. "How old are these? Were they in here when your dad died?"

October looked horrified. "No. I bought those last week to snack on and brought them up here from my office while I spied on you talking to my ex-friend."

Joey nodded as if her betrayal didn't exist. "I like Wilder. You're right. He's a nice guy."

"Nice guys don't call their friends creepy," October pointed out.

"People make mistakes, October." Joey looked at her, and October felt like she was looking at her soul. She felt too exposed. "I sincerely hope you don't hold me to that standard. Because I'm a person. I'm going to hurt you at some point. And you'll hurt me. That's okay. I forgive you. Unless you spearhead a campaign to remove *The Haunting of Hill House* from Netflix. Then we can't be friends."

"Oh my God I love that show," October interjected.

"Right? Isn't it amazing. And the twist at the end." Joey kissed the tips of her fingers. "Perfection."

"This is different," October insisted.

"How? How is this different?"

"Because." *I don't have feelings for you. I wasn't imagining my life with you.*

"Because you don't want to date me? October Manning, I'm hurt. Apologies can be submitted in writing within twenty-four hours. Acceptable forms of apology include chocolate, binge watching the latest show together, or talking all night on the phone."

"Noted. We can watch *Hill House* tonight if you want."

"Apology accepted. I'm a delight. You'd be lucky to have me."

"But you said we aren't dating," October pointed out as she grabbed a cookie out of the box and sat down across from her friend.

"We aren't. But, I acknowledge you are quite an unusual catch. If Wilder is worth his salt, he won't let you go so easily."

"Unusual catch. Should I take that as a compliment?"

"I would. I didn't mean it as anything else."

They munched in silence until Joey reached for another cookie. "October?"

"Mmm?"

"If he called you, would you tell him your secret?"

October didn't hesitate. "Nope."

"Why not? You told me right off the bat, a total stranger. Did you tell anyone else at the event that night?"

"No."

"So, why me?"

"Because I liked you. And if you were going to be scared off, I wanted to know early. Before I could get more attached." Saying it out loud made it sound really dumb. She felt small and stupid and immature.

Joey reached for her and put her hand on her arm. "You don't feel the same way about Wilder?"

"It's too late. I got attached."

"But, you're already apart. It's over. Right?"

She nodded. It was over. He'd called her creepy and there was no taking that back. Was there? If he wanted her forgiveness, would she give it to him? Before she'd even finished the thought, she knew she would.

"He doesn't want it," October whispered, leaving 'it' undefined.

"How do you know that?"

"Because he walked away."

"Maybe he needed time to think. Or space to make a mistake," Joey offered.

"Why are you sticking up for him?" October demanded, suddenly frustrated with her friend again.

"I'm not. I'm just pointing out he's human, as I hope his friends would point out for you."

October scoffed. "His friend is an ass."

"His good friends."

October thought of Tim and wondered if they'd talked

about her at all. She didn't know how she felt about that. Joey was right. October *was* the villain here.

"I just think, if the opportunity presented itself, maybe you should consider telling him your why."

"My why?" October asked.

"Why you got scared. Why you pushed him away."

"My secret." The thought made the cookie in her mouth difficult to swallow.

"What have you got to lose? You can't possibly make it worse."

October thought of all the ways she could make it worse. What if this nugget of information was what he needed to push him over the edge? Mrs. Davis said he was already as bad as he was before he went into rehab. What if the knowledge of his dead girlfriend following him pushed him over the line. What if he…

She shook her head.

"You catastrophizing?" Joey asked.

October nodded.

"Okay. Tell me the worst case."

"Apparently, after Abby died, Wilder spiraled a bit. Nearly died. Finally went to rehab and got on the right track again. His mom says that's happening again. He's circling the drain. What if the truth is what pushes him over the edge, and this time, he succeeds? Then it's my fault."

Joey's face turned serious. "That's a lot to take in. Certainly, that could happen."

October wilted. She wasn't expecting Joey to validate her concerns. "You're supposed to say something reassuring like, 'oh, you're overreacting. It'll be fine. The truth will set him free.' Or whatever." Was she crying? She swiped away the hot tears and looked away from her new friend.

"I won't ever lie to you, October. I value honesty in my friends, and I hope they value it in me. What you're considering *is* a risk. If he's mentally unstable, that might be a concern. However, I will say he didn't seem that irrational to me just now. Broken? Absolutely. Unstable? No."

October didn't respond, so Joey pushed her a little more. "So, the worst-case scenario is you're responsible for his death. Does that mean the best-case is equally dramatic?"

The best-case scenario. She hadn't even considered that. What would that even be? That he tells Abby to go away, and the two of them live happily ever after together? It seemed so far-fetched.

"The best case is a fairy tale." October's voice was as cold as the ice forming on the window as she watched Wilder walk out to his truck.

"So, then the most likely scenario is something in between. Maybe the truth sets him free, but he doesn't want to be your friend because of it. How would you feel about that?"

How would she feel about that? Mrs. Davis could be at peace finally. That would be good right? And Wilder could be happy after all that time.

"That would be okay, I think."

"Is it worth the risk?"

"I don't…" October trailed off. "What about Abby? What if she lashed out again?"

Joey nodded. "Another risk, for sure."

"I thought you were supposed to be telling me I have nothing to lose."

Joey laughed. "Well, as far as your friendship is concerned, you don't. There is no friendship currently. But you're right, there are other variables at play."

"Comforting," October said flatly.

"I just think you should consider your options if he comes back to you," she pointed out.

"What makes you so sure he'll come back?"

"Because, October. He was downstairs shoveling snow that hadn't even built up yet. He was looking for a reason to be near you."

"Or, he had some nervous energy he needed to burn off. He did that after his mother died too. Pulling weeds, mowing around here. Stuff like that. It doesn't have anything to do with me," October pointed out.

Joey smiled lovingly and shook her head. "Or, it has everything to do with you."

CHAPTER 18

*H*er time with Joey was perfectly imperfect. They had their own opinions. They were their own people, but it didn't matter. Joey loved her anyway, and October loved her for it. Joey made no bones about telling her what she thought she should do about Wilder one more time before she got on the train, and October promised to let her know if she heard from him, but she didn't think she would.

As she left Joey at the train station, she felt like she was leaving part of her heart behind. Over the course of the next two weeks, their bond only grew. Even though they couldn't spend Thanksgiving together, they texted constantly, and video called when they could. In less than a month, Joey had become a staple in October's life.

Joey spent Thanksgiving upstate with her mom and grandmother, who was too ill to come to her opening, so she took pictures of what she'd be displaying the following week. Pictures she refused to show October, because she didn't want to spoil the big reveal.

October spent Thanksgiving with Mrs. Davis and her

dad. They watched the parade, and October made a hen and all the fixins for herself. She'd have leftovers for weeks but they froze well. She'd lived alone long enough, she knew how to keep food.

When the time came for Joey's opening, October packed an overnight bag and headed into the city. Joey met her at the station, and they walked to her studio apartment above a pizzeria. Joey's place was really small, but functional and clean. Joey didn't have a couch, so they'd be sharing the bed in the far corner by the one and only window in the apartment. October didn't mind. They hadn't slept much when Joey stayed over anyway, seeing how they stayed up all night talking and watching Netflix. The kitchen was by the front door, and included a fridge, a hot plate, a sink and a few cupboards.

"So, are you ready?" October called from the bathroom small enough to crap, shower, and shave while standing in the same spot.

"I think so!"

October popped out of the bathroom and hit Joey with the door. "Sorry."

Joey laughed. "That's fine. I didn't need the mirror anyway. Or my nose." She rubbed it tenderly. "Is it bleeding?"

October checked. "No."

"Good."

"How do I look? Acceptable?" October asked doing a tight twirl.

Joey caught her by both arms and looked at her face, not her outfit. October looked down at herself, trying to get her friend to tell her if she was okay to go. She'd never been to an art opening before, and she had no idea what was appropriate attire. Mrs. Davis tried to help her pick something out, and reassured her what she'd settled on was perfect, but she was still unsure. They'd settled on a pants suit, but made it look a little less stiff with a long, flowy black cardigan.

"You look wonderful. You look like I'm so glad you're here."

"You didn't even look at my outfit. Is it too undertaker-ish?"

Joey beamed at her, refusing to give her clothes even the smallest glance. "I don't care what you're wearing, my favorite undertaker. You're here."

October leaned over and hugged her new best friend. She felt like she'd found a piece of her soul that day in the book shop, and she wasn't about to miss something this important for her.

"You look absolutely ethereal," October commented as she appraised at her friend. She held out her long green skirt which sparkled when she moved, and was complimented with a lighter green tank top, and matching green eyeliner and green glittery eye shadow. It was just perfect for the evening.

Joey beamed. "Why thank you."

"It's going to be great. I just know it," October encouraged.

Joey sucked in a breath through her teeth. "We'll see!"

But October knew there was nothing to worry about. Her forest sprite had a magic about her that was sure to charm anyone who came into that gallery.

THEY WALKED to the gallery just as the sun was setting. Joey wanted to get there a little early to make sure the lighting was right, and everything was in its place. The gallery was small, with huge glass windows inviting people inside to get a closer look at Joey's art.

The gallery owner was a woman in her sixties, wearing a

long and colorful skirt, a white top, and a lace cardigan that hung down to her knees. She held her arms wide and Joey went into them gladly.

"Joey. My favorite. Who've you brought?" The woman's voice was soft, as if she wanted you to lean in close.

"This is my friend October. She lives outside the city. She came in for the opening."

"I like you already." She pulled October into a warm embrace, and October soaked it in. She never realized how much she missed human contact, until she had someone touch her.

The woman squeezed her and pulled back, holding her at arm's length, scrutinizing her with light grey eyes. "Are you lonely, child?"

October chuckled. "Not with Joey around."

"No, of course not. But you seem...haunted by something," she offered, and Joey laughed out loud.

"How right you are," Joey quipped, and October glared at her friend. "October, this is my fairy godmother, Ruby. She owns the gallery and gave me a shot tonight."

Ruby waved her off. "You earned your shot, my dear. Now, please make sure everything is just how you want it. I got cookies from Mister Kinsman down the street. You like his bakery don't you?"

Joey snatched a cookie off the plate and dug into it, gesturing for October to do the same. "You know I do." October could barely understand her friend through the cookie in her mouth.

"October, you make yourself comfortable. Enjoy a private viewing while Joey and I finish up."

"Is there anything I can do? Joey, need me to run and get drinks or something?" October offered.

"That's very kind of you, but we have a lemonade machine there, and water. My granddaughter, Ruby, is in the back arranging another platter of cookies, and looking for more cups."

October brightened. "Beautiful name."

Ruby smiled warmly. "Yes. She's a real gem, just like her name. You should talk to her if you can. She's just visiting for a bit. But I was so glad she was here to help tonight. For now, enjoy yourself. Take in the quiet before guests arrive."

They left October alone in the space. It was mostly white, which left very little distraction for Joey's art. And her art was breathtaking. She'd used a mix of mosses, glass, leaves, and other organic materials to create beautiful forest portraits. They weren't paintings, but three-dimensional pieces that invited you to come closer, but also step back and take the whole picture in. She'd created a lovely waterfall in one with shards of blue and clear glass. She'd painted a unicorn bent and drinking from the pool below. Moss and leaves created the forest around her, leaving October spell bound.

She had six main pieces on display, with three other smaller ones scattered around on pedestals or a small end table. Each had a small sign telling customers the name of the piece, the medium of art, and the price. None were priced high enough October thought.

Joey told her she worked in mixed media, but October didn't know what that meant. She'd Googled it, but it seemed like it could mean anything. Metal work, sculpture, plastics, anything was fair game. Her art was beyond anything October had imagined, and it was so unbelievably Joey.

Each piece she walked by told a different part of the same story. It was about the forest. And for a city girl like Joey, she told it awfully well. One had a fairy sitting on top of what looked like a real mushroom. Another had a painted mouse reaching for a real berry.

Joey walked up behind her, but October was too mesmerized to look at her. "How do you preserve the…well the organic matter for lack of a better term?"

"It's dipped in a few things. Resin type stuff. But less shiny," Joey answered. "It'll preserve it forever. Possibly not environmentally friendly. But, it's nice to know my art will last the ages."

"It's beautiful, Joey. I had no idea."

"Because I didn't tell you. I wanted you to be surprised," Joey interjected.

"Fair enough. And I am. Although, I don't know why. I can tell right away this is your work."

"Really? How?"

"Because. You're a forest sprite." October hadn't meant to say the phrase out loud. It just came out.

Joey's laugh came out a little sad and October felt compelled to apologize at once. "I didn't mean anything by it, Joey. It's just what I thought the first time I met you. You're ethereal, ya know?"

"No. It's fine. It's just…It's what my dad used to call me before he left."

"Oh." There were no other words to respond appropriately to that statement. It was too heavy already to add more to it.

"Sorry, didn't mean to be a mood killer. Ruby's opening the doors. Come stand with me?" Joey's smile was filled with nerves and excitement, so October took her hand and went to the door. She manned a high-top table and offered to hand out cards for those who might want to purchase a piece later.

"Ready, my dear?" Ruby asked as she stood at the door.

"As I'll ever be." October had never seen her confident friend so shaken. But she understood. Her heart was on display. And some people were bound to say something rude. But Joey had thick skin, and an amazing gift. October couldn't believe she was fortunate enough to witness the beginning. She knew as Ruby unlocked the door and set a folding sign outside urging people to come in for free refreshments and art that this was the start of something big for Joey. This would be the moment that defined her life, and October got to witness it.

"Let your night begin," Ruby announced when she came back in.

The first few minutes, they stood quietly. No one came in, and October chewed the inside of her lip, letting Joey's nerves rub off on her. But then there were people, and soon the little gallery had a line about five people deep waiting to get inside. Joey was too busy to think, let alone worry about naysayers as she flitted from group to group answering questions. Someone bought the waterfall piece right away. They'd only been open about thirty minutes when the mouse piece went as well.

An hour in, October was talking with a lovely older couple visiting from Scotland who just happened to walk by, and wondered if they could ship overseas, when a commotion interrupted her train of thought.

"October, come here!" Joey insisted.

"I'm so sorry. Please, enjoy yourself. Take a card, and I'll try to find out for you," October offered. They smiled warmly.

"I was trying to make you an internationally famous artist when you so rudely interrupted me. What is it?" October demanded, with only a hint of seriousness in her voice.

"This is my old friend Will from art school. And his wife, June," Joey was bouncing with excitement. "They came up from Florida for my opening. But you're going to stay and see a show or something right?"

Will nodded. "Yes. We're seeing Phantom tomorrow. But then we have to go back."

"Oh my gosh, that's amazing," October held out her hand and June took it first. "You'll love Phantom."

June looked around unsure. "I'm a bit out of my element here. Perhaps you could help?"

"Nope. You and I are in the same boat. I'm no artist," October replied.

"Ha, wonderful. Two peas in a pod."

"Joey," Ruby called. "This couple has some questions about one of your pieces."

She looked at Will apologetically. "Quit talking to the people you know and go enjoy your time in the spotlight," Will teased Joey. "But I am hoping you'll have dinner with us when you're done? I'd love to catch up with you."

"Of course," Joey said. "You came all this way. We'd love to. October is staying with me tonight since she came in for the opening too."

"Did you? That's wonderful," June said. Her smile was so disarming, October couldn't help but smile foolishly back at her.

"It was a no brainer. I had to be here for this."

"You're a good friend," June said as Joey walked away.

"I try to be." They wandered away to take in Joey's art, and October looked over at her friend in her element and beamed with pride. Then she spotted a man who looked out of place. He was wearing a long-sleeved shirt, a dark brown vest, jeans, and a herringbone-style hat. To be fair, there were all different types of people in the gallery. It wasn't his clothes that set him apart. It was the fact that he was standing in front of one of Joey's pieces, and didn't notice when people passed through him.

He was a ghost.

It wasn't often October saw ghosts outside the funeral home. She knew they were there, but usually they chose to stay hidden. They rarely knew she could see them, and she suspected if they realized it, she'd be overrun with them, so she didn't interact unless they approached her. However, something about that ghost drew her to him.

October went over quietly and stood behind him. A tear trickled down his face and caught in his dark brown beard.

"Sir? Can I help you?" She offered carefully, and quietly enough that no one heard.

He didn't respond. As if he couldn't conceive of anyone speaking to him. So, October walked around in front of him and caught his eye. "Sir?"

"Are you speaking to me?" He asked, his voice harsh from disuse.

October nodded slightly and moved to his side, to look as if she was admiring Joey's art.

"How?"

"A gift, you might say."

"Or a curse," he pointed out.

She didn't want to put too much thought into that opinion. She couldn't do anything about it, so no sense in being negative.

"Why are you here?" October inquired.

"I know the artist."

"Oh really? Would you like me to tell her you're here? She didn't mention anyone dying recently." October looked at her friend with concern. She was busy taking payment from the Scottish couple and making arrangements to ship her painting overseas.

"I don't think she knows," the man admitted.

"Oh." October didn't know what to say to that. Did he want her to tell Joey he was gone? Who was he?

"This is lovely." He gestured toward the piece. It had a stained-glass rainbow in the background, shining over a mountain made of metal, and scuffed at the top to look like snow. She'd used resin colored blue for a clear mountain lake reflecting the mountain perfectly. It hadn't sold yet, despite its beauty. "I'd hang it in the living room, so everyone who came to visit would see it."

"I'm sure they would all love it."

"I should've…" the man trailed off as he looked longingly at Joey, who was living her best life. "There's so much I wanted to say. And now…"

"I can tell her whatever you'd like. If you want," October added. "No pressure."

"I don't know. This is her night."

October let him stare at Joey for a few moments, before she asked, "Who are you?"

He turned back to October and extended a hand, before looking down at it and dropping it. "Oh. I'm sorry. How rude of me. I'm Joseph Keller. Joey's father."

Of all the things he could have said, that wasn't what October expected. An old teacher maybe? A neighbor. Her dad wasn't that old. Not that October's dad had been old when he passed. It was like some kind of parental pandemic. Her dad, Wilder's mom, Joey's dad. What the heck?

"What happened to you?" October blurted, needing answers to why everyone was leaving so young.

He looked at her, surprised by how upset she was. "I took to drinking. Maybe Joey told you."

"She said she hadn't heard from you in some time. I did ask her if she wanted you to come tonight."

His eyes betrayed hope. "What did she say?"

"Honestly? She wasn't sure. But Joey is a very forgiving person. I think she'd be glad you were here, and glad you're so proud of her," October assured him.

"I hope you're right. If you think she'd want to know, tell her I came, and that I'm sorry."

"If you want to hang around, we can have a conversation," October offered.

He shook his head. "No. I don't think she'd want to talk to me," he insisted.

"I disagree, but I won't force you."

"Just tell her I'm proud of her. I am. You're right. She's perfect, and I hope she's happy."

He started to fade in front of me, a smile on his face. He was going. "Mr. Keller. Wait."

But he didn't. A few people looked at her, but she smiled and turned her eyes to the floor as she walked back to her high-top table as casually as she could. October knew Joey would have questions, and she wouldn't have answers. She might even get mad. But there was nothing for it now. She wasn't a mind reader, and knowing she would tell Joey was all the closure he needed.

She watched her friend, and wondered just when the right time would be to completely burst her bubble.

THE GALLERY WAS A TREMENDOUS SUCCESS. She sold everything but two small pieces, which Joey said were easy to store, and one large one. She'd made enough to cover her rent for the next nine months.

They walked arm in arm to the restaurant she'd suggested for dinner with Will and June. "Maybe we should take a trip with some of the money. Where have you always wanted to go?" Joey asked.

"Scotland. I'd like to see some of the castles and ruins, and the cliffs, and listen to people talk."

"Did you talk to that couple?" Joey asked excitedly.

"I did! I could've listened to them all day."

"Me too."

"I'm so proud of you," October gushed. "What's next for you?"

"One of the guys who came in gave me his card. He

suggested an online shop. Especially for the smaller pieces. I might do that. We got talking about more utilitarian pieces. Vases, lamps, stuff like that. I thought it was a good idea."

"It's a great idea. Make things people can't live without."

The restaurant was a midgrade place. Not a dive, but not somewhere that would require black tie. Muertos it was called.

"Bit morbid to name your restaurant Muertos isn't it? Are they absolving themselves of liability if I die from food poisoning? Like, we warned you kind of a thing?" October asked.

"It's a Mexican place, and I have a feeling you're going to love it."

"I'll take your word for it."

Joey was one thousand percent right. They walked into an explosion of Day of the Dead décor. There was even a black light highlighting the intricate paintings on some of the figures.

"Joey," October breathed.

Joey took her hand excitedly. "I know! Come on, there's Will." She waved at him, but October was rooted to the floor taking it all in. There was a small waterfall in the corner, with beautiful tropical flowers planted all around. Orange petals cascaded around the rocks. And there were little alcoves in the stone walls with photographs and candles lit. Some were black and white, and clearly very old. And some were tragically new. October wondered if she should light a candle for Joey's dad.

Someone played guitar softly in the other corner on a small stage, and Joey tugged at her arm again. Reluctantly she let her friend lead her to the table.

"Well, this place is amazing," June said from behind her menu. "I have no idea what to order. I assume everything is good?"

"Oh, absolutely. I'm getting the street corn appetizer, so you'll have to try that," Joey said.

"Perfect," June said as if that narrowed down her options.

October wasn't huge on Mexican food, but the place was so charming, she didn't care. And it turned out, it was amazing. Full of flavor and the meat was so tender it melted in her mouth. The cheese sauce was to die for.

The four of them barely talked until the food was gone. They were so quick about bringing the street corn out, all they could do was say "oh my God" over and over. Honestly, it sounded a little like an orgy at their table, and October didn't even care.

When they were enjoying some after dinner drinks, October finally had the wherewithal to start being social with their guests. "So, Will, you went to art school? Do you have a gallery in Florida then?"

June gave him the most intense side eye October had ever seen, and she knew she'd touched a button.

"No. I'm an accountant actually. But I did start renting some space at a studio in town," he answered, without looking at his wife.

"That's great, Will. Send me some pictures of your stuff," Joey demanded.

"Oh right, because he'll be so quick to send pictures like you were?" October teased.

"It's different, artist to artist," Joey insisted.

"Mmm," Will agreed as he put his drink down. "That's true." June gave him that side eye again and he shrugged. "It is," he insisted a little too forcefully.

"How did you end up being an accountant Will?" Joey asked. "You did so well in school, and then dropped off the face of the planet. I couldn't believe it when you reached out to me."

"That's a long story," Will said with a chuckle. "But June here has me back on track."

"That's wonderful," October smiled. Their love was so obvious. They were like two magnets drawn to each other. Even when June was exasperated with him, she didn't pull away. She pulled closer. October wondered if she and Wilder could ever look that easy together. Not with Abby around that was for sure.

"Something on your mind, October?" June asked.

October shook her head. "Sorry. You guys are so perfect together."

June snorted. "Oh right. We're so perfect and everything is sunshine and roses with mister childhood trauma here."

October choked on her drink. "Well, that was honest."

Joey beamed. "Oh I like her a lot, Will. I approve."

Will's eyes narrowed. "Remember that discussion about oversharing, June?"

A laugh escaped October as June turned innocent. "Please," October said. "Everyone has childhood trauma. I see ghosts because of mine."

She slapped her hand over her mouth. How had that just popped out? Joey clapped and giggled. "Oh, this *is* a fun night."

The conversation settled into easy banter after they all got over the shock of October's declaration. She couldn't tell if either one of them believed her, but it didn't matter. They didn't get up and leave, and they didn't treat her differently either. Joey knew how to find good people it seemed.

"Well, thank you for this, Joey," Will said as he held up his nearly empty glass. "Congratulations on a wonderful opening."

"It really was," Joey agreed.

"Yes, thank you for giving us an excuse to get away. Will's

Grandfather is wonderful, but it's nice to get some time to ourselves."

"Your Grandfather?" Joey asked.

"He lives with us. My Grandma died years ago, and he had a series of strokes that left him blind. He's a handful, but he's good company."

"You don't mind living with his Grandfather?" Joey's blunt question didn't startle June at all.

"No. I'm a home healthcare worker. That's how Will and I met. I was there for Ron. And he's come so far in just a few short years. He's even learned a little bit of braille, so he can play cards. He plays Euchre at the library with some of the seniors once a week. I'm pretty sure he's the favorite down there." She said it with such affection, it made October want to meet him while he was still among the living, even though she knew that wasn't very realistic.

"He sounds wonderful," October said, and meant it.

"He is," June and Will said together.

"Especially when he brings home dinner. Think he caught anything today?" Will asked.

June shrugged. "I'm sure he did. Whether or not he managed to reel it in and bring it home is a separate question."

"Quite the angler, I take it?" Joey asked.

"He takes himself as one. Sometimes he brings home some snapper that's good," Will said. "But mostly he just brings home stories about the one that got away."

"God, remember that time he hooked another fisherman?" June asked and they all started laughing.

"Not really?" October asked.

"Oh yeah. Missed his eye by like an inch. Of course, Ron's blind so he said he didn't know what he was complaining about. He left the guy with two good eyes."

Joey laughed. "I bet that went over well."

"It did actually. They're best friends now. I bet Marvin has kept the bench out back nice and warm in our absence," Will explained.

"And the beer supply dangerously low," June added.

They laughed and chatted until their drinks were gone, and the bill was paid. "It was so nice to meet you both," October said.

"You too," June shook her hand with a warmth only a caretaker could have. There was a genuineness to her that made October want to know her better.

"Will," Joey shook his hand as if she was suddenly some kind of professional. "I expect you to drop me a line when your opening comes around. You always had more talent than I did. I know you'll be a smash."

He eyed her skeptically. "Ha. Don't count your chickens, Joey."

"Chickens huh? I remember you were into watercolors. But, whatever twists your Twizzler, man."

They all laughed and parted ways. As they walked arm in arm back to Joey's apartment, October thought about how wonderful the evening went, and when she should pop their little bubble. Maybe she should wait until the morning, so if Joey got mad she could just pack up and leave. Was there a train out that evening? It was getting late. If she got that mad, she could always go to a hotel, October supposed.

"You've gone quiet," Joey observed as they walked up the stairs to her place above the pizzeria.

"I have something I need to tell you. I just, don't want to burst your bubble is all." Whelp. It was out there now.

Joey laughed once. "No time like the present. Burst away, my friend."

"I saw your dad tonight."

"You did? How was he? Why didn't he come say hi?" The questions rapid fired so fast, October struggled to keep up.

"He…he was a ghost, Joey."

She blinked at him. "He what?"

"Sounded like some kind of complication from drinking not long ago," October explained as she closed the door behind her.

Joey sat down on the bed without taking her coat off. "What did he say? Why was he there? Where had he been living even?"

"I don't know. He didn't say. He did say he was so proud of you. He loved the one of the mountain, and said he'd hang it in his living room so everyone would see it as soon as they came in."

Tears started to form in Joey's eyes. "Did he?"

October sat next to her and took her hand. "He also said he was sorry."

"For what?"

October shrugged. "Everything? He didn't really say."

"Did you tell him he could talk to me? Why didn't he come talk to me?"

October nodded vigorously. "I did. I offered to translate, as it were, but he didn't want to. He didn't want to steal your night. And he didn't think you'd want to talk to him."

Joey's voice deepened with a hint of bitterness October had never heard from her. "That's a cop out."

"Probably," October agreed.

"Do you think he'll come back?"

October cringed, hating to squash the hope in her friend's face. "No. He left right there in the gallery."

"Left?"

October sighed. "It's what happens when they're done I guess. They move on."

"To where?"

"Whatever's next. Heaven? Hell for some I'm sure. Although, I'm glad it's not my place to decide."

"I didn't realize they could move on. Why hasn't your dad?"

October cringed again. "I don't really want him to," she admitted.

"Wow. That's a little selfish."

October wanted to blister at that. To rage at her friend's inaccurate assessment. But it wasn't inaccurate at all. It was just Joey showing her a truth she didn't really want to see. Again.

"I know. But, before Wilder, and now you, I was alone. Like alone alone. I didn't have friends across the country like Will. Or connections like Ruby. People who'd look out for me. Who cared. I had Dad and he had me and that was it. When he died, and he stayed, I didn't tell him to move on, and he didn't ask. Sometimes, I think he might want to. But…"

"You're too afraid to tell him it's okay?" Joey filled in.

October nodded, joining Joey with her tears.

Joey laughed. "Well, we're a couple of sad sacks aren't we?"

"Welcome to the dead dad's club," October said, rather insensitively.

"I don't know that I want to be a member of that club," Joey admitted.

"Me neither. It sucks."

Joey leaned her head on October's shoulder, and she put her arm around her friend. "I'm sorry this happened," October said.

"Me too. But I'm glad you were there. More than ever."

"Hey Joey?"

"Yeah."

October let out a breath. "Thanks for not being mad."

Joey pulled away. "Why would I be mad?"

October turned and looked out the window, unable to

make eye contact with Joey. "Because I stole your thunder? Ruined your night? With my weird, creepy ghost stuff."

Joey got up and plopped down right in October's line of sight. "You did no such thing. You gave me closure I never thought I'd have. I didn't know where he was, or what he was doing. Wait until I tell Mom. She probably won't be surprised. I think he was drinking before he ever left us, but Mom tried to hide it from me."

"Your Mom knows I can see ghosts?"

Joey shook her head. "Not yet." She had already taken out her phone to text her mom. She'd been texting her all night, pictures with people she sold art to, and pictures of the gallery before everyone came in. She was upset she had to miss it, but her Grandmother was too sick to be alone.

October chose her words carefully. Her instinct was to keep her secret close. Despite how she'd blurted it out with Will and June, she'd been trying to make him feel better about whatever his childhood trauma was. This was a little different, finding out your ex was a ghost. "Do you think you should tell her? Maybe just tell her you found his obit or something?"

Joey looked up at her and blinked. "I don't lie to my Mom."

Suddenly, October felt like she was in fifth grade again, and Rosie was sitting across from her. "Of course." She felt defeated. Everything had gone so well. And that was where it would end.

"I'm just going to call her," Joey declared, giving up on texting completely. She had the phone ringing on speaker before October could protest.

"Joey, my love. It looks like it was amazing. Tell me everything. Grandma's here too."

"Hi angel," an older woman's crackly voice called.

"Hi grandma," Joey said.

"We're telling them both?" October whispered, pleading with Joey not to.

She waved October off, holding the phone just out of reach as October tried to calculate how hard it would be to overpower her and hang up. A desperate move to be sure, but...

"Dad was there," Joey blurted out.

"What? Oh my God. What did he say to you? Did he want money? How did he look?" The familiarity of the rapid-fire questions made October smile.

"October saw him. He didn't talk to me," Joey explained.

"Of course he didn't. Coward," her mother declared. Clearly she had some healing left to do.

"Mom. He didn't come talk to me because he couldn't." Joey paused and looked at October, who buried her face in her hands. "He died."

"What happened?" Her mom asked, horrified. "Did he get hit by a car outside the gallery? That must have been horrific for you!"

"Nope. He was dead when he got there." Joey was having way too much fun, and October just wanted to crawl into a hole and die.

Her mother didn't say anything.

One Mississippi. Two Mississippi. Three Mississippi. October got to eight before Joey's Grandmother finally piped up.

"I'm sorry dear. Maybe we have a bad connection. Or maybe my old brain just can't keep up. It sounded like you said he was dead when he got there?"

"That's right. He spoke to October."

"He...spoke to October," her mother repeated slowly. This is how people usually took the news. Processing until they decided October was crazy and didn't want to come within a thousand feet of her.

"October, dear. Are you there?" Joey's grandmother asked.

October peeked out from behind her hands. "Yes Mrs. Braverman. I'm here."

"I think Joey is having a bit of fun at our expense. Would you please explain what your friend is so poorly trying to tell us?"

"I'd rather not," October revealed.

"Why?" Mrs. Braverman asked.

"Because. You'll think I'm crazy, and tell me to stop hanging around your granddaughter."

The burst of laughter was so unexpected, it actually startled October. Joey nearly dropped the phone laughing at October, joining in with her grandmother's rather contagious laugh.

"Oh, my darling girl. Thank you for that. I haven't laughed like that in ages, isn't that right, Matilda?" Mrs. Braverman blew her nose. "Who on Earth have you encountered in your life that would make you think an old bat like me would react that poorly? *And*, furthermore, even if I did think you're a bit...unhinged," she said carefully. "Which I *won't* I assure you, who cares? I'm eighty-five with eight toes in the grave. What difference does my opinion make?"

"Well...I know Joey thinks very highly of you both. Should you think poorly of me—"

Joey cut October off. "I'd know they were either hangry, distracted, or upset about something else. Because you are an absolute joy."

"Enough sap. Someone tell me what is going on," Joey's mother insisted.

"I'm afraid I can see ghosts, Mrs. Keller." October braced herself.

"Right. Naturally. Of course you can. Don't you run a funeral home? Isn't that annoying, having ghosts hanging around all the time?" Mrs. Keller asked.

"Well, sometimes it can be a lot. But I've always been fine with them. Plus, my dad helps," October explained.

"Oh, that's nice. I was thinking Joey said your dad had died years ago. Must have gotten mixed up," Mrs. Keller said.

"No. No you didn't. He died ten years ago. He stays around to help me out."

"Oh." A pause. "Oh. As a ghost. Of course. How silly of me. I'm sorry. I don't mean to be rude," Mrs. Keller blustered. "What's socially correct in this situation? Sympathy? Interest? Humor? I've never known someone who could see ghosts before."

"You know, do you remember old Mrs. Castillo? She said the place at the end of the street was haunted. I caught her sprinkling holy water around the front gate one time." Mrs. Braverman said, adding a click of her tongue. "Superstitious old woman."

"I don't think October is being superstitious, mom," Mrs. Keller offered.

"Oh no. I'm sorry dear. I didn't mean to imply that you were. That's just…well, it's my only experience with that sort of thing. Between your mother and I, we hung around with a pretty good variety of folks. None claimed to actually see ghosts, except for the superstitious type. And even they didn't claim to see them. Just sort of, knew they were there and wanted them gone."

"Again, it's not a claim, grandma," Joey explained. "She can see them. I've talked to her dad. Seen him move things. It's remarkable really."

"That is something," her mother said breathily, as if the conviction behind what Joey said took her breath away.

"So, you actually saw Phillip?" Mrs. Braverman asked. "How did he look?"

"He looked, well good I guess. I didn't know what he

looked like in life so I have no basis of comparison I'm afraid," October admitted.

"Mom. Who cares how he looked? What was he doing there? What did he want? Just to bother Joey I'm sure. Distract her on the most important night of her life. Steal the spotlight. Typical Phil." October felt sad for how much he'd clearly hurt Joey's mother. Maybe he should've hung around and apologized to her too.

"He wanted me to tell Joey how proud he was of her. And that he was sorry."

"Sorry," Mrs. Keller scoffed. "For what? Leaving us in the lurch? Never once reaching out in a genuine way in thirty years? Being the worst possible father and husband he could be?"

"Yes. That exactly, I think."

October's statement was a bit of a conversation stopper, and she cringed at Joey, who just smiled back like all of it was good.

"Well, I don't know who he thinks he is, just showing up from beyond the grave and expecting forgiveness," Joey's mom insisted, not ready to let go of her bitterness.

"Matilda. I don't think he thinks much of anything anymore. He's dead," Mrs. Braverman countered.

"Is he just going to pop into Joey's life whenever he feels like it now? All the major events? Now I have to compete with him for attention?" Her mom's voice had turned a little desperate, making Mrs. Braverman laugh.

"You're worried about sharing custody with a ghost?" Mrs. Braverman finally got out.

"Well. Mom! He doesn't have to worry about travel arrangements and sick mothers. He could be there any time!"

"Back the guilt train up there, mom," Joey interrupted. "It was fine that you weren't there tonight. There will be others, and I had October with me. And Will came. Remember Will?"

"No, not really," her mom admitted.

"We went to art school together. Anyway, you were missed, but it was such a wonderful night, and I can't wait to share the next one with *both* of you."

"And, just to set your worries at ease," October added. "He left. He won't be back to visit any of you."

"Ever? Where did he go?" Mrs. Braverman asked. "You can understand why an old woman would want to know."

"Where they all go. Depends on what you believe I suppose." October wasn't prepared for another spiritual debate on the afterlife. Explaining her ghosts was more than enough for one evening. "All I know for certain is, once they go, they don't come back."

"And your father, he hasn't gone?" Mrs. Braverman asked.

"No. I was telling Joey, who thinks I'm terribly selfish, he stays for me. I wasn't ready when he died. I was alone managing the business, and didn't have any friends or family around. So, he stayed."

"I see," the old woman chewed on that for a bit. "So, you can choose to stay."

"I think so, yes."

"Interesting."

Joey's mom piped up at once. "Don't you dare think about hanging around haunting me, you old bat."

Again, the laughter that had Joey and October in stitches rang through the phone. "I think I'll do what I want," Joey's grandmother argued.

October couldn't help but laugh. What was happening? How had she found such a wonderful group of people? Maybe they didn't understand, but they cared. They genuinely cared. Her dad was right.

After the laughter died down, Joey's mom asked a serious question. "Joey honey. Are you okay?"

"I'm great mom, why?"

"Because you just found out your dad's dead." October shouldn't have been surprised by Mrs. Keller's matter-of-fact tone. Joey had to have gotten it from somewhere.

Joey chuckled. "I'm fine mom. I mean. We have closure finally. We know what happened to him. And he's at peace. If he can have that, I think we should too."

"That's very healthy." Her grandmother's approval made Joey smile.

"Plus, it was such a great night. I wanted to sell one piece. One. That was my goal. I sold almost all of them you guys. I have rent covered through next summer basically. I'm financially stable!" The way Joey said it, like she'd leveled up or something made October burst with pride.

"We are both so proud of you, my darling," her grandmother gushed. "I can't wait to see the next one. It will be even bigger and more successful, and have more glitter, and more treats, yes?"

"Absolutely, Grandma. I'll get whatever you want."

"Wonderful."

"We'll let you go then. October, it was wonderful chatting with you," her mom added.

"You too, Mrs. Keller. Thank you for understanding."

"Only a troll wouldn't. I can't believe you haven't made a fortune. Like that woman in the movie Ghost? People would pay good money to commune with their loved ones I'd think," Mrs. Braverman added.

"I like what I do." October didn't want to go into the predatory nature that line of work had, so she kept it simple.

"Mom. Let them go. They don't have much time left together," Mrs. Keller prodded.

"Bummer. Going home tomorrow, October?" Mrs. Braverman asked.

"I am. I have a service to get ready for on Monday."

"Oh, I've backed myself into a corner again. Help an old woman out, dear. What's the appropriate encouragement for you then? Good luck? I hope it goes…smoothly and there are no fights between in-laws?"

October laughed. "Anything is fine. I know your heart is in the right place."

"Oh, I do like you," Mrs. Braverman said.

"Goodbye girls," Joey's mom tried one more time.

Joey laughed. "Bye guys. Love you both."

The women blew kisses through the phone and Joey hung up. "See? That wasn't so bad."

"You enjoyed torturing all of us a bit too much if you ask me," October pointed out.

"Oh please. Why do it if it isn't fun?" She tossed her phone aside and laid back on the bed.

October grabbed a nearby pillow and hit Joey with it. Things devolved from there. They didn't sleep, and October was just fine with that. She could sleep later. That night was for making memories with the best friend she'd ever known.

IN THE MORNING, they had breakfast at a lovely little café near the station, and she bid Joey goodbye.

"Take care," Joey commanded. "You take a piece of my heart with you, every time we part ways."

October felt exactly the same way.

"I wouldn't have you being careless with it," Joey added, making October laugh.

"I would never."

"See that you wouldn't," Joey ordered.

By the time she got home, they'd texted more than a

dozen times. She walked into her house, greeted by silence. She'd left Queso with her dad, just in case Abby decided to come back around. It was unsettling as she set her keys down on the kitchen table.

Her phone rang just as she was setting her stuff in her bedroom. "Ms. Manning. I have an intake for you. Thirty-five-year-old male. Died in a horrific car crash. Lucky he only hurt himself. Body's pretty banged up. Family will likely want cremation. I've scheduled a meeting with them for you tomorrow morning, but he will arrive there shortly."

"Okay, thank you so much." She hung up, glad she'd come home when she had, and headed down to the funeral home. Maybe the dead would wait, but Queso wouldn't.

CHAPTER 19

"*N*ever did care much for that boy," Mrs. Davis said as October thanked the delivery men and looked at Colin laid out on her table.

"Oh Colin. What happened?" He was barely recognizable. In fact, she'd double checked his name twice to be sure. Had Wilder told her his last name?

"Are you sure this is Wilder's friend?" October asked Mrs. Davis, just to be sure.

"Yes. He's been hanging around Wilder more lately. Since you…well, since…" she frowned. "There's no good way to finish that sentence without sounding like I'm annoyed with your choice, which I'm not, so I'm just going to stop talking."

"What should we do?" October asked as her dad frowned down at the body.

"You haven't seen the ghost?" Her dad glanced around, as if mentioning him would make him appear right then and there.

October shook her head. She was glad she hadn't seen Colin. She couldn't imagine he'd be any easier to deal with in death than he was in life.

"Someone should call Wilder. Make sure he knows," Mrs. Davis suggested.

"Me. You mean me, don't you?" October pinched the bridge of her nose.

"Lucky he wasn't in the car with him." Mrs. Davis looked like she'd seen a ghost herself. She was clutching the neck of her shirt, and Steve was at her side.

"Wilder's fine. You've just been to visit him. He was wallowing, but alive," Steve reassured her.

"He'd been joyriding with Colin not that long ago, you know? In that horrible death trap of a car," Mrs. Davis explained. "Said it was quite a rush."

"I bet it was," October surmised.

"Well, well, well. What have we here?" Colin's voice echoed off the sterile space, and October squeezed her eyes closed.

"Colin. I'm...well, I'm sorry this happened," October mustered.

"I told him you were a weirdo, but I had no idea how weird. You're some kind of ghost collector? How morbid. Who are these poor folks you've got trapped here?" He demanded.

"What?" October asked.

"I beg your pardon," Steve demanded as he stood straighter and puffed out his chest.

"Calm down old timer. If she's not keeping you here, what are you doing here?" He asked as he leaned on the table where his body lay.

"I believe we ask the questions." Steve didn't back down, and took a step toward Colin.

Colin held up his hands. "No need to get prickly with me. Don't you think it's bizarre the local undertaker can see ghosts? Not only see us, but talk to us?"

"Never gave it much thought. What are *you* doing here?" Steve asked.

Colin shrugged. "Just thought I'd take a look around before I move on."

"See that you do. Move on, I mean. Rapidly." October had never heard her father's voice so cold.

Colin looked to October. "What's with him?"

"You've been rather rude to me, in my place of business, in front of my father."

"Your dad? That's even weirder. Come on. And who's this, Wilder's mom? Oh my god. Is *that* how you're trying to get to him? Jeeze. I knew Wilder should've run from you like the plague. Does he even know you're batshit crazy?"

October had enough. "You know, I'd be careful. I'm not the one on the wrong side of the dirt, uncertain of what happens next."

"What do you mean? I know what happens next. I go to heaven and get my forty virgins or whatever."

"You honestly think you've earned some kind of paradise? You know, ghosts aren't all I can see. I see where they go. Sometimes it's lovely. It's warm and golden, and they run into the arms of their loved ones. But others," she clucked her teeth. "Those are the ones that keep me up at night. Promise me something?"

"What?" His voice seemed less sure than it had moments ago.

"When they come for you, don't hang around here. I don't want to see another one dragged into the darkness screaming."

"You're lying." He backed away from her and she advanced.

"Am I?" The two words were all he needed to turn and run from the room. Somehow, she knew she wouldn't see him again after that.

"Well. That was…" Mrs. Davis trailed off as she visibly relaxed.

"Unpleasant?" October asked as she pushed Colin's body into a refrigerated drawer, so she didn't have to look at him anymore.

"I was thinking of a few other words to describe that guy, but man. I'm proud of how you drove him off, Boo," her dad beamed.

"I should feel terrible. I shouldn't have lied to him," October said as she left the basement, with two ghosts in tow.

"You don't *know* it was a lie," Mrs. Davis said carefully.

"Mrs. Davis," October chastised. "Are you encouraging my terrible behavior?"

"Lord knows the boy could use a bit of a come to Jesus. Seems he's going to get the real thing," Mrs. Davis shrugged, as if October had nothing at all to feel guilty for.

What bothered her was she didn't feel guilty at all. She hadn't ever lied to a ghost like that before. She'd always tried to help them when she could. She'd never done them harm that way. But Colin pushed one too many of her buttons. She shook her head, deciding to stew about her behavior later. As she sat down at her desk, she knew she had to call Wilder.

Her phone beamed at her, waiting for instructions before going dark. "What will you say to him?" Mrs. Davis asked gently.

"I'm not sure. Your jerk friend is dead seems a bit tactless."

Her dad coughed to cover up a laugh, and Mrs. Davis gave him a sidelong glance. "A bit," she confirmed.

"I don't know. Hopefully it'll come to me." She dialed his number before she could chicken out, set it to speaker and pushed the phone away, so she couldn't hang up in a panic.

He answered halfway through the first ring. "October?"

How did he sound? It was hard to tell from one word. Not normal. But not a broken mess either. Maybe she was just being hopeful.

"Hi Wilder. I'm sorry to bother you."

"It's no bother," he insisted quickly.

She took a steadying breath. "Have you talked to Colin lately?"

The question seemed to catch him off guard. "Colin? Why?"

"I…I don't know how to tell you this. He's passed away, Wilder. I'm sorry. Terrible car accident it seems. I'm meeting with his family tomorrow. If you'd like, I can let you know when the service will be."

"I don't believe it. A car accident?" Wilder processed, and October gave him the space to do it. The phone was silent and she chewed the inside of her cheek.

"Wow," Wilder breathed. "I went with him in that car not too long ago. He seemed to have good control."

"Seems no one else was involved," October added, although she didn't know why.

"Well, that's good." The relief in his voice made her wonder if he was thinking about Abby. "Um…yeah. Geeze. I had no idea. Thank you for calling me. And yes. Yes, I would like to know when the service is, if you're all right with having me there."

"Yes, Wilder. Your friend has died. This isn't about me. Or us. It's about Colin."

Wilder turned quiet. "Right. Talk to you later then?"

October tried to ignore the hope in his voice. "Of course. Again, I'm very sorry Wilder."

With nothing left to say, he hung up.

. . .

"You said *what*," Joey demanded when October explained what had happened. Which took some doing. She'd never mentioned Colin specifically to Joey before. Didn't really see a need to. "I'm so proud of you!"

"I'm not sure I am," October admitted.

"Why not? Don't even tell me you're riding that guilt train because that train is full of people who are no fun."

"Well," October insisted. "This gift, or curse as your dad suggested it might be—"

"My dad told you it was a curse?" She scoffed. "That figures."

"He didn't mean anything by it." October immediately regretted mentioning that tidbit. Joey had already forgiven him and moved on, and here she was giving her a reason to dive back into his imperfections. "He was concerned is all."

"I'll allow it, if for no other reason than I don't want to devote any more brain power to it."

"Fair enough," October granted. "Anyway, this ability if that works better, should be used for good right?"

"Who says what you did wasn't good? It spurred him to move on right? And quit torturing you. How is that in any way bad?"

Joey's argument was sound, but October couldn't quite get on board with it yet. "It's not. And that's probably why I don't feel guilty. And that's what I feel guilty about."

"Was your mother Catholic? I've never heard someone justify their guilt in such a bizarre way."

"Joey come on. I made him think he was going to hell," October reasoned.

"So. Maybe he was."

"I hope not."

"Really, October? After everything he said?"

"Joey. You are one of the most immediately forgiving people I know. You even reminded me to forgive you better than I had forgiven Wilder if you ever made a mistake. I am not the one who judges the ghosts, and I'm glad for that. I don't want the responsibility of that. Do you?"

Joey was silent on the other end of the phone while October waited for her to respond.

"I don't know. It might be fun for a minute or two," Joey admitted. "But then I'd cave and send everyone to heaven so it's probably best I'm not in charge, you're right. But, you still don't need to feel bad for not feeling bad."

"I suppose not."

"Colin was who he was, and is where he is regardless of what you said to him," Joey pointed out.

"Yes. You're right."

"Obviously."

"How did I ever befriend someone so wise?" October quipped.

"We got lucky that night."

"Yes, we did."

"So. How was Wilder?"

October wondered when she would ask about that. "I'm proud of you. That showed remarkable restraint."

"Thank you. I wanted to ask as soon as you told me his friend died, *ten minutes ago.*"

October laughed. "We didn't talk long. He wasn't his normal self, for sure. But he didn't sound horrible either. He may have been a little hopeful when we hung up."

"Hopeful? How?"

"He asked me to call and let him know when the service was, if it was okay he came."

"Mmm," was all Joey said.

"Mmm? Is this a croissant you're enjoying or my life in upheaval?" October asked.

"Oh stop. Your life is not in upheaval. Maybe this is the

opportunity you need? To tell him?" And there it was. What Joey was itching to say all along.

"Feel better?"

"God yes. And you will too if you get it out in the open."

"Maybe." October wasn't so sure. Although, Joey's argument was solid. He seemed okay on the phone. "Maybe if he comes to the service, and seems okay, I'll go from there."

"Good," Joey latched onto that like a hungry baby taking a bottle. "I think that's a great plan," she encouraged.

"I'm sure you do," October teased.

"Just because I'm right, you don't have to be so bitter about it."

"We'll see who's right in the end."

"Only if you actually tell him," Joey pointed out.

"True. That's the rub, isn't it."

Joey yawned. "A problem for another day, I'm afraid. Promise me you won't lose sleep thinking about Colin and what you didn't do to him?"

"I promise."

"Okay. Goodnight." Joey hung up abruptly, like she always did, and then texted her three more times before she must have fallen asleep, because the messages went quiet.

October kept her promise. She didn't lose sleep over Colin. It was Wilder that was keeping her awake, and all the what-if's that went with him. Was she ready to be free of those? The limbo was hard, yes. But once she moved forward, the what-if's would be gone. The potential. The hope. There would be no room for any of that. There would only be...whatever she'd done or not done. And that thought terrified her.

CHAPTER 20

*W*ilder had no idea what he was doing. He'd parked his truck ten minutes ago. The service would start in five minutes. If he didn't go in soon, he'd be interrupting. If it was at any other funeral home, he wouldn't think twice about just going in.

But he felt glued to the seat. There weren't too many cars in the lot, which made him wonder if the family had bothered to call anyone. Colin had a lot of friends. Well. Maybe not friends. People who knew him? His coworkers must have known what happened. But maybe they didn't hear when the service would be. Or maybe, they didn't want to come. Maybe they were busy at two o'clock on a Thursday.

It didn't really matter. What mattered was Wilder was trapped in his truck in the funeral home parking lot that belonged to a girl he didn't know how to act around.

Taking a deep breath, he hauled himself out into the cold, early December air and went inside. October was stationed by the door and greeted him warmly, but not like she had before. It felt just like the first time they'd met. Like there was an unfamiliarity between them. A distance.

"Wilder. It's nice to see you," she'd said.

"You too," he echoed.

"It's just through those double doors."

"Same room mom's was in?" It came out judgier than he meant. Obviously, she couldn't have a special room for each client. It just felt weird to be back in there so soon.

October's expression softened. "If you'd rather not, I'd be happy to tell the family you stopped in and sent them your sympathies."

He shook his head and tried to stand a little taller, but it felt like there was a weight around his shoulders, making him want to hunch over.

"Would you like a cup of coffee or something to warm you up before you go in?" She offered.

"Isn't it about to start?"

"It is. But it'll just take me a second to get it."

"No. That's all right. I'd spill it on my pants."

"They do look nice," she observed with a smile, before schooling her face as if that comment was too friendly.

"Thanks. I couldn't bring myself to wear my suit again. I might not wear that ever again. I should probably donate it and get a new one that hasn't seen the inside of a funeral home."

"You saying something about my funeral home?" She teased, and he loved her for it. Which made his heart ache even more. He opened his mouth to say something, but she reached for the door.

"His parents are just up there if you want to say hello." She pointed to the couple lingering near the closed casket.

"Thanks." It came out flatly, with very little gratitude behind it. He didn't want to go in. He wanted to stay out and talk to her. Colin hadn't been a great friend. He'd been a man child with too much money, and it seemed like it had killed him. The news had sobered Wilder up, and he hadn't had a drink since October's call. But he still felt like something wasn't right, and a part of him understood Colin's need for fast cars and nice things. Distractions from the darkness in his head. It was probably best he didn't have the kind of money Colin had.

He approached Colin's parents quietly. "Mr. and Mrs. Dupris? I'm Wilder Davis. I went to school with Colin. We were friends. Had a drink with him about a week ago in fact." Wilder didn't know why he added that.

"Yes. Well. He was fond of that," Colin's mother commented bitterly.

His father held out a hand. "Sorry. Colin was drinking and driving, so you touched a nerve there. He's lucky he only hurt himself."

"I apologize. I'd had my suspicions, but…" *Stop talking*, Wilder scolded.

"We all hoped it was innocent fun I think," his dad offered a consolation Wilder didn't think he deserved.

"How did you even hear about the service? His phone was destroyed in the crash. All his contacts were gone. We had no idea how to let his friends know." His dad leaned in close. "Cheryl didn't want a lot of people gawking anyway."

"Of course not. I apologize. I didn't come to gawk or whatever. I just wanted to pay my respects."

Colin's dad started to sputter. "Of course, of course. I didn't mean. I'm sorry. This is all very—"

Wilder interrupted him. "You don't need to apologize to me. Ever. My mom died a few weeks ago. I know what this is like. Not knowing what to say. Or how to act. Or what to do. Or what tomorrow will bring, now that this chapter is over."

Cheryl let out a sob, and Wilder felt out of place as Colin's dad put his arm around her. "I'm very sorry this happened." Wilder offered, and went to take a seat near the back.

There were only about twenty people there, and Wilder knew Colin would've hated it. Way too understated and solemn for him. He would've had music so loud you could hardly hear. And kegs. Wilder shook his head. But that life-style is what got him to Manning Funeral Home in the first place.

October wasn't in the room. She let the family have their privacy during the service. But when it was over, she somehow knew, and opened the doors quietly.

He heard Colin's words, echoing in his mind. That she was creepy. No good for him. But he wasn't exactly perfect either, was he? He'd been mad at Colin the last time they'd talked. But his death somehow softened those emotions, now that Wilder couldn't make it right. It didn't matter. None of it did. What he'd said, or done, or the kind of friend he'd been. He was gone, and October was talking to the family.

Wilder sat with his thoughts, letting people pass by him until the room was empty. October didn't come back in, but she didn't shut the door either. She knew he was still there, but didn't want to bother him. Either she was giving him space, or telling him to leave her alone. Once he was sure Colin's parents had left, and October's attention wasn't needed by them, he got up and wandered to her office.

He found her at her desk signing paperwork. He knocked on the doorframe and she looked up. Her smile looked genuine, but her expression was difficult for him to read. She seemed distracted, looking over to his right. It was a quick glance, and maybe he'd imagined it, but the frown he'd glimpsed seemed real enough.

"Can I come in?"

"Of course. Would you like something to drink?"

He shook his head and sat on the couch where he'd watched the leaves blow by not all that long ago. So much had changed, but somehow he'd ended up just as lost and forlorn as he'd been the first time he'd been inside Manning Funeral Home. How had he let that happen?

"You were right about him. He did think you were creepy," Wilder admitted.

She walked around her desk and sat in the chair across from him. "I know."

"How?"

She scoffed and shook her head. "Call it intuition."

"We'd had a fight not too long ago. He said some…unflattering things about you and I stormed out."

She shook her head again and held up her hands. "I can only imagine. But it's probably not polite to speak ill of the dead. He was your friend, and that's what matters."

"You didn't care for him, did you?"

"It doesn't matter."

"No, I suppose it doesn't now, does it?"

October chewed the inside of her cheek, and Wilder made an effort not to stare at her. She really was beautiful. Her hair was pulled back into that severe bun she liked while she was working. He much preferred when she let her hair down. It suited her better, he thought. But he understood her practicality.

"Thanks again for letting me know. His folks said his phone was destroyed in the wreck, so they didn't have any of his contacts."

"Of course. I thought you'd at least want to know about it, even if you decided not to come."

"Definitely."

He bounced his leg until it felt uncomfortably cold. That happened a lot. He should probably see a doctor about it but never got around to it.

"October, can we—" he started, but stopped when he saw her looking at his leg like there was something there.

"Abby? Can we talk?"

215

Wilder couldn't breathe. There was no air. Had she said what he thought she'd said? Was she being cruel? She wasn't even looking at him. She didn't see his panic or the pain she'd caused. She was looking into an empty space next to him. Maybe she really was crazy. And if she was, what did that make him?

CHAPTER 21

*A*bby stood up and the lights began to flicker. "How dare you talk to me." Her voice was young, and the threat came out more bratty and entitled than the terrifying statement it was meant to be.

"What…" Wilder trailed off as he looked at the lights.

October glanced around the room, spying all the breakable things that could be thrown at her head and was suddenly desperate to go outside.

"Wilder, do you mind if we take this conversation somewhere safer?"

"What is going on?" He demanded as he stood up too. Not because he intended to go anywhere, but because he needed to move. Why had she brought Abby up? When she knew he wasn't over the trauma of it. Especially with everything that was going on.

"Wilder?" October was already at the door when a vase on her desk broke spilling water and flowers dangerously close to her computer.

"Oh," he said going to it, looking for paper towel or something to wipe it up with before it got on her laptop.

"Leave it. Please?" The way she pleaded made him move towards her. She was holding the double doors open, and he then followed her out to the field behind the funeral home.

October looked around. The breeze picked up a little, and she wrapped her blazer tightly around her as she eyed the tree line near the edge of her property, seeming to look for projectiles maybe? But why?

A branch went sailing past and she shook her head. "Abby. Is all this really necessary?"

"Have you lost your mind?" Wilder exclaimed before he could regret it. He'd called her creepy, and then crazy. But what else was he supposed to think?

"I'm sorry Wilder. I should've told you already. I can see ghosts. And Abby never left you. She hurt me that night. It's why I pushed you away. I was scared."

"What?" Wilder couldn't get his brain to work. What had she said? Abby hurt her? But she died. A lifetime ago. She couldn't hurt October any more than she could hurt Wilder.

"Are you okay? Like...mentally?"

The wind picked up, and almost sounded like a cackle, but it faded as soon as he'd heard it, and he shook his head. The weather really was being weird. "Maybe we should go back inside. That branch nearly hit you," he suggested.

"No. I really do think we're safer out here," October insisted.

Wilder eyed the skies, but they were blue and clear, which puzzled him further.

"October. Tell him something for me," Mrs. Davis said. October had no idea when she'd joined them. But her dad was there too. They made quite a motley crew standing in the field.

October winced and lowered her voice. "I don't know if that's a good idea."

"Who are you talking to?" Wilder took out his phone. "If

you're having some kind of psychotic break, I want to help you. Who should I call?" He looked down at his phone, not even sure what to Google.

His mom went to him and stood in front of him, tears streaming down her face, as Abby moved in closer to stand possessively by his side. "After Abby died, do you remember the day I found you? The day you'd decided this world was too much? That everything was just too much?"

Abby stopped. "What?"

"Wilder, your mom has something she'd like to say."

"No, I'm not listening to this. I'm not buying into this. You're sick. You need help."

"Just tell him."

"She wants to know if you remember the day she found you. They day you decided the world was too much."

He eyed her but said nothing.

Mrs. Davis went on. "We were two peas in a pod, and I didn't want to be a lonely pea."

October repeated it, and Wilder started to cry. "Now I'm one pea."

"I know, and I'm sorry. But you don't have to be. October is right here." Mrs. Davis gestured toward her, as if Wilder could see what she was doing.

October said everything except for the last sentence.

Abby took two steps back. "He tried to…"

Mrs. Davis finally looked at her. "He did."

"When?"

"How did you not know? I assumed you'd been hanging around him all this time."

She shrugged. "The beginning is a little fuzzy. I know I stayed with my folks some. I visited him occasionally. I didn't start staying with him until he started drinking so bad. I didn't think he could be left alone."

"Did it ever occur to you he started doing that because

you were hanging around?" Mrs. Davis accused, the venom dripping from her words.

Abby jerked back as if she'd been slapped.

Wilder stood, his head in his hands, trying to get his head around what was happening.

"I didn't…" Abby trailed off. "He was…And *she…*" Abby turned to October.

"What about her?" Mrs. Davis asked.

"She wanted to take him from me." Abby's voice sounded small, and young. Just as she was.

Mrs. Davis' expression softened. "What kind of life did you imagine for yourselves, Abby? Was it this? The solitude? The drinking? The depression? He doesn't even know you're there."

"I…" Abby looked at Wilder, as if seeing him for the first time. Broken. She reached out and touched him, and a sob escaped his throat, making her pull back like she'd been burned.

She smiled sadly. "I thought we'd get married, ya know? Go to college together. I had no idea what I wanted to do, and neither did he. But we'd figure it out together. I thought we'd have a few kids. A house with a swing on the porch, like my parents had. Do you remember?"

Mrs. Davis nodded. "I do. You and Wilder spent a lot of time in that swing."

Tears streamed from Abby's eyes. "I never meant…I thought I was helping. I thought he needed me. That we were soul mates."

Mrs. Davis went to her, and took the girl's hands. October was shocked Abby let her. The wind died down, and Wilder looked around.

He sniffled. "What's happening?"

October didn't know what to say. Her dad stood by her side, and he nodded encouragingly.

"Your mom is trying to help Abby."

Wilder shook his head, like it was too unbelievable.

Mrs. Davis folded the young ghost into her arms. "Your soul wasn't meant to be on this Earth this long, baby girl."

October relayed everything, and Wilder took one step forward, and then another until he was in front of October, his cheeks wet with tears. "How is this possible?"

"I don't know," October shrugged. "I never asked how. I just accepted it."

"This is why you don't have friends, isn't it? You tell them and they think you're crazy?"

October nodded.

"I'm sorry." Wilder took her in his arms and hugged her like he never intended to let her go. She squeezed her eyes closed tightly, and willed it to be true.

And in that moment Abby left them.

CHAPTER 22

A sense of relief Wilder couldn't ever remember feeling washed over him and he let out a breath.

"What?" October pulled back from him reluctantly.

"I don't know. I just feel…like a weight has been lifted off me."

October looked around. "Abby is gone."

"Where did she go?" Wilder looked around as if he could see where she'd gone, which was ridiculous, and he stopped as soon as he realized what he was doing.

"Where they all go."

"Did my mom go too?" A sense of panic gripped him. Was he truly alone?

October looked lovingly to his left. "No, she's still here."

"I have so many questions," he began, but October stopped him.

"I'm sure you do. Can we talk about them inside? Maybe over a cup of hot chocolate? Because I'm freezing."

Wilder's protective instincts kicked in and he rubbed her arms vigorously. "Of course, let's go."

Once they were settled into her dad's apartment, the questions began.

"Is mom trapped here? Is your dad here too? Is that why you kept this place? What do they look like? Is it sort of *The Sixth Sense*? Or *Beetlejuice*? Gosh I hope not. That would be disturbing. Maybe I don't want to know the answer to that question. What's it like to die? Why was Abby here? And why did she hurt you? And how did she hurt you? Have you been hurt by the ghosts before?" Then a look came over him. "Colin. You saw Colin didn't you?"

She nodded.

"He was a jerk to you, wasn't he?"

She nodded again, and he reached across the table for her hand. "I'm sorry. For everything."

"There is nothing to be sorry for. If I had told you the truth from the beginning, none of this would have happened."

"Maybe. Or maybe I would've stayed away from you. Can you imagine that first meeting?" He changed his voice to a more falsetto version of his own, doing his best impression of October. "Hello, Mr. Davis. I have your mother here and she has some specific requests."

A lightbulb went on. "The flowers...she told you didn't she?"

"She did. She also forced me to bring Mission to you that first night. She showed up at my place a bit distraught."

"Mom, you meddled?" Wilder demanded.

October translated for her. "She says in her defense, you were in a worrisome place."

"Yes. Well. It would've been more worrisome if I'd been happy, don't you think?"

October snickered. "You've been scolded."

Wilder shook his head. "I can imagine. All right, get back to my questions. I need answers here."

"Oh gosh. I'm not sure I remember them all."

"Fine. I'll refresh you."

October held up her hands. "One at a time please."

"Torturer Is mom trapped here?"

"No. She can move on any time."

"Is she going to?" He cast around the room looking for her, hoping she'd stay a little longer, but feeling guilty for it at the same time.

"She says she's staying put for now."

"Is your dad here?" Wilder pressed. "Is that why you kept this apartment like this?"

"Yes. And yes. He helps me manage the ghosts. Before he died, I managed the ghosts and he did the paperwork and prep work. We were a perfect team. Now I have to do all of it."

Another lightbulb went on. "Oooh. And the ghosts are why you can't hire someone else. Got it."

"It would be very hard to keep that secret with an outsider here. Yes. Even if I just had them upstairs handling the families. The ghosts aren't patient. I can't be talking to an outsider when a ghost is vying for my attention. It wouldn't end well. If it went badly enough, I could lose everything. My reputation. The home. Everything."

"You're right to keep it to yourself, for now at least. Maybe someday the right person will come along."

"Maybe. Joey certainly has given me hope."

"Joey knows?"

October nodded and sipped her hot chocolate. "I told her immediately. Dad encouraged me to. After everything that had happened with you, your mom was begging me to tell you my secret, and that Abby was making you miserable. I was resistant. And just as I was about to, you lost patience, called me creepy and stormed off."

Wilder cringed. "Possibly not my shining moment."

October shook her head. "Any normal person would've done the same. Point is, when I went to make a new friend at the friendship event downtown, I decided to experiment. When someone came along that I actually wanted to talk to again, I told her everything. Joey's such a different person. She didn't even question me. Believed me immediately."

Wilder smiled to himself. "I can believe that. She seems...special."

"She is. I feel very grateful to have her."

"That's funny. I think she feels the same way."

October scrutinized him. "What exactly did you two traitors talk about that day?"

Wilder put a hand to his heart, as if wounded. "Traitors?"

"That's right. Gossiping about me like schoolgirls."

Wilder turned serious. "October. We weren't gossiping. We were both a little territorial I think, and sizing each other up."

October laughed, which caught Wilder off guard. "What?" He demanded.

"Like I belong to either one of you?"

"Well," he insisted, as if the single word justified their actions.

October looked down at her mug. "She thought I should tell you my secret too. What did I have to lose she asked."

"She said the same thing to me. Not about telling you a secret. But about asking you what happened. Giving you more time to explain. What did I have to lose?"

"Now who's the meddler?"

In the silence that followed, Wilder tried to absorb everything. Ghosts were real. His mom was among them. His girlfriend had been hanging around him for over twenty years, and was the cause of his depression. As much as logic

225

demanded he question the information staring him in the face, it made sense.

"Abby made the light burst to hurt you. She spilled the water that day. And she made it so windy just now." Wilder put the puzzle pieces together in his mind. "You stepped away because you were worried for your own safety."

October looked away, but nodded, as if she was ashamed. "That's right. I wanted to help you. I did. I could see she was casting a cloud over you and your life. But she wouldn't talk to me or your mom. My dad went over in a rage after she messed up my face. You know she protected you when that happened, so all the glass went on me?"

"She did what?" Wilder was horrified. "How is that love?"

"It is love. At sixteen, love is irrational and emotional and hormonal and all the most intense things."

"She was still sixteen?" He just couldn't get his brain around it. He thought of that picture October had rescued from the box. "Did she look sixteen?" He wasn't even sure he wanted the answer.

"She did." October softened her voice. "She was lovely. I recognized her picture as soon as you pulled it out of that box. She looked exactly the same."

"So, it's not a *Sixth Sense* sort of situation then. That's a relief."

October laughed. "Indeed. That would leave me with a lot more sleepless nights."

The phrase triggered something else. "The break in. That was her, wasn't it? The police even said it was like the robber was a ghost."

"It was her. And I knew it right away, which is why I didn't push the police to find the person responsible. But, that's also why I stayed here for a few nights. Until I was convinced she felt like she got her point across. She didn't seem to bother me as long as I had another ghost around."

Wilder didn't know what to say. His girlfriend from his childhood had been terrorizing a woman he could love. He did love. And he'd called her creepy for it.

"Um…" He didn't understand how to digest it all. "If I accept all of this as the truth, and I think I do, I just…" He looked into her blue eyes, knowing he could lose himself in them, and the thought didn't scare him one bit. Not like living another day without her did. "I'm sorry."

She seemed confused. "For what?"

"For Abby's behavior. For not understanding. For putting you through physical harm and expecting you to come back for more." The more he talked, the worse he felt. But he needed to get it out. "For telling you I was your friend, and turning my back when it got hard. For everything."

She stood up and went to him, stood behind him and put her arms over his shoulders, leaning her chin on him. She was warm and smelled like cinnamon and fall. "I'm sorry too," she whispered. "I should've been honest and trusted you. Dad, you were right."

"Ha, don't hear that every day," her dad gloated and Mrs. Davis smacked him before his chest could puff out too far.

"Your dad," Wilder processed. "I could meet your dad?"

"I mean. He's known you for some time," October pointed out. "But yes. He's here."

Wilder started to stick out his hand to shake, but then thought better of it. His back straightened as if he was formally meeting his girlfriend's father. Was October his girlfriend? That was water they'd wade into later he supposed. For now, the man who loved her first was somewhere in the room, assessing the man Wilder was now.

"Mr. Davis." Wilder did his best to sound strong and safe.

October giggled. "Davis is you, Wilder."

"Oh God. I'm sorry. Mr. *Manning*. Geeze."

There was a pause before October exclaimed, "Dad!" Clearly embarrassed.

"What?" Wilder asked, following October's horrified gaze to a spot over near the fridge, wondering if that's where the ghosts were standing.

"My dad wants you to state your intentions," October mumbled.

"Oh. Well," he debated what to say. A joke to lighten the mood? Something romantic to let her dad know how he felt about October? A promise to show he wasn't going anywhere this time?

"Dad," October chastised again. "Now he's laughing. He's enjoying this."

Wilder relaxed. "I like a man with a sense of humor."

"My dad does too." October clearly wasn't amused. "He says he's happy to 'meet' you with the air quotes. He's quite proud he knows how to use those."

"Oh, I'll take her word for it," Wilder gestured toward October.

They spent the rest of the night talking and laughing. He talked to his mom for hours with October's help, and learned more about her dad. October never got tired of his questions, and he never got used to her answers. It was real. All of it. At 2 a.m. he glanced at his watch, and was shocked by how late it had gotten.

"Geeze, I should go."

"Your mother says you can stay here if you're too tired to drive home," October offered.

"I'm sorry, since when does my mother have any jurisdiction over your funeral home?"

October shrugged. "It's fine. You can stay here if you like. I need to go home though. Poor Queso."

"I'll drive you," Wilder offered as he stood up.

"Oh. My dad would like to shake your hand." October offered an unsure grimace, but Wilder acted quick and stuck out his hand randomly, hoping to hit the target. He moved it up and down. "Pleasure to have finally known about your existence, sir," he added for good measure. He felt an alarmingly real, but cold tap on his shoulder and whirled around.

"Sorry, he's over there," October explained, as if that had been obvious.

Wilder felt a strong hand in his, unnaturally cold, but there. It was real. Just when Wilder thought he believed, he believed even more. He felt overwhelmed, and tried to put his other hand on top to hold tight, ground himself, but it passed through.

"Oh. Dad says he's sorry. He's not as good at it as Abby was."

"Abby?"

"Yes. She had a lot of advanced powers. Breaking stuff, flickering lights. She could touch you too. She was always hanging on you," October explained.

"She was?" Wilder shivered. No wonder he always felt so heavy. "Is that why my house was always so cold?"

October shrugged. "Maybe? Probably?"

"Might save a mint on heating this year," he speculated, then looked in the direction he hoped Mr. Manning was standing. "Thank you for your hospitality tonight. I'm sorry for keeping you up so late." Then he remembered his mom. "Mom? Is she still here?"

"She is," October offered.

"I'll see you again?" He asked, not ready for this second chance to be over.

"You will," October assured him. "She wishes she could touch you too, but she hasn't gotten the hang of it. She's blowing you a kiss."

"Thanks mom. See ya," he looked into the empty apartment wishing he could see them like October could, but also grateful he didn't have to carry that burden.

They rode to her house in companionable silence, and when he parked the truck, she didn't move to get out right away.

"Wilder?"

"Yeah."

"Thanks."

"Sure. It wasn't that far." He really didn't think it was that big of a deal.

"No, you goon. Not for the ride. For believing me."

"Oh, well, if you're going to be ungrateful, maybe you can walk next time." He laughed as she tried to shove him, but the truck door prevented him from going too far.

"I mean it. You believed me without question." Was she getting misty eyed? He looked away, not sure how to handle himself.

"I don't know what you're talking about. I had lots of questions. And I'll probably think of more," he joked.

"But you're open to the answers. Everyone except you and Joey didn't want to hear it. They all decided I was crazy, so they felt bad for me, or were plain scared."

"Yeah. I mean, I can relate to that. There were more than a few moments in that field when I waffled between those two conclusions. Even got out my phone to call someone, but I couldn't settle on who. A mental hospital I guess? I don't know. I may not be who you want to call in an emergency," he pointed out.

She threw herself at him, and he put his arms around her as best he could in the truck. "You're exactly who I will call. Every time. From here, until one of us is a ghost."

He looked down into her eyes. Her once very orderly bun was pulling out and looking frazzled in places. A few stray hairs were framing her face. He couldn't help himself, so he leaned down and kissed her softly, slowly, letting her know he was in it for good.

When he pulled back, she still had her eyes closed. "Until we're both ghosts," he corrected.

CHAPTER 23

*O*ctober slept in. She thought she'd have a hard time falling asleep after everything that had happened, but when she hit the pillow, she was out. She woke up around ten, blinking and trying to figure out what happened. Why was it so late, and why was she still in bed?

Slowly, the events of the previous day came back to her. Had it been real? She reached for her phone, just to double check she didn't have any appointments she'd missed that morning, and found a hilarious meme of a ghost leaning against a doorframe. "I'm waiting," the caption read.

It was real. She'd done it. She'd told him her secret, and he hadn't run from her.

Before she even got out of bed, she called Joey and told her everything. About Abby, and how she was finally gone, and about Wilder and how he'd believed her.

"I knew he would," she dismissed.

"Oh, and he kissed me."

"Shut the front door, why wasn't that the *first* thing you told me?"

"Um, because there were angry ghosts, and stuff to talk about."

"Kissing trumps everything. I knew you'd set everything right. I did *not* know he'd kiss you already. Tell me everything. How was it?" October could picture her sitting on her bed, legs folded in close, settling in for a good story.

"It was amazing. Soft and comforting. Safe."

"Well, that'll set your panties on fire." Joey added a snore for good measure.

October laughed and wished they were together so she could throw popcorn or something at her unruly friend. "All right. I should get to work."

"Yeah, yeah. The dead don't wait and all that."

They said their goodbyes, and October couldn't help the smile that was becoming a permanent fixture on her face. It didn't fade the whole time she was getting ready for work, or when she grabbed something to eat. She held it on the walk to the funeral home, and even when she sat at her desk making phone calls.

She was between clients, so it was the perfect day to oversleep and ease into her day. She was on the phone with Hospice when Wilder knocked on her doorframe.

Waving him in, she couldn't help but light up. Even the Hospice worker noticed the change in her voice and commented.

"Well, you better tend to whatever just walked into your office." Her southern drawl made it sound almost scandalous.

"Miriam, it's not like that."

"Mmhmm. And if I believe that, I bet you've got some land in Florida to sell me too, huh?"

"*Anyway* I have Joe down for a drop off at four today."

"Yes ma'am. So take care of whatever business you've got goin' on before then." Miriam couldn't help but giggle, and October hung up shaking her head.

"Who was that?" Wilder pointed to her face. "You're blushing."

October covered her cheeks. "No one. One of the Hospice workers. She's really nice, but I've never met her in person. She could tell when you came in is all. She was teasing me."

"Oh? About what?" Wilder pried.

"Nothing. Forget it. I'm not talking about this. What did you bring?" October asked, desperate to change the subject.

"Oh, I brought lunch. Want to take it upstairs and eat with your dad?"

"Oh, uh sure. Yeah, I'm sure he would like that." She hadn't had lunch with him in awhile. She didn't usually on workdays. She ate at her desk, and he'd keep her company if he wasn't busy with one of the other ghosts.

They walked upstairs, and just as October was about to knock, she thought she heard something, and stopped her hand just before she made contact with the door.

"What?" Wilder asked.

"I'm sorry, I thought I heard...something," she censored herself. Had that been moaning? It couldn't be. Just in case though, she knocked quickly and loudly, announcing their arrival.

"Dad?" She called for good measure. "Wilder brought lunch and thought you'd want some company." *Although maybe you don't need it?* She thought with a cringe.

She heard a lot of shuffling behind the door.

"Does it usually take him this long to answer?"

October laughed nervously, and hoped he didn't notice when her dad came to the door. Wilder startled at the sudden movement. To him it must have looked like the door opened by itself.

"Dad's here," she explained.

"Right. Of course."

Her dad was disheveled. Like actually mussed. His hair

was a mess, his shirt was nowhere to be found, and his pants were pulled up, thank God, but undone. A disturbing detail. In all the years he'd been a ghost, she'd never seen him like that. He was always dressed, salt and pepper hair combed to the side, and all the buttons done up thank-you-very-much.

"I'm sorry, Dad. Did I wake you up?" The question was ridiculous. He was a ghost and didn't sleep. But her brain was casting around for an explanation, and even the outrageous would do.

"No. Sorry, I was just trying a workout." His voice was unsteady, and he looked nervously over his shoulder before turning back to her with an unconvincing smile.

"You're a ghost. Your body never changes. You don't need to exercise," October pointed out.

"Well, when you're off galivanting with your boyfriend I get bored."

"What's going on?" Wilder interrupted her interrogation. "Are we having lunch or what?"

Her dad eagerly jumped at the chance to change the subject. "Oh, that sounds great, come on in." He pushed the door open wider and revealed Mrs. Davis looking every bit as mussed as he was. Her buttons were all kitty wampus, and her hair looked like a bird nested in it.

October stuck out her arm, blocking Wilder from going in. "Hang on." She looked back and forth between Mrs. Davis, looking rather sheepish as she slowly approached and put her arm around Steve's waist. "Were you two...oh my God. If *I* was off galivanting, I'd hate to know what *this* is."

October turned around, covering her eyes. Wilder was completely bewildered.

"What seems to be the problem, October?" He didn't seem concerned, just confused.

"It seems that your mom, and my dad are...something of an item."

Wilder actually laughed. He thought she was kidding. "No way. Mom doesn't date." He pushed through the open door, walking right through her dad before he could step out of the way. He caught himself when he felt the cold air pass over him. "Sorry, whoever that was. Didn't mean to step on any toes. But our food won't be warm forever, and you can tell me jokes like that while I eat."

"He's getting hangry," Mrs. Davis explained as Steve went to look for his shirt.

"Maybe she didn't date in life, but it seems like she is now." October insisted as she looked at the food he was unpacking. Suddenly she wasn't sure she was all that hungry. Had they been on the table? Oh Lord. She scrambled over to the sink and grabbed a paper towel and the Lysol she kept under the sink.

"Pick that up," she ordered before nearly spraying their food with disinfectant and wiping down the table. And both chairs for good measure.

"Geeze October. You're going to sterilize me. Come on. This is a joke. You're getting all wrapped around the axle about nothing. They're ghosts. They don't date."

"Apparently they do. Your mother has her arm around my father."

"In the friendliest way, I'm sure." He didn't sound sure though and his eyes searched the room for any sign of their affair. "It's friendly, right mom? You were always too busy to date after dad died. And by the time I was older, and you had time, you didn't want to compromise. That's what you said when I asked you. You liked your independence."

"Things change, Wilder. Obviously. And honestly, if I'd met Steve in life, I might have been willing to compromise."

The thought was so sweet, it almost took the edge off how alarming the situation was.

"What did she say?" Wilder asked while October tried to decide if she wanted to fawn, or vomit.

"She said she might have compromised for my dad if they'd met in life."

Wilder sank back into the chair she'd just finished wiping down. "Did we interrupt something?" The horror of what they'd stumbled into was finally settling in. He sprang back up out of his chair. "Mom!"

"What? Ghosts have urges too."

"I don't need to know, Mrs. Davis," October refuted.

"I don't think I do either." Wilder put a hand on his stomach.

"I tell you what. Let's take lunch back downstairs, give these two a chance to…look presentable, and they can meet us down there when they're ready," October offered.

"Great." Wilder was out the door with the food like his pants were on fire.

"Boo, listen," her dad tried, but October held up a hand.

"Dad. You're a grown man. What you do is your business, and for the love of God, please attempt to keep it *your* business. I'll meet you downstairs." She started to leave, but stopped before she got to the door. "If you take too long, we'll know why."

Mrs. Davis giggled as October left them to fix themselves.

"I don't believe this. I mean, this is harder to swallow than the fact that ghosts are real, and you can see them," Wilder babbled.

"I know. I'm not sure I would've believed it myself, if I hadn't seen them…"

"Stop right there. I have no desire to know what you saw."

Unpacking the food had been completely forgotten as

they both threw themselves on the couch, trying to absorb their parents dating.

"If they date, can we date?" Wilder blurted out.

"I don't see why not. A. They're ghosts. And B. We aren't siblings just because our dead parents are shaking the sheets so to speak."

Wilder laughed once. "It works because they're ghosts."

"Thank you for the explanation," October responded flatly. "Your mom actually seems pretty smitten."

"She does not. She doesn't get smitten," Wilder argued.

"She's a grown woman. She can do what she wants," October defended.

"And your dad? What exactly are his intentions with her?"

Now it was October's turn to laugh. "He asked you that same thing last night, if you'll recall."

"He did, didn't he? This is so *weird*!"

October shook her head. It was weird. But that was the literal definition of her life. Weird. "Wilder. I'm a funeral home director who sees ghosts. Weird is just another Tuesday for me."

"Fair enough." He leaned forward, apparently ready to unpack the salads and sandwiches he picked up from a new bistro downtown.

"I think they might even be happy," October said as she watched them walk into her office hand in hand.

"Happy?" Wilder said through a mouthful of sandwich.

October set two more chairs around the coffee table, but they didn't take them. They snuggled up next to each other on the couch, as if relieved their secret was out.

"Yes. They seem very happy."

The sight of them put all the panic out of her brain. Her dad, after all this time, was happy. He had his arm draped over her shoulder, and she reached up and laced her fingers through his. Like they were a young couple or something. It was actually adorable.

"I'd like to set some ground rules though, if you please," October suggested.

"Are they here? Who are you setting rules for? I'm no rule follower," Wilder pointed out.

"Not for you. For the love birds sitting on the couch next to you."

"Oh geeze. They're not making out are they?" Wilder protested.

"No. They're holding hands. It's rather cute."

"Ah geeze," he repeated as he folded the wrapper around his sandwich and moved to the chair over by October. "Safe to sit here I take it? No stray ghosts joining us for lunch?"

She didn't even try to hide her smile. "No stray ghosts."

He sat down in a huff. "I'd like to finally eat this now, if that's okay with everyone."

"Hangry," Mrs. Davis repeated.

"Seems that way," October confirmed.

"What's this about ground rules?" Her dad asked.

"Well, have you thought about the other ghosts? What if one of them comes across you two?"

"Hasn't been a problem so far," her dad assured her.

"Good. Even still. Maybe keep the…shenanigans to the hours when the funeral home is closed? Particularly not during a service if you please?"

Her dad was affronted. "We have a little bit of respect left, October."

"Excellent."

"We didn't mean for you to find out that way," Mrs. Davis insisted.

"Oh really? So, this little afternoon delight during my office hours was a surprise encounter?" October raised an eyebrow.

"Well," her dad said defensively. "You haven't come upstairs for lunch in some time."

October laughed at the sight of her flustered father. "Oh I see. The interruption is my fault entirely?"

He stuck to his guns. "That's right."

"Noted. And I promise I will always knock. If you're... busy...just holler that you'll be right down. No one needs to see that again."

"You didn't see anything indecent, stop being dramatic," her dad insisted indignantly.

"Did they agree to those entirely reasonable, and lenient to the point of negligent, rules?" Wilder asked as he moved on to his salad.

She looked at her dad and Mrs. Davis. "Of course we do. We did mean to tell you in a more..."

"Clothed way?" October filled in.

Mrs. Davis giggled again. "Proper was the word I was looking for, but clothed works."

"Indeed."

They ate and laughed again, and October watched them as the moments passed. The two ghosts loved each other. It was obvious. She wondered if they knew, and supposed it didn't matter. Her little family had an eternity ahead of them.

CHAPTER 24

*T*he next week passed by in a bit of a giddy blur for October. Her last ghost even commented on how odd it was to have such a Suzie Sunshine directing the funeral home. She decided to take it as a compliment from the cantankerous old man.

October and Wilder spent every moment they could together between work and sleep. They didn't sleep over again, but they did watch movies, ate way too much take out, and laughed.

With three weeks to Christmas, it was time to put up the ten-foot tree in the lobby. She always kept the decorations simple and coordinated. And she also set out a menorah, so as not to offend anyone, although she didn't celebrate herself. Christmas had always been a magical time for her and her dad. In fact, the ten-foot tree came the year after her mom disappeared. He'd wanted to make the season special for her, and he did. He'd gotten her a black motorized pony to ride that year.

She and her dad had picked out the current tree together the year before he died. When the original started looking raggedy, she floated the idea of replacing it. He'd been resistant at first, but liked the idea of making new memories with her, so he relented. She'd ordered it online after Christmas, and they'd hauled the beast of a thing to the storage closet together. The next Christmas, she'd had to get it out on her own. And she had every Christmas since then, until Wilder came along.

He huffed and puffed as he dragged it upstairs. "Don't you have an elevator?"

"I do. And I usually use it. Wasn't sure you'd want to though. It's how I get the caskets up here."

"Good call." He heaved it up the last stair. "Any chance you think it looks good there?"

She laughed and dragged the bag over to where she wanted it. "That's the easy part. Now we have to get it out of the bag and put it together in the right order."

He sat down on the floor. "You go ahead and get started. I'll be right there."

"You really do need to get out in the field more," she teased. "You're getting out of shape!"

"If I had the energy, I'd refute that untruth right this instant."

"Well, when you regain your energy, be a dear and bring up the ornament boxes would you? And the lights? It's all labeled down there."

"I had no idea you were such a work horse, October Manning."

"Your willful ignorance isn't my problem, Wilder Davis. You know I run this place by myself. Of course I'm a work horse."

"True. Damn it." Reluctantly, he stood up and went back down to the storage closet to retrieve the bins she'd asked for. It took him three trips, and by the time he had them all, she had the tree put together.

"Wow," he breathed as he sat on top of one of the bins looking at the huge tree.

"Wait until I get it all decorated."

It took all day, but without Wilder it would've taken even longer. Simple was a look that took an annoying amount of work, it turned out.

But when they were done, it really was magical.

Wilder hugged her from behind as they looked at its twinkling lights casting a warm glow on the lobby.

"So, listen." Wilder seemed hesitant, and October pulled away so she could turn to face him. "I was wondering if you'd like to help me pick out a Christmas tree. Seeing how it's my first Christmas without my mom, I thought it might be fun to start a new tradition. Go to an actual tree farm maybe?"

"Absolutely. I don't have anything Friday evening, if that works."

"Like a date, October," he clarified.

She stopped. A date. They'd touched on dating once, when they were hit with the fact that their parents were doing a little more than dating. And they'd kissed. But they had yet to formally define their relationship. October wasn't sure how she felt about it. Excited scared was a thing, right?

"Tell me the terms of this date," she demanded.

"Terms?"

"What are your expectations?"

"Oh, sex definitely."

October shushed him and looked around, although her father wasn't really in a place to judge her exploits. "Wilder Davis. I'll have you know," she wound up, but Wilder cut her off with his boisterous laughing.

"October Manning. I have no expectations. I like you, and I'm pretty sure you like me. I want to spend time with you, and be more than your friend." He bent down to her. "I'm quite fond of you actually."

For a moment, her brain went fuzzy and words escaped her.

"You're not saying no," he pointed out.

"True," she offered when the words came back to her. "I'm not saying no."

SHE SETTLED on jeans and the warmest sweater she had layered over a long-sleeved shirt. Her jacket and hat finished the ensemble, and when she looked at herself in the mirror, she wasn't exactly looking like sexy dating material, but she refused to be cold on their date.

She promised to tell Joey everything when she got home, and she filled Queso's food dish early, just in case she was late. He was none too happy with her the night Abby left and she came home so late. She heard about that infraction for at least ten minutes straight.

He purred as she scratched him on the head while she waited for Wilder to pick her up. He meowed in protest when Wilder knocked on the door. "Be good," she called to him as she grabbed her keys and left.

They drove north and west, away from the city where the snow was white and the trees weren't so manicured. It was lovely.

"What were our folks up to today?" Wilder's completely natural question struck October, and she smiled. No one had asked her what her dad was up to in ages.

"I don't know. I didn't ask."

"Probably best."

"Where is this place? New Jersey? We've been driving forever." October tried to fake complaint, but her contentment was too obvious. The truck was warm, Wilder was holding her hand, and the scenery got more and more lovely as they drove. The road was lined with trees dusted with snow, a sample of what was to come as winter pressed on in the northeast.

After another half hour or so, they pulled into the tree farm. It had twinkling Christmas lights lining the road, leading you to the entrance, and a sign out front. "Papa Jack's Trees" it read in bold green letters that looked like they'd been painted by Papa Jack's grandson.

Wilder parked and when they got out, October was glad she'd dressed sensibly. It was cold up there, and a thin layer of snow crunched beneath their feet as they walked to the main building, what appeared to be an old barn.

"Welcome," a bearded man called. Possibly Papa Jack. "How can I help you today?"

"Just looking for a tree," Wilder called back.

"Well, I'm afraid all I have are flamingos." The man kept such a straight face, October started to doubt they had any trees left. "But if you're interested in a flamboyance, I can give you a discount."

Wilder laughed and looked to October. "We were looking to start a new tradition. You game?"

"I…" she was so out of her depth, words escaped her.

The man laughed boisterously, and although his beard was brown, the sound of his laughter reminded her of Santa.

"Jack Decater at your service." He walked around the cash register and shook Wilder's hand heartily.

"Wilder Davis, and this is October Manning."

"Pleasure to meet you both. I love traditions. Let's see if we can't get you set up with our finest flamboyance available, hmm?"

"What is a flamboyance?" October whispered.

"A flock of flamingos, of course," Papa Jack responded, making no effort to keep his voice down.

"Of course," Wilder nodded. "What else would it be?"

Papa Jack showed them the lay of the land. Pointed out

where the best trees would be. "Once you find one you like, just holler and I'll come help you."

"You got it." Wilder threw in a thumbs up for good measure, and October eyed him.

"What?" He asked.

"Like you're some kind of pro with that thumbs up?"

"I want him to like me, okay? He's cool. So we need to be cool," Wilder insisted.

"Do you have a man crush?"

"That is not a real thing." Wilder disappeared behind a lovely fir tree, but October knew he was just hiding from her.

They wandered for about ten minutes, enjoying the sounds of nature you couldn't hear as much in their small town. True, they weren't in the thick of the city, but the tree farm was a type of country October wasn't used to, and she didn't hate it. The air smelled so clean, she couldn't take a deep enough breath to satisfy herself.

All the trees were a bit smaller than she expected. Most were shorter than she was, with the taller ones way off in the distance. But she wasn't bothered. They didn't need a giant tree like she had at the funeral home. They needed something small that they could manage.

A cardinal landed on a nearby tree, and she went to it. It was a lovely tree, not quite perfectly shaped, but none of them were. And October loved that. The little tree had character.

"Wilder, what about this one?"

Wilder popped out from between two trees with snow in his hair. "Hm?"

October gestured to the tree with the cardinal in it.

"Well, that handsome boy seems to be making it his home. Wouldn't want to disturb him, would we?"

October hadn't thought of that. She assumed he was

helping them. She'd heard once cardinals were the spirits of those gone before, and she always loved them. "I don't know. I think he's showing it to us. Mister Jack?" October called, hoping he could hear her. They'd wandered a long way from the barn.

"On my way," he hollered back, but he sounded a long way away.

"It is a nice-looking tree," Wilder observed. "I like how this little bit bumps out. Like the tree is looking for a handshake."

"I know. He just looks like he belongs with us."

"He?" Wilder eyed October.

"Yes he. The girl trees are much more feminine and proper looking." She pointed to one three trees away. It was lovely but very stiff looking. "See?"

Wilder actually nodded. "You know what, I do. You're absolutely right."

"Good man, knowing when his woman is right." Jack leaned in close to Wilder. "Which is always, my friend. Always."

"Good tip," Wilder matched Jack's low tone, but October could still hear them both.

"You've picked out Gus. I do love him."

October beamed. "What did I tell you?"

"I never should have doubted you," Wilder acknowledged.

"Now, here at Papa Jacks, we do things a little differently. I'm not going to cut old Gus down. I'm going to dig him up and put him in a big pot. You take him home and care for him for the season, and bring him back. Then I plant him back in his spot, and you can come get him next year too if you want."

"I love that idea." October stopped herself from clapping out of sheer excitement.

"Talk about a tradition. Can we reserve this tree for next year?"

"You sure can. But why don't you take him home first, see if he's a good fit. Young Gus won't get his feelings hurt if you decide you want Pricilla next year instead." Jack gestured toward the female tree they'd been looking at earlier.

"She is gorgeous," October complimented. "But Gus is more our style. He's unassuming. I think he'll fit in wonderfully." Part of October wished they were putting him up at her house. But she already had a small tabletop tree she'd set up in the living room last weekend. The thought reminded her Gus wasn't her tree. She'd hijacked the whole process. "Wilder? What do you think?"

"I think Gus and I will be fast friends. How can I help?"

Jack handed Wilder a shovel and they started digging around the bottom of the tree. Jack explained how he worked to keep the ground from completely freezing up so he could dig up the trees. It was all news to October, but Wilder was very interested, and wondered if the process of warming with solar blankets and tilling to keep the soil moving could be applied to landscaping.

While October admired their passion, she couldn't help but let her mind wander. The cardinal had fled to a different tree that she didn't know the name of, but he still watched them. She wondered if Abby had returned, and approved of their choice. She hoped so.

Jack helped load Gus into Wilder's truck, and bid them farewell.

"You take care. I like Gus so treat him right."

"Yes sir." Wilder stopped short of saluting Jack, but October could tell he wanted to.

"Be cool," October whispered.

Jack slapped the back of the truck, and Wilder took that as his cue to leave. They were starving, so the first sign of civilization, they took Gus for a bite to eat. They offered him a burger, but he declined.

"Must be watching his figure," Wilder speculated.

"Well, he should know he's perfect how he is, and doesn't need to buy into any such social media nonsense," October insisted.

"Absolutely."

They took him home, and got him settled in Wilder's living room, off to the left of the fireplace. The pot Jack planted Gus in was dark green, and complimented the red tree skirt Wilder produced from an old box nicely.

"This was all my mom's. Figured we could put it to good use," he explained. "We don't have to use all of it. But she had some nice stuff."

"Of course." October peered into the box and saw carefully boxed ornaments, a history of her memories set out before them both.

They started with lights, and picked out about a dozen ornaments for Gus' small frame.

"He looks a little sparse." Wilder picked through what was left of the ornaments, but they all meant something to Mrs. Davis, not them. One from a trip to the Grand Canyon, for example, didn't feel quite right on Gus.

"I might have a solution." October grabbed her purse and pulled out a bag from Hobby Lobby.

"What is that?" Wilder's skepticism slipped into horror as she pulled out the ornament kits.

"I thought it might be fun to make our own ornaments for your tree," October explained as she pulled out brushes and everything they would need.

"I'm not crafty." Wilder said it like it was a get out of jail free card.

"I'm not either. Which will make it even more fun. Too bad we don't have nieces and nephews to blame them on,"

October joked. He stood there watching her, but she wasn't going to let him off the hook. She set everything out on the floor near the tree, and then looked at him expectantly.

He cast around the room, looking for a way out. But there wasn't one. So he sat down next to her and dug in to the plastic wreath they were to paint.

His turned out looking like a green blob with muddy brown dots on it. Turns out he needed to wait a little longer for the paint to dry before adding the red. But he wanted the glitter to stick. "Who invented glitter?" He'd been trying to get it off his pants for the last two minutes straight. "I hope they're in hell."

"Wow." October was busy putting the finishing touches on her much more recognizable ornament. "Tell me how you really feel."

"It's everywhere! Look! It'll never come out of the rug."

"Oh come on. It'll just add a bit of sparkle to your life," she insisted.

"I'll add a bit of sparkle to your life." With that, he attacked her with tickles. She crumpled beneath him, and reached for a nearby paint brush so she could dot his nose with green, and hopefully glitter.

They were both laughing so hard, tears streamed from their eyes as they rolled around on the rug in front of Gus, hoping for the higher ground. Until at last, Wilder looked down at her, and her beauty struck him. She was mid laugh, and the sparkle in her eye wasn't from glitter.

He had her hands pinned to either side as he straddled her. He leaned in without thinking and kissed her deeply. Although she was caught off guard, her body knew what to do, and responded immediately.

The kiss was more urgent than any of their others, and soon his hands weren't pinning her wrists down, they were in her hair, giving her goosebumps.

He pulled back and turned to Gus. "Sorry Gus. You may want to avert your eyes."

She giggled, and he cut her short with another kiss that told her what he wanted, and she wanted it too. She was breathless as he pulled her shirt over her head. She couldn't imagine wanting something more, but it wasn't the sex she wanted. It was Wilder. And the way he pulled her close to him, she knew he felt the exact same way.

CHAPTER 25

*C*hristmas was magical for them. They agreed not to go all out for each other. But didn't listen. Wilder gave her a set of dishes that looked exactly like the ones Abby broke. The ones her dad had picked out for her. Flowers and all. She'd cried. She'd been eating on paper since the incident, unable to bring herself to replace them.

Her gift for Wilder felt inadequate in comparison. She worried she'd overstepped. But Nikki seemed excited when she'd talked to her. And if he didn't like it, Nikki said she understood, and there were no hard feelings. She really was a gem, and October hoped Wilder knew what he had with her.

"What's this?" he asked as he opened the envelope. "It looks like a contract."

"It is."

"Uh huh. For what?"

"For Nikki. She's agreed to be your manager if you'd like. So you can be out in the field more. You'll still need to be in the office once or twice a week to sign checks and stuff like that. But, she's willing if you are. I added a bit of a raise for her of course."

"I see that you did. Very generous of you with my money," Wilder quipped.

October backpedaled. "If you aren't ready, she said she didn't need it right now. No hard feelings, those were her words."

"I…" Wilder looked at her with a shine in his eyes that hadn't been there a moment before. Was he getting emotional? "Thank you, for giving me a gift I didn't have the courage to give myself."

He hugged her, and their parents held hands happily watching their kids make a life together.

JANUARY RANG IN COLDER than October could remember.

"When can I see you? I missed you at Christmas, but mom needed me." It had been a few weeks since October and Joey were able to see each other. The longest stretch they'd had since they met.

"Of course she did."

"This had better not become a thing, now that you have a boyfriend, October. I know dating is new to you, but you don't throw your girls aside just because a man comes in."

"I know that, Joey. But as you said, your mom needed you. That one wasn't on me," October pointed out.

"Ug, true," Joey conceded.

"I was actually hoping to come see you this weekend, if that's okay."

"That's great! I have plans with a guy I want you to meet."

"A guy?"

They proceeded to gossip about Joey's new interest, although October didn't think she seemed very interested in him. More in the idea of him. October made a note to ask her about that over the weekend.

After work, she met Wilder at his house for dinner. It

seemed so empty without Gus, and she found herself looking forward to December in a way she never had before. October was always her favorite month. But having someone to share the season with made it so much more magical.

"I'm going to see Joey this weekend," October announced a little more forcefully than she intended.

"Oh yeah? What are you gonna do?" Wilder asked.

"Not sure. Apparently she has a new boyfriend she wants me to meet. Although she doesn't seem real into him."

"No? What makes you say that?"

October shrugged. "She just didn't talk about him much."

"So what you're saying is, you talk about me all the time."

"Possibly."

"Maybe I should go too. Meet this guy. Size him up. Tell him to treat Joey right and all that."

"You don't even know Joey. You can't claim ownership of her like that." October stopped short of saying that was her job, but she wanted to.

"You don't want me to go?" Wilder's genuine hurt stopped October short.

"What? I didn't say that."

"But…" Wilder waited for her to fill in the truth.

"Joey and I are used to girl time. You'd be bored, don't you think?" And then she thought of something. "Shoot. Also, Joey and I share a bed. There's nowhere for you to sleep."

"On the couch?" He proposed with way too much confidence.

"She lives in a four hundred square foot studio. The bed is the couch."

He shrugged, unbothered. "Mom has an air mattress at the house I can grab. If Joey will have me."

October couldn't see any reason to tell him no. Except that it might cramp their style. But that was just mean to say out loud. And she did want to spend time with them both.

"Okay. I'll call her."

Wilder looked at her expectantly. "What are you waiting for?"

"Oh. Uh, okay. Apparently I'll call her right now."

"Didn't I just talk to you?" Joey hardly ever answered the phone with a hello. Often she was mid thought, as if half the conversation happened before October called. But she was getting pretty good at catching on.

"Wilder wants to come too. Is that okay?"

"Oh. Well, I refuse to reenact whatever weird fantasy he has about what we do during our sleepovers."

"For the record, my fantasies don't include you," Wilder said.

October cringed. "You're on speaker Jo."

"That's fine. I'm a little hurt, Wilder. I'm gorgeous."

"True. But you were pretty prickly when I met you the first time."

Joey interjected before he could say more. "Ditto."

"That's fair. My point is, that set me on a path to not fantasize about you. Anyway, I don't need it. I have October."

"Oh gross. No, he can't come if he's just going to be mooning over you the whole time."

"Fine. I'll be perfectly aloof and won't pay attention to either of you," Wilder offered.

"Well, don't be a jerk to her either," Joey countered.

Wilder turned to October. "I have no idea what I'm allowed to do."

"Stay home?" October mouthed, and he scowled at her.

"Are you planning to come every single time, Wilder?" Joey never was one to mince words.

"I don't know. Maybe. October is pretty important to me."

Joey chewed on that for a moment. "What if I said no, would you respect that?"

"I would. But, I would like you less," Wilder answered honestly.

"Why?" She fired back.

"Because. A girl who wants to make things hard for her best friend doesn't seem like a great friend at all. And you seem like a really great friend, so I'd be kinda sad if you made that choice."

"October, am I making this hard for you?" She asked.

October had her head resting in her arms on the table. "You can both take equal responsibility for that." She didn't bother to pick up her head.

"What do you want?" Joey asked.

What did she want? "I want to be able to see Joey without you. But I also want to spend time with both of you. I want flexibility without drama."

"Fair enough. Yes, Wilder you can come if October wants you to. You'll be on the floor though." And that was that. Joey didn't sound the least bit upset or resentful. She was completely accepting of whatever October wanted, as long as it made her happy. And, she was also willing to change if it didn't make her happy.

Wilder turned to October. "So can I come?"

"Sure. It'll be fun. Thank you Joey. We'll take you to dinner to thank you, okay? Wilder's buying."

He choked on his drink, but regained his composure quickly. "I heard that Day of the Dead place was pretty cool. Wanna go there?"

"No. I had another spot in mind. And I'm bringing my boyfriend for dinner too, so you boys can split it. Wilder, you can buy breakfast somewhere. Deal?"

"Deal. On one condition."

"I make no promises," Joey countered.

"I want to see your studio. October talks so highly of your art. I want to see."

October was shocked. He wasn't into art at all. He was an outdoorsy guy. She had no idea he was interested in seeing what Joey did.

"Oh. But I don't have a show going on. And the studio is a mess," Joey protested.

"Even I haven't seen the studio, Wilder. Don't take it personally. She's very protective of the space."

"That's silly, isn't it?" Joey asked.

"No. You have a process that's working great for you, ya big shot," October reassured her.

"True."

October could picture Joey chewing her nails, and shook her head at Wilder.

"When's the next show, Joey?" He asked.

"Not sure yet. I need more art. Kinda got cleaned out from the last one. Four months at the earliest."

"Okay. I can wait."

"Thank you," October mouthed to him, and he smiled winningly back at her.

They hung up a few minutes later, after ironing out a few more details. October found herself excited. She hadn't been there when Wilder and Joey met, and she couldn't help but want her two favorite people in the same room. What could go wrong?

FRIDAY AFTER WORK, Wilder and October took the train out to Joey's. October really loved her slower pace at work, and people were adjusting well to it. She couldn't have every weekend off, but it sure was nice to have one occasionally.

All their stuff made it look like they were staying with Joey for a week, with their clothes, the airbed, and sleeping bag. And, once they managed to make their way to her apartment and set everything down, it legitimately looked like too much.

"Wow. You weren't exaggerating about the size of her place." Wilder looked around desperately for a place to set his things down that wasn't in the way, but came up short.

Joey eyed him. "Thanks?"

"No. I wasn't. Thanks Wilder." They'd been there five minutes and already October was flustered and stressed.

Joey grinned. "Well, that was fun. Maybe it wasn't such a bad idea having you here." She and Wilder actually high fived.

"Did you plan that ahead of time?" October demanded.

"Absolutely not." Wilder put a hand on his chest, as if he'd been wounded.

"I don't actually have his number," Joey pointed out. "Although, I wouldn't mind planning future pranks."

"Excellent," Wilder agreed as he took out his phone and she snatched it to put her number into it.

October flopped onto the bed. "Oh, good God."

"Quit moping. We're going to dinner with Blaire."

Joey took them to another very unique place that served Pho. October wasn't sure about it, but ended up liking it quite a bit. Wilder wasn't as picky and loved it. However, Blaire was a bit of a dud. He answered all their questions with one word answers, and looked at his phone more than he looked at Joey. More than once, October caught Joey's eye and glanced back to Blaire. Joey only shrugged.

They walked to a bakery a block down and all got the most delicious, buttery cupcakes October ever had. She ended up getting three more they could eat later. Blaire didn't order one.

He left after that, with a peck on the cheek for Joey and a grunt in October and Wilder's direction.

"Nice to meet you," Wilder called after him, but he didn't look up or wave over his shoulder.

"Wow," October let out before she could stop herself.

"I know. He's not great. But, it's fun to remind myself occasionally what's out there and why it's better to be single," Joey admitted. "And he does pay for food." She was right about that. Even though he didn't get a cupcake, he did buy Joey's.

October hooked her arm through Joey's as they walked. "You're amazing."

"I know that. You're just now coming to that conclusion?"

"No. Maybe someday it won't shock me every time you do something awesome. But it's not today apparently."

"I do like to be surprising," Joey admitted.

"In Blaire's defense, if you're not into him, maybe you should stop getting free meals from him?" Wilder, ever the devil's advocate, chimed in.

"Eh. He must get something out of it too, or he wouldn't ask me."

"He asks you for that…whatever that was?" Wilder couldn't comprehend. "He acted miserable that whole time. Like he couldn't be bothered."

"To be fair, I did ask him if it was okay if you were there. He said it was fine," Joey explained.

"Is he not always like that then?" October was hoping she'd say no, and Blaire could redeem himself. Meeting two new people could be overwhelming after all.

"Yeah, he is. When it's just the two of us, that's when I text you the most."

"It is?" October didn't even try to hide her horror.

Joey shrugged again. "Hey. It's a free meal. If he wants to ignore me, that's fine. Better than small talk."

"How many times have you been out with him?" Wilder

was still trying to get to the bottom of Blaire's thought process.

"That was the third. But I don't know if I'll go again. Depends on how hungry I am and where he wants to go I guess. I'm not really a starving artist anymore," she reminded herself.

"Well, I don't mean to talk you out of something. But he is a little lacking in…"

"Interaction?" Joey asked.

"I was going to say personality, but sure," October filled in.

"He certainly isn't the one," Joey confirmed as they went up to her apartment.

WHEN THEY GOT BACK, October got in the shower, and Joey took the opportunity to accost Wilder. He'd had a blast so far, and was working on blowing up the airbed when she came and flopped down onto the half inflated mattress.

"Slept on one of these for about a year until I could afford a real mattress. Took me two more years to get a frame for it." She said it so flatly, Wilder knew he wasn't supposed to feel sorry for her. In fact, he felt proud of her hard work.

"It's sort of nice to not be hungry kids anymore, isn't it?"

"What are you talking about. I was still a hungry kid a few weeks ago."

Wilder laughed and turned off the pump.

Joey looked at him steadily, and he stopped what he was doing.

"What are your intentions with October?"

"Why is everyone asking me that?"

"Who else asked you that?" Joey wondered.

"October's dad."

"Isn't he great? I love him. And Mrs. Davis. Your mom, I

guess? I hear they're quite an item. That must be a little weird."

He was having a hard time keeping up with her stream of consciousness, but he thought he got the gist. "Yes, Mr. Manning is nice. I liked him better though when I didn't have to wonder whether or not his hands had been on my mother."

"Oh they definitely have," Joey confirmed.

Wilder gave her his most serious side-eye. "Thanks for your words of comfort."

Joey was unmoved. "Well?"

"Well what?"

"You didn't answer my question," she pointed out.

"Which one? There were so many."

"You danced around all of them didn't you? Except it seems pretty clear you're uncomfortable with your mom getting involved with October's dad. Is that just because they're ghosts? Or because you have a problem with Mr. Manning? Or because no one is good enough for your mom?"

"Geeze. Your questions are a little intense." Wilder distracted himself with getting the sleeping bag out of the bag. It was in there so tightly, he had no idea how he'd stuff it back in, but that was a problem for tomorrow.

She blinked at him, and he could tell he wasn't going to get out of answering any of her questions so he took a deep breath. "As for Mr. Manning, I like him a lot, and deeply respect him for hanging around so long to watch after October. Soon, I hope he hangs around because he wants to, not because he's worried about her."

"Oh really? You planning on taking that spot for her?"

"Her father's place? No. That's weird. Why did you make it weird, Joey?" He teased.

She smiled wickedly at him. "Nicely done. Back to my question."

Wilder eyed the bathroom door, which he could reach out and touch if he wanted to. The water was still running, so he felt safe enough telling Joey, but still lowered his voice. "I plan to marry her someday."

Joey flew up off the bed and Wilder threw up his hands, casting the mangled mess of a suitcase aside. Silently, he begged her to be quiet. Her cheeks were bursting with her exclamations, but she held them back.

"This is her first serious relationship. I intend to take it slow, and give her time to make sure this is what she wants."

Joey came over and swept the tangled sleeping bag away from Wilder, and laid it out flat on the airbed next to him in one fell swoop like she was some sort of camping wizard.

"You know, I didn't know her before you came along. But she seems pretty sure to me."

"What makes you say that?"

Joey shrugged. "She's happy."

"Uh huh. So am I. Life changes have a tendency to mess happiness up, ya know?"

"Yes. Chaotic life changes can do that. Positive life changes don't. Job changes, moves, marriage, kids. If they're right, they build on the happiness. They don't destroy it, weirdo."

"It's too soon," Wilder insisted.

"If it is, do you not trust her to tell you that? To know her own heart? Bit insulting don't you think?" She scowled at Wilder. "And arrogant on your part, to think you know better than her on this."

"Now wait just a minute," he protested, hearing the water turn off, and knowing he didn't have much time left.

Joey held her hands up in surrender. "You're right. That was too far. All I'm saying is, Valentine's Day is a very romantic time of year. One that might be perfect for proposing?"

Wilder looked back at the bathroom door, still closed. "I'll think about it if you'll quit talking about this."

Joey fluffed him off. "She's oblivious, don't worry."

"Because she isn't in the same head space. If I spring this on her—" He stopped himself. They could go round and round all night. "You know what, never mind. I told you I'd think about it, and I will. End of discussion."

Joey smiled like a Cheshire cat.

"You haven't won," Wilder insisted.

"We'll see. She just may be more sure than you realize."

That night, Wilder didn't sleep. The girls stayed up late watching Netflix, and talking low. Not because they were keeping secrets, because they thought he was sleeping. But he wasn't. He couldn't stop thinking about what Joey said. Wilder knew the night Abby left. The night he felt free for the first time. He knew he didn't want to waste another moment of his life.

He had no idea if October wanted kids, or what her future looked like to her, but he knew he wanted to be a part of it. Was six weeks enough time to learn what she wanted, and if she had him in her plans?

He sure hoped so.

CHAPTER 26

*B*efore he knew it, February was upon him, and in spite of himself, he was making plans. He knew October didn't love the idea of Valentine's Day. She thought they shouldn't need a designated day to show each other basic kindnesses. That they should be doing that every day. And if he was honest, he agreed.

So, he made plans for the Wednesday before. A totally innocuous day. He texted Joey his plan, and she approved whole heartedly. Even sent him a Michelle Tanner "you got this dude" gif. She was speaking his language. Man was he glad he got her number when he was there. He sure as heck wouldn't be doing this so soon without her planting the seed.

He picked out one of her favorite movies, *Get Out*, and ordered sushi from Spice Thai. He was going to make it a special night.

But when she showed up, she burst into his house full of emotions he didn't know how to deal with.

He watched her yank her bun out of her hair and toss her purse on the chair by the door, and knew something was up immediately. "What's wrong?"

"I haven't seen my dad all day. Or your mom for that matter."

"I'm sure they're fine," he tried to comfort her, relieved it wasn't anything serious.

"You don't understand."

No, apparently he didn't. "Well," he stifled a laugh when he saw the expression on her face. "It's not like they're just going to disappear, October."

She looked at him with such fear, he stopped what he was doing. "It's *exactly* like that. They'll move on. Leave us here, and we'll never see either one of them again."

He stopped. Had they gone without saying goodbye? "Um. Okay. I have food on the way. When it gets here, let's go to your dad's and see if he's there."

"I knocked on the door before I came over and he didn't answer."

"Maybe they were out for a stroll," he offered. "It's not time to panic." He wasn't sure what to think. This is what everyone went through when someone died, and October never had to with the person closest to her. Would she finally have to truly grieve? And if she did, he knew it wasn't the time to propose.

October paced around, and he went to her. He put his hands on her shoulders, trying to ground her but she looked like a trapped animal. When Abby left him, he felt such freedom. But her father wasn't torturing her. He was nurturing her. Making her who she was in a positive way. Not dragging her down the way Abby had done to him.

He thought about how he'd feel if he never got to talk to his mom again, but it was different for him. He'd already said goodbye to her, and lived without knowing she was a ghost for weeks. True, they'd had some great talks since he found out, and he was grateful to know what she wanted him to do with her house when he was ready, but he wanted her to be happy. He also hadn't had contact with her as a ghost for the last decade, and was under the impression that she would move on at some point.

October was aware on some level her dad would move on, he knew. But he also knew when her dad did move on, it would be a huge change. And he wasn't sure she would ever be ready for it. Sort of like ripping a band aid off. If the band aid had been holding your heart in one piece for the last ten years or so.

He crushed her into a hug, forcing her to relax. It took longer than he thought it would, but eventually, she did. Her breathing slowed, and he couldn't feel her heart about to pound right out of her chest anymore. Those had to be good signs. At least until the Uber Eats guy rang the doorbell. They both jumped at that.

"It's just the food. I'll grab it and we can hop in the truck and go over."

She only nodded, because apparently words escaped her. If they had gone, he had no idea what he was going to do. He was holding on to the idea that they wouldn't go without saying goodbye. Abby had. But that was different. He hadn't even known she'd been hanging around, claiming ownership of him.

They didn't speak on the drive over. She held onto her phone with a death grip, but he didn't know why. Who was she going to call?

"Did you talk to Joey?"

She shook her head. That surprised him. She told Joey everything. "Why not?"

"I didn't really want to breathe life into it."

"But you told me…"

"I couldn't hold it in anymore. I've been worrying about it for a few days. Seeing them both less and less. Like they're slowly stepping out. This is the longest stretch yet. I haven't seen either of them since yesterday at lunch. What if…" She trailed off.

"Nope. We're not catastrophizing. They're around." He felt like if he said it out loud, it would have to be true. As much as she didn't want to voice her concerns for the same reason. They couldn't be gone. Not yet.

He thought about his proposal that wouldn't happen, and how he'd imagined telling them both their plans after she said yes. If they'd gone, none of that would happen. Some of her panic started to leech into his own mind as he pulled into the funeral home.

Before he could even put the car in park, she was out. He parked under the overhang right by the front door, rather than choosing a space to save time. They took the stairs two at a time, and she pounded her heart out on the door.

"Dad? Please. You have to be there." She pleaded, fresh tears streaming down her face.

The door opened on its own, or so it seemed, and Wilder let out a breath he hadn't known he'd been holding.

She looked like she was hugging air, and he knew Mr. Manning was holding her. One side of her face was even flattened, her hair pressed up against it like she was leaning on an aquarium or something.

"There, now. You see. They haven't gone anywhere." Saying it out loud slowed his racing heart that much more. They hadn't gone.

"Where have you been?" She demanded. Wilder had never seen her so upset, and he knew it was only a taste of what would come when they did move on. He hoped he could be the man she needed when that time came.

She seemed to be ushered into a seat, and Wilder got out some mugs and made some hot chocolate for them both. He remembered their food in the truck, and wished he'd thought to grab it. Now that he wasn't panicking, he remembered how hungry he was.

He wanted to let them talk, but he also wanted answers. Where had they been? Why weren't they around as much?

After a few minutes of listening to a one-sided conversation, in which October only got in things like "but" or "I'm worried," he finally asked what the heck they were talking about.

"Dad said they're enjoying their time together, that's all. And that they aren't moving on. Yet."

The way she put emphasis on the word yet made him feel edgy. Like he was out of time to tell them about his plans. But he couldn't do that without telling her what he wanted to do. And she was so preoccupied, he knew it just wasn't the right time. He'd just have to pray they'd hang around until she settled down. They wouldn't leave her in such a state would they?

By the time they went back to his house, she seemed more calm, but still chewed the inside of her cheek.

"What aren't you telling me?" He asked when they got back to the house. He was too scared to eat the sushi he ordered, so he tossed it out and got down some cereal bowls for them.

"He said he hadn't moved on because I wasn't ready."

"You're not," Wilder said without thinking.

"I know that," she spat back. "I didn't want him to know that. I don't like the idea that I'm keeping him here. That he's missing out on his peaceful eternity because of me."

"Woah there. Back the massive eternal guilt train up there, undertaker. He's not missing out on anything." He took her in his arms, and she let out a shuttering breath. His heart broke for her, and he hoped his words could hold her together, at least a little bit.

"In fact," he added. "He met my mom because of how you

kept him here, as you put it. He seems pretty all right with that."

"Do you think I'll ever be ready? You seem ready."

Well, that felt like a trap, and he had no idea how to answer without hurting her feelings. "Um…do you want me to make you feel better, or tell you the truth, because I'm afraid I can't do both." He hoped it sounded like a joke to her. He cringe-smiled down at her, and she giggled through her tears.

"The truth. Of course."

"No. I don't think you will. Losing a parent is something no one is ever ready for, whether your thirty-five, or seventy."

"I've been handling the clients on my own more and more lately with him hanging around your mom so much. And it's gone okay. I think the business will be fine. But it's lonely, ya know?"

The ring weighed heavily in his pocket. But he left it there. He wanted to tell her she wouldn't be alone. He would be with her, if she'd have him. But it just didn't feel right. She was distraught. And he wanted her to be overjoyed. So, in his pocket the ring stayed.

"I know," was all he could think to say back to her as he held her.

She stayed over that night, and she fell asleep in his arms. Once he was sure she was out, he reached for his phone. He had about eighty-six-thousand messages from Joey demanding news. By the end, she was panicking since she hadn't heard from October. But she thought if it went badly, she would've heard something from her. A sobbing call.

What the heck happened? She demanded.

Glad he'd silenced his phone before October ever came over, he finally responded to Joey's slew of messages, explaining what happened.

Well that sucks, she responded.

Yeah. I'm not sure what to do. I don't want them to leave before I can get to it. But I don't want to do it when she's so distraught either.

I get it. You're in a tough spot. But that's life. Always stuck between a rock and a hard place, she typed back. She even added a gif of a bug skooshed between a rock and the sidewalk.

You're always such a voice of comfort, Joey.

Thank you.

He fell asleep with no solution to his problem, but with October sleeping soundly beside him, he tried not to worry about it too much. The operative word there was tried.

CHAPTER 27

*S*pring can be an odd season for an undertaker named October. She much preferred fall's crisp air and falling leaves. But that spring felt like a fresh start. A rebirth. And she found herself enjoying the flowers.

Wilder had planted new ones around the funeral home, and it looked lovelier than ever. She couldn't help enjoying the season. They'd even taken to hiking around the area, and had found some gorgeous streams to hike to. He liked the fresh air, and she liked the green scenery, in spite of her Wednesday Addams roots.

She tried not to think of how little she'd seen her dad lately. They would go days without each other. Like he was trying to prepare her to be without him. But it was agony. He said he wouldn't leave without saying goodbye, and she'd asked if he had that much control over it. He thought he did, but she knew darn well he wasn't sure.

The ghosts had the best time traveling all over. They'd gone as far as Maine to see the lighthouse iced over. Her dad said it was quite a sight. That spring, they planned to go out west to see the mountains and the wildflowers. Things he hadn't gotten to see in life. October really was happy for him. But the longer he was gone, the more she missed him.

The ghosts could tell too. A few encouraged her to get some help. Said it was too much work for one person. And she explained her dad was just on vacation. And he'd be back. One older gentleman scoffed at that.

"Let your poor father enjoy his life."

"He's a ghost like you are."

"Well for heaven's sake child, let him enjoy his death. If you need help, you need to hire someone. You seem perfectly capable to do this on your own though," he added.

"I am, thank you Mr. Feldman."

He smiled warmly at her. "Call me Artie, dear. And go easy on that powder stuff. Men don't wear makeup."

"I will. I promise," she assured him.

Bringing help in was just too complicated. She'd be fine. She just needed to…what? Get over her dad? She'd never do that. Grieve? Hadn't she already done that?

Spring was a new beginning. Maybe all she had to do, was grab at that.

THAT AFTERNOON, Wilder came inside the funeral home after planting a particularly lovely rose bush on the corner of the building.

"I put that trellis behind it. Hopefully it'll climb that and be beautiful by the summer," he said as he walked to the bathroom to wash up. "Hey, are you busy?"

"I am. But I won't be in a few minutes."

"Great. There's something I want to talk to you about."

She stared at her computer screen. He hadn't sounded anxious or upset. He'd sounded excited. Was there a trip coming up he wanted to go on? She couldn't think of anything he'd mentioned. She tried not to let her mind run away with itself, but as the cursor on her computer blinked at her, she knew it was too late.

He sat down on the couch and surfed his phone, waiting patiently for her to finish. But she couldn't.

After about thirty-eight seconds, her curiosity got the best of her. "Forget it. Tell me what's up."

"You sure?"

"I can't focus thinking about the possibilities."

"Nothing is wrong if that's what you're worried about," he offered.

"Just tell me. Good God man."

He laughed. "Okay. I can see you're a little wound up. That's not how I wanted this to go. But I seem to be committed to it now. I was thinking. Maybe. We should… move in together."

She froze. Move in together? Is that what he just said? Her heart screamed yes, but a small voice that was growing louder by the second screamed no. All she could think about was her mom, and how she'd left them in the lurch. She didn't want to be like that.

Wilder watched her cautiously. "October?"

Don't panic, she told herself. This is what she wanted. So why did the thought of it suck all the oxygen from the room?

"What about Queso?" She assumed he was okay with living with a cat, but they'd never discussed it. There was kindof a lot they'd never discussed. Shouldn't they do that before they live together?

"What about him? Kick him to the curb."

Wilder's straight face wasn't helping her panic. He got up and knelt down beside her while she sat at her desk and stared at the spot he'd been sitting. "October. I'm teasing you. I don't know why you're freaking out. Queso is wonderful. Bring him. I just want to spend more time with you, that's all."

"Where would we live?" Her voice was shakier than she'd meant it to be. Betraying her.

"Wherever. Your place is a little far from my office. Maybe mom's house? Since I haven't listed it yet? We could ask her."

"Would that be weird?"

"Not sure. Worth asking though. It is kindof halfway to work for both of us," he pointed out.

Perfectly reasonable. And his mom's house was so much bigger than hers. "But the haunted house. All my neighbors…"

"We'll put up signs in October telling them where you went. If they want to come, they will. And mom's neighborhood is full of kids. Her house is so great for something like that. You've seen it. The architecture is perfect." He sounded excited. Like the more he thought about it, the more he was sold on it.

She chewed the inside of her cheek. "You know what, nothing needs to be decided today," he offered. "Why don't you think on it?"

Despite the fact that she nodded her head, she'd never felt so unsure about anything.

THAT EVENING, she told Wilder she had some work to catch up on, so she'd see him tomorrow. He seemed concerned, but gave her space.

She texted Joey, who was way too excited, and did not understand her panic. She'd never lived with anyone other than her father. What if her habits were annoying and ruined everything? Joey said she was being ridiculous, and October had no argument for that. She also didn't seem to have a cure for it.

Silently, she prayed her dad would be in. She hadn't seen

him in over a week. Seemed Spring was bringing new beginnings for them all, whether October liked it or not.

"Dad?" Her voice was barely above a whisper as she knocked. She wasn't sure her heart could take it if he wasn't home. She started to open the door, but he opened it for her.

"Boo! What a wonderful surprise. We just got back from Tennessee. What a beautiful area in the Spring."

"Can we talk?"

He assessed her face, and the smile he wore faded. "Of course, come in."

She spied Mrs. Davis, who rose to greet her, but she couldn't bring herself to smile back at her. "Hi Mrs. Davis. Could you maybe go visit Wilder? I'd like to chat with my dad. Alone." She heard how curt she was being and tried to backpedal. "I'm sorry. That was rude of me. How was your trip."

"Of course, dear. I'm happy to. When I get back, all four of us can chat about the trip together, okay?" Mrs. Davis promised.

October was so overwhelmed with gratitude for the woman, she nearly started crying right then and there. Mrs. Davis looked to her dad with a little bit of pity in her eyes. "Good luck, Steve. I think you're going to need it."

But Mr. Manning had been handling his daughter on his own for over thirty years. He kissed Mrs. Davis gently on the cheek and bid her goodbye, before ushering October over to the couch.

"Now, what's this all about?"

"Wilder asked me to move in with him."

"Well, that's wonderful," he said before he saw her face. "I mean what a presumptuous jerk. How could he ask you such a thing?" He watched her. "Nope. Still not right. Wait, I'll get there." His eyebrows knitted together, trying to read her face, but coming up short. "He's such a pig, how could you ever live in such a mess?"

"Dad."

"You're going to have to help me out here, Boo."

"I've never lived with anyone except you. I…what if I turn into mom?"

"Your mother had blonde hair, are you planning on dying it?"

Her dad just wasn't following her. "DAD."

"What, honey? I'm genuinely trying here. Wilder is a good man. What's the problem here?"

"I've always been single. Always. I never dared to dream I'd have a life with someone. And now…this is moving so fast. I don't want to mess it up. What if I mess it up? What if I panic and leave?"

"Sort of like you're doing right now?" He ventured. October glared at him. "Okay. Not ready for jokes. That's fine." Mr. Manning cleared his throat and sat up a little straighter, trying to get to business. "October. Your mother was…" he hesitated, searching for the right words. "Well. She was a bit haunted I think. But not like you are. There were things that happened to her. I only knew bits and pieces of it to be honest. And I think a family scared her. She went along with me when I floated the idea of having a family. I thought she would bond with you ya know? But she never did. She disappeared a lot. But she always came back. Until she didn't."

October hiccupped through her tears. "I don't ever want to do that to Wilder."

"And that's exactly why you won't, Boo. Your mom never talked to me about it. She wasn't open with me, like you are with Wilder."

"Is that…is that why you wanted me to tell him my secret?"

"Well. I guess so," her dad squeezed her hand. "But I also don't think you can have a healthy relationship with secrets. And that's what I wanted for you. Something healthy."

She let that sink in for a minute. Was it really that easy? Did she just have to talk to him?

"What if he doesn't like what I have to say?"

Her dad laughed. "He won't always. And you won't like what he has to say either. That's what a relationship is. Working through those differences. Compromising. And moving in together will be full of that. It'll be good practice, I think."

"Practice for what?"

"Marriage, I assume."

"Right. Marriage." October hadn't dared to think past the fact that she wanted to spend her life with him. She hadn't dreamed about the logistics of how that would actually play out. Sharing space. Sharing meals, well they already did that. Sharing money? Would they do that? She frowned.

"Don't get caught up in the logistics of it, Boo. Let it happen, and take it as it comes."

"When have I ever been able to do that? When you died, I did everything but take it as it came. I was a mess, and you were still here to tell me what to do!" Panic rose up again, and it tasted like bile. "And what will I do when you go for good? Who is going to talk me down then, huh?"

"Oh, my Boo." He folded her into his arms and waited until her breathing slowed down. "My girl. Listen to me. Did you ever consider Wilder might be the one to talk you down from now on? That maybe he *wants* to be that person?"

"I…" she hadn't considered for a moment he would *want* that. "No one *wants* that."

"And yet, you did it for him when Aurora died."

She had done that for him. But it wasn't work. She'd been

happy to do it. Is that how Wilder felt? Abruptly she stood up, startling her dad.

"I should talk to him."

"You should," her dad agreed.

Then she turned to him. "Thank you, Dad. For everything. For all these years you stayed. For me. I know it's not easy."

"Don't even think on it, Boo. I'm happy to do it. And, I got Aurora out of the deal. You have to admit, that makes it a lot sweeter."

October pretended to gag. "Dad. I don't want to know how sweet she is. She was my friend before she met you. Don't taint her."

"Oh believe me. She's been tainted."

"DAD."

His laughter chased her all the way to the door. "Good luck, Boo!" He called behind her.

When she got to Wilder's house, her brain was running a mile a minute. She didn't even know where to start.

Mrs. Davis was sitting with him on the couch, but he wasn't talking to her. She wondered if he knew she was there. He was watching a landscaping show on HGTV, and criticizing how much they were spending. It was one of his favorite things to do.

"Oh hey." She'd let herself in with the key he'd given her just after Valentine's Day. They'd traded them. That was something she felt comfortable with. But this…

"Are we ready to live together?"

"What's this we crap? I can't speak for you," he joked.

She took a deep breath as Mrs. Davis gave her a thumbs up and silently excused herself. "Fine. Are you ready?"

"I asked you, so I'd say yes, I am ready."

"I don't know if I am," she admitted.

"Why? You don't want to spend your life with me?" He braced himself for the answer, and she went to him, taking both his hands in hers.

"That is *not* it at all. I've lived alone most of my life. What if I'm horrible to live with?"

"I think Queso would let you know."

October nodded. "You're right about that. But what if we fight?"

"Oh, we definitely will. You'll finish my cereal without letting me know. And I'll leave beard stubble in the sink." He smiled so brightly at her, as if he didn't see these things as deal breakers. Maybe that's because they weren't. "It'll be great." The look in his eyes told her he really meant it. He didn't think it would be great, he *knew* it with every fiber of his being.

"Yeah. Okay. It'll be great."

He lit up, and surprised her by picking her up and spinning around. "It *will* be great! You'll see. What do you think? Mom's place? Or somewhere totally new?"

"Let's talk to her about it," October suggested.

He set her down and looked deep into her eyes. Honestly, she couldn't think of a time she'd seen him so happy. "Great. Oh my gosh, I can't wait to live with you, October Manning."

Falling into his arms, feeling the weight of him surrounding her, making her feel safe and loved, October finally knew she couldn't wait either.

CHAPTER 28

*M*rs. Davis was thrilled about them using her home that way, and making memories of their own.

"What about sleeping in your room?" October asked.

Wilder waited for the response. He'd gotten used to listening to their back and forth, and he loved how October worked to help him feel included.

October shifted. "We haven't talked about that yet, Mrs. Davis. One step at a time please."

She looked over at Wilder, and he could tell she was one toe away from backing out of the entire thing. "Mom. Whatever you're telling her, you're about to scare her off. Look how uncomfortable you're making her. October, what is she saying? She should be ashamed."

October hid her face behind her hands, muffling her voice a bit. "She said it's fine to sleep in her room, as long as we give her grandkids while we're at it."

Wilder doubled over with laughter. "Mom. Mind your business. Geeze. We aren't even married. You want a grandkid out of wedlock? I'm shocked and appalled," he teased.

"To be fair, you aren't getting any older either," October pointed out. Wilder could only assume his mother had claimed she wasn't getting any younger.

"If it's our house, we can use it how we want, mom. We will have sex in your kitchen. If you aren't okay with that, we'll get our own place." October shrank into her seat, clearly uncomfortable having this conversation with their parents.

She turned to him, and whispered. "Maybe we should just get our own place. Or wait. Maybe we should wait." The way she added it so quickly made him glare in the direction he hoped his mom was.

"Mom. Fix this now. If you don't want us to have the house, that's fine. I understand. But a gift is a gift. You can't dictate how we use it."

Silence. His leg bounced as he waited for October to show some sign of a resolution. Eventually she nodded. He felt a chill near him, and she visibly relaxed. Maybe her dad had put a hand on her shoulder.

"That's a good question. I'll probably rent the duplex out for now. Don't you think? And Wilder could do the same if he wanted. I certainly don't think selling is a good idea right away."

The statement caught him off guard. "You don't?"

She blinked at him, trying to calculate what had hurt him. "No. What if we don't get along and need someplace to retreat to?"

He chuckled and took her hands. "We won't need some-place to retreat to. But if it makes you feel better, and like less of a flight risk, we will keep the houses. I'm not going to mess around with renting mine, but certainly you can rent yours."

"Dad," October scolded.

Wilder cringed. "What did I do?"

"Dad just said of course she can rent hers. It's hers."

"Exactly my point. I don't have a say in what you do with your own home," Wilder tried to smooth over.

"Well, I'd like your input when we get there."

Wilder's smile was warm and full of affection. "I appreciate that."

FIRST, they had to move his mom out of the house, which turned out to be a bigger project than either of them had imagined. He wasn't prepared to part with most of it, but he made himself make hard choices. Stuff they couldn't use, went. Her couch was nicer than either of theirs, so they kept it. Her bed went, because October was uncomfortable sleeping in it, let alone doing anything else. They agreed to get an entirely new mattress to sleep on, and kept October's bedroom set, because it was the nicest. And that's how it went. Keep, sell, donate. And his mom kept quiet through the whole thing. He thought she felt guilty about making October uncomfortable, and rightfully so. He hoped she'd just been teasing, but October was so uncomfortable about all this, she wasn't in a teasing place.

He found himself wishing he could talk to her dad about it. Ask him what made her so uncomfortable. She'd mentioned her mom, and not wanting to be like her, but October was so little when her mom left. How could she have any concept of what her mom was like? It baffled him, and he tried to make her comfortable, but as they got closer and closer to moving in, she got more and more anxious.

Finally, they moved the last of her things in, and she found a realtor to help her find a renter for her duplex.

Their first night, he just held her, hoping to ease her

nerves. He thought she slept eventually, but he wasn't sure. He in turn, dozed off blissfully, holding the most precious thing on earth in his arms.

As the weeks went by, he thought she relaxed some, but not as much as he did. He understood, it was his mom's house, so he was never uncomfortable in it. But he didn't think that was it. She'd get frustrated looking for a mug, or watch TV with the volume too low to even hear it, for fear she was disturbing him if he was in the other room. She scooped the kitty litter constantly, and vacuumed relentlessly, for fear he would get annoyed by Queso. He'd never seen her so uptight.

Joey wasn't able to help either. She'd told October how proud she was for pushing herself, and to give it time. She'd find her stride. Wilder could only hope that was true. He'd texted Joey in a desperate plea for help after about two weeks of watching her torture herself.

She is so uncomfortable, and I am so happy. I feel guilty, he explained.

She'll settle in. Give it time.

Maybe we shouldn't have done this, he speculated.

Quit it. You don't have time for that. What can you do to make her comfortable?

I don't know, he typed frustratedly mashing the screen. *I never snap at her for being loud, but she thinks she is. I'm genuinely not bothered by her the way she thinks I am.*

I never said you were. I asked how you could make her comfortable.

He stared at the screen for a moment, and an idea hit him.

Joey, you're a genius.

She typed something back, but he didn't read it. He had work to do.

. . .

He took the next day off to get ready. Lucky for him, with a service the following day, October had a full day at the funeral home. She had florists, caterers, and other arrangements to coordinate. She apologized for her long workday when she left, but he hadn't been bothered. Then he thought he'd be giving his surprise away, so he doubled back and probably overacted. It was fine. She'd left with a confused look on her face, and asked if he was okay. That was fine by him. Keep her on her toes.

She got home after dark, which was perfect. The purple string of lights he'd hung outside were already on.

When she came inside, she gasped. "What did you do?" But it came out breathy, not accusatory. Slowly, she made her way around the house and found every Halloween decoration they owned carefully placed in all the nooks and crannies he could find. A lot of her outdoor decorations he put in the back yard so she wouldn't see them when she pulled in, and ruin the surprise. Tears streamed down her face as he took her from room to room. He even got out her Halloween bedding, and dressed their bed, hung orange lights around the vanity, and lit her black candles.

By the time they got to the back yard, and she saw the makeshift haunted house he'd set up, she was a snotty mess.

"Do you like it?"

"It's May," she pointed out.

"That's not an answer."

"I love it." Tears streamed down her face. "I love it so much. Thank you, Wilder."

For the first time since they'd moved in together, she relaxed in his arms. If he had to have Halloween decorations out all year to make her happy, he'd do it. She was worth it.

"I can't believe you did this for me." She blew her nose on a Kleenex she'd grabbed from the kitchen before he brought her outside. "Wilder. I love you."

Warmth filled his chest until he thought he might burst. "I love you too, October. I love you so much. We can have Halloween all year for all I care. I just want you to be happy."

"I am. I am so happy with you. I was being silly. This feels like home. With you. We can do this."

He laughed, and suddenly, his emotions caught him off guard and he tried to swallow them down. "Yes. Yes we can, my love."

"Wilder, can I ask you something?"

She looked up at him with those blue eyes he never wanted to look away from, and they were shining with emotion and happiness. He knew he'd say yes to whatever she asked.

"Anything."

"Will you marry me?"

CHAPTER 29

"**W**hat?"

She'd thrown him off. Clearly, he hadn't been expecting the question, but after spending the last six weeks being unsure about everything, and afraid to destroy it all, everything seemed crystal clear. Wilder was the man for her. Simple as that.

"You can't steal this from me," he declared before running into the house.

Left alone in the yard, she was confused to say the least. She followed behind him, reluctantly leaving the paradise he'd created for her. If he was mad, she needed to fix it, but she knew she would. For the first time, she wasn't worried he'd abandon her, or she'd abandon him. She knew with such peaceful certainty they were it. Fixtures in each other's life.

He nearly knocked her over in the kitchen in his rush to get back to her.

"Whoa." She held out her arms, as he slid on his knees toward her. She couldn't process what he was doing. Kneeling in front of her, a small box in his hands.

"You can't steal this from me," he repeated.

Slowly, she lifted a hand to her face, unable to take her eyes off the small box. Was that what it looked like? It was black velvet on the outside, with a small black clasp holding it closed.

"October Manning, I love you. I've loved you since the day we met, I think. I just didn't realize it. I need to spend my life with you, if you'll let me." He opened the box and she gasped.

The ring was black gold, with a leaf pattern, holding a purple diamond. It was perfect. The most perfect piece of jewelry she'd ever seen. She threw her arms around him and sobbed her answer into his neck.

"Yes. A thousand times, yes."

THAT NIGHT, they went back to the funeral home to tell their parents, but Steve and Aurora weren't there.

"That's okay. I'm sure they're having an adventure somewhere. We'll tell them when they get back," Wilder calmly suggested.

But October was bothered. She hadn't seen either of them in about a week, and they hadn't mentioned where they were going.

"They promised not to go without saying goodbye. They're around. Just not here." She wanted to believe his promise. She had to. Her dad *had* promised.

It was three more days before they showed up. And Wilder wasn't there. Mrs. Davis had surprised her while she was working in the basement.

"Where do you think you'll do it?" Mrs. Blackman asked while she watched October blow dry her beautiful red hair.

"Do what?" Mrs. Davis asked.

Thankfully, she didn't wear her ring when she was working in the basement. It was safely in her pocket.

"Well, hi stranger." October turned, trying to hide her surprise. "Where have you been?"

"Tahiti. Absolutely lovely this time of year."

Her dad came in and blew her a kiss. "Hey Boo. Long time no see. Who's your friend?"

"This is Mrs. Blackman. She was a nurse," October explained.

Her dad held out his hand and Mrs. Blackman took it. She was glad for the distraction. "Lovely to meet you. You're her father? You must be thrilled."

October's eyes grew to the size of dinner plates and she shook her head no as discreetly as possible.

"About what?" Her dad asked.

"About…" Mrs. Blackman looked at October and way too slowly got the message. "About her taking over this place, and handling it so well on her own."

"Oh. I am indeed. She does a great job with it," her dad proudly boasted.

"And you are?" Mrs. Blackman held out a hand to Mrs. Davis.

"Oh, I'm Aurora Davis. October did my service awhile ago. Turned out I liked it around here, so I've stayed."

"I see. You can stay?" Mrs. Blackman pondered.

"You can. But most don't. I stayed because October was alone. Although she isn't anymore. Aurora's son has taken a shining to her. They moved in together not too long ago." Her dad beamed with pride, and October was still surprised by it.

"Ah, now it makes more sense why you both stayed. I don't think I will. I want to see my family one more time, but then I'm happy to move on." The old woman looked up at October. "I've lived a good life. My kids are good people. They love me, but they don't need me."

"You don't have to justify your choice to me. I'm happy for you," October offered, and the woman smiled.

"Well, I'll leave you to your reunion. It was nice to have met you both." Mrs. Blackman excused herself as politely as ever.

"So, how are you?" Mrs. Davis asked.

"Good. Really good. Would you guys be willing to hang around for dinner tonight with Wilder and I?" October hoped her eagerness didn't give anything away. "I know we'd love to hear about your adventures."

"Sure," her dad and Mrs. Davis said in unison.

"Why don't you come over after I'm done here? Around sixish sound good to you?" Her heart hammered. She desperately wanted to tell them their news, but couldn't do it without Wilder.

Her dad eyed her, but only said, "That sounds great, Boo. Looking forward to it."

"Great. Let me finish up with Mrs. Blackman here, and maybe I can duck out a little early."

"What's the rush?" He inquired, watching her even more closely.

"Nothing. I'm just excited to see you guys, and don't want to be working is all."

"Mmhmm." October could tell he didn't buy it.

"You're not pregnant are you?" Mrs. Davis burst out.

"Oh my gosh, no. I...no. And I can't even bring myself to apologize to you for it. I started to, but no. I won't. We've only been living together for a few weeks, Mrs. Davis. Let it go please, and let us move at our own pace." She clamped her mouth shut, unable to believe her outburst.

Her dad beamed at her. "Well said. Although, I wouldn't mind a grandkid, this is all happening a bit quickly. I don't mind pumping the breaks a bit."

Anxiety threatened to steal her joy. Were they moving too

quickly, getting married? Of all the things that had happened in the last few months, she hadn't been sure of any of it, except marrying Wilder. So no, she couldn't bring herself to doubt that. Whatever her dad thought, she knew it was right.

"Well. Keep your secrets. We'll let you work, unless you need help?" The way he asked, he seemed to be probing her. Almost like he wanted a task. But she honestly didn't have anything for him. Mrs. Blackman had been content without him, and the ghosts were all he could help with.

"Nope. Thanks Dad. See you tonight. Don't be late," she warned.

They left her in peace, and even though they kept out from under foot the rest of the workday, she didn't put her ring back on until she got home that night.

"Dad and your mom are coming for dinner tonight," she burst out as soon as she got home.

"Oh, they're back?" Wilder had been setting plates around the table when she came in. He'd grilled something out back, amidst their haunted house. She'd take the decorations down eventually, but not yet. They just made her happy. "What did I tell you?"

As she hung her purse on the hook by the front door, she shook her head. "You know, smug isn't a great color on you."

"Oh really? I beg to differ." He walked over and kissed her on the cheek, holding a bag of chips and container of dip.

"Clearly."

"Where have they been?"

"Fiji? Maybe we should ask them about it, and see if they notice my ring? Make them wait a little?"

Wilder looked at her, noticing it was missing. "Where is your ring, by the way?"

"Oh my gosh. I took it off when I was working on Mrs.

Blackman, and they showed up while she was asking me about our plans. How she didn't blow our secret is beyond me. They know something is up though. Your mom asked me if I was pregnant for heaven's sake." She flounced down in the chair where he'd set a full glass of wine by her plate. "I was too scared to put it back on after that, for fear they'd notice, but I'm putting it on now."

"Good call. Mom is like a dog with a bone, what the heck?" He grabbed a plate and disappeared out the back door for a minute, returning with two burger patties. "They coming soon? These are ready."

"I think so. I told them six." A glance at her watch told her it was five fifty.

"Well, let's get started while it's warm. They won't mind."

At precisely six o'clock their guests arrived.

"Knock, knock," her dad called as he and Mrs. Davis walked through the front door. "I see you waited like pigs."

"Well, not like you're going to eat anything," October countered.

"Fair enough. So, tell us this secret." Clearly, her dad was too anxious to let her tease either one of them.

"Your daughter got impatient and stepped on my pride a bit," Wilder explained.

Her dad raised an eyebrow. "You invited me over here so he could tattle on you?"

"Wilder," October scolded. "No dad, that isn't why we invited you over here."

Mrs. Davis was awfully quiet during the exchange. Something caught her eye. "What is that?" She gestured toward October, who looked behind her.

"What?" October asked, looking out the window over the kitchen sink. "Our Halloween decorations? Wilder thought it would help me feel at home. And it did." She didn't even try to hide her smile.

"No, not that. Although I did wonder why it was so Halloweeny in here in the middle of May." She pointed to October's hand. "That."

October looked over at Wilder. "She wants to know what's on my hand."

"That would be why we invited you here," Wilder explained.

Mrs. Davis flew up out of her seat and was nearly on top of October. "Let me see! Oh, it's gorgeous and so perfect. I love it. Tell me everything."

October's dad smiled wryly. "So, when you say she got impatient, did you wait so long, she proposed to you?"

October chocked and reluctantly relayed what her dad asked.

Wilder set his beer down hard. "Hey! I didn't wait so long! We've only been dating a few months! I've only known her since October!"

October's dad looked at Mrs. Davis in a way October had never noticed. Like he only had eyes for her. "When you know, you know, Wilder."

Wilder looked over at October who was half listening to Mrs. Davis' rapid fire questions, and half listening to Wilder and her dad.

"I did try in February. But you sir, foiled my efforts," Wilder accused.

Her dad was affronted. "Excuse me?"

Wilder went on without needing to hear her Dad's defensive response. "You'd disappeared, and October freaked out. Thought you'd left for good. That was the night we showed up at your apartment and made you promise not to go without saying goodbye."

"You were going to propose that night?" October asked.

"I was. Had the ring ever since. So, when you asked, I was ready."

"Congratulations." Mr. Manning pulled Wilder into a man hug and slapped him on the back three times. Wilder looked bewildered when he let go, having been unable to see any of it, but October knew the cool feeling of a ghost's embrace well by then.

October struggled to focus on Mrs. Davis. "I'm sorry, what was that last one, Mrs. Davis?"

"What did Joey say?"

"She is thrilled. Bugging me relentlessly to come dress shopping."

"That will be a blast. Can I come too?"

The thought hadn't really crossed her mind, but when it did, she was delighted. Her mom had left so long ago, she never imagined doing any of that girlie stuff. "I would love that, Mrs. Davis."

She beamed. "Wonderful. When can we go?"

They made plans. And more plans. And October soaked every one of them up. Her life stretched out in front of her, and she was ready to live every single moment of it.

CHAPTER 30

*O*ctober Manning would have nothing but an October wedding, and the fall day was absolutely perfect for them, as if Mother Nature was showing off. The sky was that gorgeous shade of blue only fall could offer, set off by the red and yellow leaves that had yet to fall.

Despite the chill, they were married outside, near a stream with the woods all around them. It just felt right. Tim McDee was surprised when Wilder asked him to be his best man, but didn't hesitate to step up. Turned out he and Wilder had a lot in common, and the more time they spent together, the more both Wilder and October liked him.

Joey had handled everything perfectly. October let Joey pick out her Maid of Honor's dress, and Tim's complimenting vest and flowers. She'd chosen a short black lace dress with long sleeves, and picked out a black lacy flower October had never heard of and a purple accent to match October's bouquet.

October was a vision as she walked down the aisle. She wore a simple white sleeveless dress under a long black lace piece with long sleeves that belled out near her hands. It buttoned with an antique button just below her bust and was accented with a beautiful purple jewel. The piece had a train that trailed out behind her, making her feel like the queen of fall. Her hair fell in loose curls down to her shoulders and she'd opted not to wear a veil. Instead, she chose a black hairpiece adorned with purple jewels.

Mrs. Davis dabbed at her eyes in one of two seats in the front row that appeared empty to everyone but October. A memorial to their parents the guests assumed.

Her dad walked with her, whispering how much he loved her the whole time, making it hard for her to hold back her tears. Without missing a beat, he kissed her on the cheek and patted Wilder on the shoulder. "I'm so proud of you both. I love you, Boo." He blew her a kiss and sat in his seat next to Mrs. Davis. She blew him one back and the very small crowd made up of mostly people Wilder knew from work quietly said 'aww.'

"Fancy meeting you here." Wilder took her hands in his with the biggest smile she'd ever seen, and she knew hers matched it.

The ceremony was a beautiful beginning of their life, perfect in every way. Near the end of the small reception, when people were busy chatting, her dad asked her for a dance.

He walked her, hand in hand, to a back corner of the room, where no one would notice October dancing alone.

"Thank you, Dad. For everything."

"Of course, Boo. I wouldn't have missed it."

They danced for a few moments, and she rested her head on his chest.

"Boo?"

"Mmm?" She wished she could smell him. His aftershave.

His fabric softener. His deodorant. Something. But all she felt was the chill of his embrace, and she knew that had to be enough.

"You're ready."

She'd been waiting to hear it for weeks. Even though they'd both been around more than normal in the last month or two to help with wedding preparations, she knew. A part of her thought they might hang around for grandkids, but another part was glad they didn't want to. She wasn't sure she could handle that kind of pressure.

Despite the fact that she'd been expecting it, the tears came quickly. "I know."

He squeezed her hand, but said nothing.

When she could find words again, she said, "Thank you. For everything, Dad. For taking care of me all these years." Before he could protest, she went on. "And I do hope this isn't goodbye forever. I don't even know if you can, but maybe we'll see you again? Maybe you can visit us?"

The only promise he would make her was, "It definitely isn't goodbye forever." Even his voice was full of emotion as he kissed her hand, and didn't let her go when the song finished. They danced that way for two more songs. Until Wilder came over, and cut in.

Mrs. Davis and her dad danced next to them until the end of the night. When it was time to go, and there were no words left to say, Wilder and October stood hand in hand crying happy tears as their closest friends waved sparklers at them. They watched Mrs. Davis and her dad walk away, hand in hand. Just before they disappeared, her dad turned around and October blew him a kiss. He caught it in his hand and held it to his heart. When October blinked her tears away, they were gone.

The Mannings got their happy ending after all. Both of them. October couldn't speak for her dad, and she couldn't ask him anymore, but as she got into Wilder's truck and they drove away, she didn't feel like she'd lost her dad. She felt like they had both gained their happiness. As she held Wilder's hand, she knew she wasn't ever going to let it go.

THE END

The following is an unedited preview of March Hair, coming March 1, 2024. A preorder link will be available soon! Until then, enjoy the first few chapters with March, Stella, Alice, and Robin.

CHAPTER 1

*D*o you ever walk by someone on the sidewalk, completely unaware of your face, until the person mirrors it? That's how March Wilson started her day. Staring at a rather large man's moobs trying to read his shirt.

She didn't realize she'd been scowling at the effort until she looked up to his face, and he was scowling back at her.

"Sorry," she offered. "Your shirt's funny." But seeing the expression on his face stole the laugh that had been bubbling up.

Currently unsupervised (this should frighten you), was emblazoned across his chest. It really was funny, if not hard to read. Maybe if the font hadn't been so scripty it would've been better. But March kept her constructive criticism to herself.

His expression softened. "Thanks."

She smiled weakly and moved past him as quickly as she could without looking like she was trying to escape him and the faux pas. She sniffed as the cool spring breeze made her nose run. Or maybe it was the azaleas blooming on both sides of the two-lane street.

Most of the shops that lined the road hadn't opened yet, but that was probably best. She didn't need any more distractions. Although she didn't have any appointments scheduled for the day, she did have plenty of work to do.

When she arrived at her salon, the March Hair, she was flustered, and Stella could tell.

"What did you do this time?" Her best friend asked as she flounced into the chair in front of her mirror.

"Stared at a large man's moobs without realizing it."

"Well, he probably deserved a taste of his own medicine. Men spend far too much time ogling women." Stella punctuated her thoughts with a firm nod.

March raised her eyebrow at her only employee, a woman fifteen years her senior. "Stella, when was the last time you were ogled? I'll be honest, I don't ever remember being ogled." She used air quotes to accentuate the last word while stifling a giggle.

"Excuse me. Hank ogled me this morning while I was getting dressed thank-you-very-much."

Hank and Stella were a storybook couple. The kind of love March hoped to find some day, but wasn't sure she ever would. At thirty-five, she was single, and living in a small town where she knew nearly everyone. Encounters with strangers usually ended much like her blunder with funny shirt man. She spent too much time in her head. Too much time daydreaming. That's what she'd been told at least. By everyone except her folks, and Hank and Stella.

They'd taken her in after her folks died in a car accident. She was 14 at the time, but had known them her whole life. They'd been friends with her parents, and she'd practically lived over there before her folks died. Stella taught March everything she knew about hair, although Stella would disagree.

"That girl doesn't need to be taught anything about hair. She's a natural," she'd say. March wasn't so sure.

"Where'd you go?" Stella often used this question to gently bring Stella out of her head.

"Oh, sorry. I was thinking about you and Hank." Before Stella could offer any kind of oh-you'll-find-your-prince-soon type sentiments, March changed the subject. "Who do you have today?"

Stella sighed as she made sure her station was in order and ready for the day. "Blanch Braverman."

March chuckled, but only because she didn't have to deal with the woman. Blanch was…opinionated. Honestly, March didn't understand why she kept coming back to Stella. She never had anything positive to say, but she always tipped her tremendously, so Stella couldn't bring herself to refuse her appointments. "Don't bite the hand that feeds you," Stella always commented after the woman left.

"That woman's going to get more than a bite one of these days," March declared, after listening to a thirty-minute tirade about how her bangs were clearly uneven. March got out a measuring tape to prove they weren't, and that's when Blanch waved her away, tossed a massive tip on Stella's station, and left.

They thought they'd never hear from her again, but there they were. Five weeks later, bracing for another tirade.

"You've got this," March tried to assure her. But even she wasn't sure she could listen to her without firing back. Stella insisted they both keep their mouths shut, that they were professionals. But Blanch made it awfully hard.

March looked around her salon. She'd worked hard to make it a place everyone could be happy and comfortable. Some clients even commented on a certain amount of magic the place held. March wasn't sure about that, but she sure loved it. She and Stella bought the space between the bookstore and what had been an insurance company at the time. Now, it was a thrift store that Stella swore she could find gems in every time she went in there. To that day, March had never seen anything worth taking home. But Stella found a few paintings of gardens that hung on opposite walls in the shop, and March had to admit they complimented the salon well.

They'd painted the walls soft green, and hung plants from the ceiling, "to bring the outdoors inside," Stella justified. March had a hard time keeping plants alive, and had tried to get fake ones on more than one occasion, but Stella could always tell, and they'd be replaced with real ones. As soon as Stella took her annual three-week vacation, they'd die. They had green ivy spilling out of the pots in each corner of the room at the moment, and a few months yet before Stella and Hank's trip to Italy. March hoped ivy was heartier than anything else they'd tried.

Their stations were as unique as the two women. Stella's was very utilitarian. Nothing frilly and everything in its place. March often used a paint pen to write something inspirational on her mirror, and had a few funky comb holders she got at the local pottery shop next to Hank's hardware store. Although, her combs were often stuffed in a drawer, or laying on the counter. There was always at least one clean one. Somewhere. Maybe. She had been known to steal from Stella's stash on occasion, but her wrath wasn't always worth it.

They'd splurged on lounge chairs for clients to wait in, aiming for a relaxing getaway sort of experience when people came in. Even the chair behind the desk by the door was an upgrade Stella wasn't sure they needed. "When are we ever going to sit in that?"

March shrugged. "We'll be on our feet all day. Don't you want a divine experience when you finally do get to sit down?"

Stella couldn't argue with that.

The chime over the door let them know Hank was there with their morning treats. "Just in time, my love," Stella declared as she went to his open arms.

March went to the box of donuts he set on the desk near the front door and dug in as she raised a particularly hot cup of coffee to him. "Thank you," she tried through a full mouth of powdered sugar donut.

"Don't mention it. What would my morning be without a light dusting of powdered sugar from you, March?" He only frowned a little as he brushed off his shirt. March didn't bother to apologize for spraying him with her delicious treat. It was part of their routine, and she knew deep down, the old curmudgeon loved it.

"This is just what I needed to face Blanch," Stella declared as she took a long sip of her coffee, and picked out her apple fritter. Hank always knew what they liked, and brought it to them weekly. Although the coffee came daily, the donuts he said wouldn't be a treat anymore if he brought them every day. March wasn't so sure, but beggars wouldn't be choosers. Or so he insisted.

"Godspeed," he wished his wife, and added a kiss on the cheek before he headed for the door.

"Any luck finding help in the store?" March asked before he was out.

"Not yet. But I'm not worried. The right person will come along." The door jangled as it shut behind him.

"That person better come along soon. I'm sick of him working so much. We're too old for long hours." Stella looked over at March. "We're not kids like you anymore."

"Doesn't mean you have to act like old farts either,"

March pointed out as she settled into the front desk to tackle the paperwork she'd been saving up all month, immediately appreciating their splurge on the comfy desk chair. She dreaded paperwork day almost as much as Stella dreaded Blanch Braverman.

"Who you calling an old fart?" Blanch Braverman asked as she breezed into the salon six minutes ahead of schedule. March looked up at the woman and noticed something different, although she couldn't quite put her finger on it. Her white hair was only just starting to look shaggy. Her outfit didn't have a spot on it, despite the fact that she was wearing white capri pants just begging for dirt to cling to them. She'd even matched her pink purse to her Lily Pulitzer top. Blanch was so put together, it intimidated the crap out of March, and she found herself grateful the woman was Stella's client, and not hers. She'd never cut her hair. She'd never needed it. March didn't think the woman was capable of change.

Stella got her seated in the chair and set to work, asking Blanch about her month, if they'd taken any trips, and what they'd been up to. Yes they'd taken a trip, but it was far too buggy, and didn't Stella think it was early for it to be buggy? Stella didn't get to respond before she launched into a criticism of the hotel they'd stayed at that had a dripping tub that kept her up all night, and that reminded her could Hank stop by and check their kitchen sink? The faucet was dripping.

March shot her a look, but thankfully Blanch again didn't give Stella a chance to respond. After nearly an hour, Stella was finally finished. Thankfully, Blanch didn't color her hair, or they would've had to endure that torture even longer.

Stella and March held their breath as Blanch looked herself over. Stella gripped the cape she'd just taken off Mrs. Braverman tightly as March watched from behind the desk.

"I think that will do. I'll see you in five weeks." She tore a check she'd apparently pre-written out of her checkbook and placed it on the desk in front of March. Before she could even look at the amount on it, Blanche turned and left without further comment or criticism.

"That was odd. Don't you think that was odd?" Stella asked. "She didn't comment on a single thing I did."

"Well, what could she have commented on? It was a beautiful cut," March insisted.

"She found something the last time."

"Maybe she learned her lesson?" Even as March said it, she knew that woman was incapable of growth. Or at least she thought she was.

"Something's changed," Stella said as she watched Blanch walk to her car through the big glass windows in front of the salon.

March could feel it too. A change in the air. But she couldn't put her finger on the source of the feeling.

Stella swept up before her next customer came in, and March tried to focus on the bills in front of her. But by lunch time she needed to move. "I'm going over to the salad place. What do you want?"

Stella looked down at her watch and brightened. "I don't have anyone until twelve thirty. I'll go with you. Maybe the walk will help."

"That's my hope. I feel…itchy. No. Prickly? I don't know. I need to move," March tried to explain.

Stella nodded. "Blanch has both of us unsettled. Maybe that was her ploy all along."

March laughed. "You know, you're probably right."

Just the thought had March feeling better. She wouldn't put it past the woman to be kind to them just to make them uneasy.

As she reached for her purse, the bell over the door

jangled, and goosebumps spread across March's arms, making her hair stand on end.

"Hi." The voice was small and sweet.

Turns out, change came in the form of a ten-year-old girl with long blonde hair.

CHAPTER 2

"*I* need a haircut," the girl declared. She smelled like sugar and outdoors, and March loved it.

Stella looked at the girl, and then at March, who was quickly moving around the desk with her arms open, ready to usher the girl to her chair. Stella shook her head, knowing their lunch plans were over and done.

Stella, ever the practical one, pumped the brakes. "Where are your parents, honey?"

"Oh, my dad' in the truck." The girl gestured dismissively over her shoulder and followed March to her station.

March spied a shiny truck parked across the street. "Why didn't he park at the salon?"

The girl shrugged. "He's standoffish like that." The way she said it, like isn't everyone's dad like that, gave March pause.

Apparently, Stella felt the same, the way she looked uneasily at March. "He just let you come into a strange salon for a haircut alone?"

She shrugged again. "I can take care of myself."

Clearly, Stella mouthed.

"Why didn't he come in?" Stella pushed as March got her seated in her chair.

"He's looking for work in a paper he picked up from a box up the street."

Stella considered. March knew she wanted to suggest Hank's opening, but wasn't sure about the standoffish man who sent his ten-year-old to be with strangers in a strange town. She said nothing, at least for the moment.

"What's your name?" March asked as she draped the baby blue cape across the young girl.

"Alice."

It struck March. She did look like Alice, from Lewis Carrol's book. A beautiful girl filled with wonder in her blue eyes that almost matched the cape, and nothing but trust for the world around her. March's problem was, she was lovely. March specialized in transformations. She didn't work on kids. Kids transformed themselves every day. They grew and changed all on their own. It was adults who needed a push. Confidence to nail that interview. Or just the right look to wow their fiancé as they walked down the aisle. Or a complete shedding of the past after a divorce. Kids didn't need change like that. But Alice...

March glanced at the truck sitting across the street as she brushed Alice's long blonde hair. "What brought you here, Alice?" Maybe if she dug for a reason, she'd feel better about what she was about to do. March saw the change Alice needed as if it was already a reality. That's how it always was for her. She knew instinctively what had to happen, and she knew how to do it. But this was the first time she wondered if she should.

Kids weren't their appearance the way adults were, were they? They were chameleons. One day happy and social, the next day dark and brooding. What they looked like on the outside didn't matter. Right?

But she ached as she looked at the face in the mirror, when she realized she wasn't listening to the answer she'd asked for.

"I'm sorry. What was that?" March asked.

"Daddy wanted a change or something. I'm not sure."

March looked at Stella, who was watching in the mirror. Another dubious look from her dear friend. What was going on? Was Alice being kidnapped?

Turning the chair to face March, she looked into the girl's face. She didn't look scared, or like she was silently crying for help. She looked happy, well fed, and maybe even excited for a change. "You're safe, aren't you?" March caught herself saying out loud.

Alice blinked her blue eyes at March, clearly wondering why she'd asked such a dumb question. "Of course I am."

"Do *you* want a change?" March asked carefully.

"I do! I think it'll be fun." The girl's excitement was contagious, and March smiled.

In that moment, inspiration took over. Stella knew better than to get in the way once that happened. People came from all over the country to experience March's inspiration. And that little girl just wandered in on a day when March wasn't busy.

Lots of her clients claimed March was magic, but she was convinced her clients brought the magic with them, and Alice was no exception.

It took hours. And the whole time, the truck stayed parked out front. Her father never wandered in to check on her. March didn't have time to wonder about him though. She was too caught up in her work.

In the end, she cut Alice's blonde hair into a neat bob that stopped just above her shoulders. She also colored it dark brown, with a baby blue streak on the right side to match her eyes. When she was done, Alice clapped.

"Oh, I love it." She twirled the blue streak around her first finger.

"Do you think your dad will be upset we took so long?"

"No. He likes his alone time. Plus, he's looking for a job remember?"

"You know," Stella chewed the inside of her cheek but plowed forward anyway. "My husband owns the hardware store up the street and is looking for some help. I mean, if your dad is handy."

Alice shrugged. "I don't know what he wants to do." March couldn't tell if Alice had any intention of even mentioning the job to her dad, but decided whatever happened was fine. Maybe an aloof guy wasn't what Hank wanted in the shop anyway.

"Well," March said after a beat of silence. "Don't forget to come back in four weeks or so, so I can touch up your color."

Stella shot her a look. Usually, she did the touch up work. Once the transformation was done, Stella took over. They were a team. It was the first time March bucked their system. But it was obvious why. Alice had charmed the entire shop, and March didn't want to let go of her. How could Stella blame her?

"Oh don't worry, I'll be back before then." March couldn't help but smile at the promise. Alice produced a small wad of money and held it out to March, but March held up her hands.

"This one's on me. Why don't you treat Stella and I to ice cream the next time you're around?" March suggested.

"I would *love* that. Where's a good place?"

"Oh, you stick with us, kiddo, we'll tell you where all the best places are."

She giggled, and skipped out of their shop, and it suddenly felt emptier without her, as if the magic had gone with her.

"Well. That was different," Stella mused.

March chewed her bottom lip. "Do you think I shouldn't have colored her hair?"

"I admit, I didn't feel good about it while you were doing it. Damaging that baby hair. But once it was done, I couldn't picture her any other way. I don't know how you do it."

"Honestly, I don't either."

But, as she watched the truck pull away, she knew the how wasn't what mattered. It was the why. And no matter how March turned it over in her mind, she couldn't settle on why that child needed such a change.

CHAPTER 3

"*Y*ou know," Stella remarked while she was snipping away at her own client's beautiful silver hair. March braced herself for the lecture she was about to get. "You have to stop giving away your services. The hair color alone cost at least $50. And that fancy blue stuff? Even more!"

"She needed us, Stell. Couldn't you tell?"

"I'm not so sure about that. Seems like we needed her too." Stella commented. And the woman she was working on nodded.

"She felt magical didn't she?" Mrs. Prince said, a dreamy look in her eyes and a half smile on her face. "And when she left, she took some of the magic with her." Her cloudy eyes landed on March. "But not all of it, hmm?"

March smiled warmly. "Not all of it."

Stella scoffed. "Magic is going to put us right out of business."

March laughed. Stella was always the steady one. The one who kept her grounded. But honestly, as much as she loved to give her services away, she'd never once been worried about how to pay the bills. The money was always there when they needed it. Whether it was a generous tip, or an influx of appointments, they never wanted. And in fact, she'd given Stella a bonus every Christmas for the last decade.

"March, dear. Have you ever had anyone who came to you looking how they should?"

"What do you mean, Mrs. Prince?" March asked as she swept Alice's blonde hair from the floor.

"You specialize in transformations, right?" She said *transformations* like it was a magical, mysterious word, and she even added a flourish with her hand, which was trapped under the cape, making the gesture rather comical.

March stifled a smile. "I do."

"What if someone walks in and doesn't need it? What if they look perfect, just how they are?"

The memory was warm, and March loved it, so she didn't mind telling Mrs. Prince about it. "It has happened. Once. The woman had a huge job interview scheduled, so she called me up, wanting something to give her an edge. Apparently it was a very competitive opening, and five other interviews were scheduled that day alone. But she knew she was perfect for the position, so she enlisted my help. But when she showed up in her suit and heels, her hair was perfect. It was modern and sleek, but also healthy looking. I refused to do anything. I told her she looked great, and didn't need my help."

"And how did that go over?" Mrs. Prince grinned like she knew exactly how well that went over.

"About as well as a ton of bricks dropped on a China shop."

"That well, huh?"

"She was madder than a hornet that she drove all that way for nothing. I tried to tell her, it wasn't for nothing. She wanted every possible edge she could get, and she had it. I offered to wash and dry her hair if that would make her feel better, but it looked great as it was. I had no doubt she would get it. She stormed out, promising to tell everyone she knew, which turned out to be more than a few people, that I was a crock of you know what."

Mrs. Prince was a bit shocked. "What happened? Did you hear from her again?"

"I did actually. That evening she called me."

"Well that's ballsy of her."

March laughed at the old woman's choice of words. "It was. But she was too excited to be sheepish. Turns out, I was right. They loved her, and offered her the job on the spot. And, that extensive list of people she knew? She told every single one of them. Turns out I've gotten quite a bit of business from her after all."

Mrs. Prince laughed, delighted at the happy ending. "What a foolish woman for doubting you."

March shrugged. "It's better just to roll with it. Like today for example." She looked at the desk, and her long forgotten paperwork. "I had no appointments, and intended to do paperwork, maybe leave early to get some house chores done. But that didn't happen."

She glanced at the clock. 5:30 already. Mrs. Prince was Stella's last. Hank would be around soon to take her home. Everything March had planned would have to wait.

As March walked home that evening, she couldn't get Alice out of her head. What had happened to them before? Where had they come from, and why had they settled in Dumont, Georgia of all places? Barely a blip on the map.

March lived only a few miles from the salon, and enjoyed the walk when the weather was nice. The woods closed in around her as she got closer to home, and her driveway was barely visible between the old oaks. They made room for her small yellow cottage though, as if it belonged among the trees, and they were happy to have it there.

Her car was parked out front, and she couldn't remember the last time she'd used it. Probably to get groceries last week. Which reminded her she needed to make a trip again. She was down to cereal for dinner, and she was a little too hungry for that, after skipping lunch to work on Alice. She shook her head. She should've grabbed something on her way home. But she was so preoccupied with the girl.

The porch groaned as she stepped up onto it, and March ran a reassuring hand along the banister. "I know, old girl. But you'll have to wait."

Her next project was the roof, which she was hoping Hank would help her with. She just hadn't gotten the nerve to ask him yet. Her lot butted right up to the preserve, giving her lovely old oak trees that shaded her little house. She loved it, and the only reason she could afford it was because her Grandmother had willed it to her. Stella and Hank had helped her make it livable when she was a teenager, and as soon as they were comfortable with its condition, she moved in.

She went inside and hung her keys on the hook by the door before hanging up her jacket. She had two bedrooms, one bathroom, and barely a one butt kitchen, but it was home. Immediately she went out back to her sanctuary. She'd built a deck back there and adorned it with two Adirondack chairs and a fire pit. The wind moved through the trees as the sun set and she lit a small fire in the pit. She sat with a cup of hot chocolate, and a bag of peanut butter pretzels trying to understand her day. Possibly not the dinner of champions but it would do.

March hadn't been looking for change, but it had come in the form of a little girl who seemed to step right out of Wonderland and into their lives. What did it mean? Would she see her again? Before she was even finished asking the question, she felt sure she would. As she sipped her hot chocolate, she couldn't help but be happy at the thought. She liked Alice, and wanted to get to know her better. March wanted to know what made Alice happy, who her friends were, what her favorite subject in school was. And March had no idea why she wanted to know all that.

March didn't spend much time around kids. She didn't have any of her own, and Stella and Hank didn't either. She didn't cut kids' hair either, so the times she crossed paths with them was fairly minimal. That didn't mean she didn't like them, she just didn't have much experience with them. But she was drawn to Alice like a moth to a flame. And March knew the girl was a light she hadn't known she needed in her life.

The next day, March had a wedding appointment. She loved those. They were always so exciting and joyful. There wasn't any stress of a pending job, or the depression that surrounded a divorce style transformation. While all her appointments looked forward to the future, weddings did it with such unapologetic joy.

Judy was perfect. She talked nonstop about her wedding. It would be about two hours away, on a ranch her in-laws owned with some of the Smokey Mountains in the background. It sounded like a lovely setting. It would be in the barn with twinkle lights everywhere, and fun rustic touches all around.

March listened while she worked, smiling so much her face hurt by the time she was done. Judy's hair was almost sparkling as she turned in front of the mirror. Ringlets of brown hair cascaded down her shoulders as she beamed at herself.

She hugged March without concern for her hair, and

March loved it, hugging her back. "Thank you. I just know the day will be perfect because of you and your magic."

"I'm pretty sure your day is going to be perfect because of you, Judy," March countered. If she didn't live so far away, she'd have wanted to be friends with her. She was so positive and warm, if not at least ten years younger than March, but that was beside the point.

Judy was happy when she came in, it was her wedding day after all, but March found most of her clients had a better outlook by the time they left. They seemed uplifted by whatever March did. Stella called it part of her magic, but March wasn't so sure. Shedding an old look is a magic all its own. Something she didn't have anything to do with.

"Thank you again, March. You're amazing." Judy slipped out, leaving more than double the amount March charged her on the desk before she went.

"Well, she was a delight," March said as she spotted a man sitting in the chairs near the front window. She had no idea how long he'd been there, or if Stella had seen him. She eyed the pile of cash, but he didn't seem to notice it.

He looked...well, homeless. His beard was long and ratty. His brown hair looked like it hadn't seen a brush maybe ever as it poked out from under an old grey baseball hat with the words "gute fahrt" on it. March snickered, causing him to look over at her. His eyes were just as blue as Alice's had been, and stopped March in her tracks. Who was he and what was he doing in her salon?

ALSO BY STEPHANIE ERICKSON

June Nights - Available now!

March Hair - Coming March 1, 2024

ACKNOWLEDGMENTS

In the time I worked on October's Ghosts, my Grandmother (mom's mom) and my Grandfather (dad's biological dad) died. I spent a lot of time in funeral homes in a two month span. But my family is a bunch of weirdos that get along, so we made the best of it.

My point is, this book hit closer to home than I meant it to, and I want to thank everyone that had a hand in it.

First, of course, thanks goes to God. For giving me the time, the words, and the support I needed to finish this. I'm very proud of this book, and I hope He is too.

Second, thanks to my husband and daughter for their endless support, even when my books only make $5.72 a month.

Third, thank you to my wonderful parents for babysitting, and reading VERY early drafts and still thinking I'm amazing ::cringe::, and for being some of my biggest cheerleaders. Love you the mostest.

Thank you to my friends who've supported me through all of this. Joanna, who's always clamoring for more pages; Amber and Shelley, who remind me who I am and what's important; Dannie who lets me be part of her family. I love you all.

To the Regina Girls, thank you so much for your support! You guys are the coolest.

And a special thank you to my aunts: Karen, Sue, Marylou and my grandma. Who inspired a particularly…eye opening scene in this very book. Heehee. Love you guys!

And to you, dear reader. Thank you for staying with me. For taking valuable time away from your life to spend with me and my book. You'll never know how deeply I appreciate you.

See you in March.

—S

Made in United States
North Haven, CT
01 July 2024

54273596R00195